The boy was laid on the grass beside the pit where the night breeze ruffled his hair, blowing wisps across his pale, unlined forehead. His clothes were cut free and pulled aside so that the body was naked to the night, white marble in color and stillness. Metal glinted in the moonlight, plunging downward, entering, slicing.

When the moon rises, terror descends. . . .

"Fascinating . . . malevolent violence . . . intricate . . . strong horror."
—*The New York Times*

"A tense, chilling and satisfying blend of human and supernatural horror . . . gruesome goings-on . . . recommended for all horror fans."
—*Library Journal*

"A very scary novel . . . abundant suspense."
—*St. Louis Post-Dispatch*

MOON
James Herbert

AN ONYX BOOK

NEW AMERICAN LIBRARY

PUBLISHER'S NOTE

Onyx is a trademark of New American Library.

SIGNET, SIGNET CLASSIC, MENTOR, ONYX, PLUME, MERIDIAN
and NAL BOOKS are published by NAL PENGUIN INC.,
1633 Broadway, New York, New York 10019

First Onyx Printing, December, 1987

2 3 4 5 6 7 8 9

PRINTED IN THE UNITED STATES OF AMERICA

Before

THE BOY had stopped crying.

He lay in his narrow bed, eyes closed, his face an alabaster mask in the moonlight. Occasionally a tremor would run the length of his body.

He clutched the bedsheets, pulling them tight under his chin. A dreadful heaviness inside weighed his body down, a feeling that his blood had turned into liquid lead: the burden was loss, and it had left him exhausted and weak.

The boy had rested there a long time—how many hours he had no way of knowing, for all of the last three days had been a timeless eternity—but his father had forbidden him to move from the bed again. So he lay there, enduring the loss, frightened by the new loneliness.

Until something caused him to open his red-rimmed eyes once more.

The figure stood near the end of the bed and she smiled at him. He felt her warmth, the momentary shedding of bereavement. But it was impossible. His father had told him it was impossible.

'You . . . can't . . . be . . .' he said, his small voice a shivery intrusion on the night. 'He . . . says . . . you can't . . . you can't . . . be . . .'

The sense of loss was renewed, for now it was also within her.

And then the startled boy looked elsewhere in the room, gazing upwards into a far corner as if suddenly aware of yet another presence, of someone else watching him, someone he could not see. The moment vanished when footsteps were heard along the corridor and he looked away, for the first time real fear in his eyes. The woman was gone.

In the doorway stood the swaying shadow of a man.

The boy's father stumbled towards the bed, the familiar reek of alcohol as much a part of him as the perpetual sullenness of his features.

'I told you,' the man said, and there seemed to be guilt mixed with anger in the harsh words. 'No more! No more . . .' His fist was raised as he approached and the boy cowered beneath the bedsheets.

Outside, the full moon was clear-edged and pure against the deep blackness of the night.

At last she was dead.

Where there had been terror, there was now only emptiness.

Dead eyes. Those of a fish on an iced slab.

Her body dormant, the final spasm exhausted, the final gasp silenced. Her last expression dissolved.

Clawed fingers still held the shape about her, one thumb curled inside its mouth as though she had tried to rip away the smile.

The shape rose, releasing its grip from her throat; its breath was barely laboured, even though the woman beneath had struggled for a long time.

It pulled the thumb from its mocking lips and the corpse's hand fell away, smacking against bare flesh.

It paused, studying the victim. Smiling all the while.

It reached for the lifeless hands, gripping their wrists, lifting them. It ran the cracked nails down its own face, drawing the shock-stiffened fingers around its throat as if taunting them, tempting revenge. A low chuckle derided their inertia.

It trailed the hands across its exposed body straddled over the corpse, moving them down so that they touched everywhere, caressed every part. The deathly soft stroking incited further sensations.

The figure busied itself upon the woman's slowly cooling body.

After a while it rose from the bed, a light sheen of perspiration coating its skin. Not yet was it satiated.

Cold drizzle spattered the window in sudden gusts as if protesting against the cruelty inside. Faded curtains, closed against daylight, muffled the sound.

A bag in the corner of the dingy room was snapped open, a black package removed. The package was unrolled on the bed, close to the corpse, and the gleam of metal instruments was only slightly dulled by the poor light. Each one was lifted, examined, held close to the eyes whose gleam could not be subdued. The first was chosen.

The body, cooling to room temperature, was sliced from sternum to pubic symphysis, then from hip to hip. Blood quickly seeped through the deep cross.

The flaps were separated then pulled back. Fingers, already crimson, delved inside.

It removed the organs, cutting where necessary, and placed them on the bed covers where they glistened and steamed. The heart, reached for last and wrenched free, was tossed onto the heap. It slithered down the slippery mound and plopped to the floor. The sickly odour pervaded the room.

A receptacle made, it was soon filled.

The figure searched the room for small objects, but only after the dead woman's own appendages had been used.

When at last it was satisfied, it drew needle and thread from the wrapping on the bed.

It began to sew the flaps together again, piercing the flesh with large, crude stitchwork, smiling all the while. The smile broadening to a grin as it thought of the last object placed inside the body.

HE FINNED over the green-hued rocks, movement leisurely, relaxed, hands used only occasionally to change
direction, careful to avoid barnacles that could cut
deep into water-softened skin. His legs flexed slowly,
moving from the hips with long, graceful strokes, semi-
hard fins propelling him easily through the currents.

Coral weed waved ghostly patterns at him, and startled fish jack-knifed away from his stealthy intrusion;
snakelocks anemone seemed to beckon silently. Daylight filtered through from above, its rays dissipated,
the seabed sanctum muted and secretive. Childes could
hear only the ponderous, dull sounds of his own actions.

A tiny undulation, a scurry of sand, caught his eye
and he cautiously approached, gently placing his hands
on an outcrop of rock, bringing himself to an easy,
swaying halt.

Below him, a starfish had attached itself to a cockle,
pinning it down and prising the two shell valves apart
with tube feet. The starfish worked patiently, its five
tentacles used in relays, tiring its prey, resolutely widening the gap to expose the cockle's body tissues.
Childes watched with mild but fascinated revulsion as
the hunter eventually extruded its own stomach and
sank it into the opening to suck out the fleshy substance beneath.

A subtle displacement among the ridges and caverns

of barnacled stone close by diverted the diver's attention. Puzzled, he studied the craggy relief for a few moments before a further shifting directed his gaze. The spiny spider crab skited across the rock face, its shell and claws sprouting green algae, a natural and effective camouflage in both the shallows and the deeper waters. When still, it was virtually invisible.

Childes followed the crab's progress, admiring its agility and speed, the little multi-legged creature enlarged and brought much closer by the magnification of his diving mask's glass faceplate and the seawater itself. The spider crab stopped as if suddenly aware of being stalked; he used a probing finger to galvanise another spurt.

The diver's smile at the sudden panicked flurry was distorted by the snorkel wedged into his teeth and gums, and he was abruptly aware that his lungs were almost exhausted of air. Unhurried, he prepared to skim back to the surface.

The sighting came without warning. Just as other sightings had in the past.

Yet he hardly knew what he saw, for it was in his mind, not his vision; a confused jumble of colours, of smells. His hands tingled in the water. There was something long and shiny, coiled, red and gleaming wet. Now metal, keen-edged steel against a mushy softness. Swimming in blood. He was swimming in blood. Nausea hit him and he drew in salt water.

His body curled up painfully and bile mixed with seawater exploded from his throat, clogging the snorkel pipe. The mouthpiece shot free of his lips and more water rushed in. Childes cried out involuntarily, the sound a muffled, gurgling croak, and he kicked down, arms reaching for the surface. Wildly escaping bubbles matched the crazy disorder behind his eyes. The light-spread ceiling above seemed a long way off.

Another vision stabbed into his nightmare. Hands, cruel, blunt fingers, moving in rhythm. An insane thought-sight. They were sewing.

Childes' body doubled up once more.

He instinctively tried to close his mouth, no clear direction in his head any more, but it continued to drink in great gulps of salt water as though conspiring with the sea against him. His senses began to dim, his arms and legs felt feeble. So quickly, he thought. They warned how quick drowning could be. Yet ridiculously, he was aware of the J-shaped snorkel, tucked into the retaining band of his diving mask, scratching loosely against his cheek. He struggled, feeling himself drifting, sinking.

A slender arm slid beneath his shoulder, gripping tight. A hugging body against his back. Rising. Slowly, controlled. He tried to help, but an opaque mantle was descending.

Bursting through the surface as though shot from a black stifling embrace, life painfully thrust back into him rather than gently returned.

His stomach and chest heaved, jetting liquid; he choked, spluttered, threatened to drag them both down again. He vaguely heard a soothing voice and tried to heed the words, forcing himself to relax, commanding his lungs to take in air cautiously, gasp by gasp, spitting out residue, coughing out the last of the bile.

She towed him back to the shoreline, holding his arms above the elbows, his head cradled against one of her own arms. She swam on her back by his side, fins driving them easily through the small waves. His breathing was still laboured, but soon he was able to help by flexing his own legs, keeping in time with hers.

They reached shallower water and the girl hauled him to his feet. She pulled the mask from his face and put an arm around his hunched shoulders, hitting his back when he coughed more sea, bending with him, her young face etched with concern. Kneeling, she drew off his flippers, then removed her own. His shoulders still jerked with the effort of breathing as he stood half-crouched, hands on his knees; gradually he recovered, the shudders merging into a shivering. The

girl waited patiently, her own diving mask raised high
over her forehead, her blonde hair worked loose, darkened by the water and hanging in dripping trails over
her shoulders. She didn't speak, knowing it would be
pointless just yet.

Eventually it was the man who gasped, 'Amy . . .'

'It's all right, let's get to the shore.'

They left the water, lurching slightly as they went,
her arm beneath his shoulders, supporting. Childes
slumped onto the shingle, feeling relieved, shocked,
sickened—all these emotions. She sat next to him,
sweeping hair from his eyes, gently massaging his back.

They were alone in the small, remote bay, the steep
climb through the rock-eroded cleft too daunting for
many, a chill south-easterly breeze deterring others.
Lush vegetation spilled over the clifftops, flowing down
the steep slopes, stemmed only by an uncompromising
stone face near the base, a granite fringe washed clean
by thunderous tides. Early May flowers littered the
upper reaches, speckling the verdure with blue, white
and yellow. A miniature waterfall gushed close by, its
stream winding through the pebbles and rocks to join
the sea. Further out, little fishing boats, dinghies mainly,
bobbed easily on the slate sea, their mooring lines
stretching like grey thread to a quay on the far side of
the inlet. Access to the quay was by a narrow track, a
jumble of boulders separating it from the beach itself.
The girl noticed one or two faces peering in their
direction from the quayside wall, obviously concerned
over the incident; she signalled that all was well and
they turned away.

Childes pushed himself into a sitting position, wrists
over his raised knees, head slumped forward. He was
still shivering.

'You scared me, Jon,' the girl said, kneeling before
him.

He looked at her and his face was pale. He brushed
a hand across his eyes as if trying to dismiss a memory

'Thanks for dragging me out,' he said at last.

She leaned forward and kissed his cheek, then his shoulder. Her eyes were curious. 'What happened out there?'

His body juddered and she realised how cold he was. 'I'll fetch the blanket,' she said, standing.

Her bare feet ignored the hard shingle as she skipped over to their pile of clothing and bags lying on a flat slab further up the beach. Childes watched her lithe figure as she snatched a blanket from a hold-all and was grateful for her presence—not just because she had pulled him from the sea, but because she was with him. He shifted his gaze back to the lapping water, a white band on the horizon, harbinger of the coming storm.

His eyes closed and he tasted salt in his throat. He cast his head downwards and moaned quietly.

Why now, after so long?

The weight of the blanket over his shoulders drew him back.

'Drink,' Amy said, holding a thin silver flask under his nose.

The brandy loosened the salt inside and he relished the sudden inner warmth. He raised one arm and she joined him beneath the blanket.

'You okay?' she asked, snuggling close.

He nodded, but the shivering had not yet ceased.

'I brought your glasses over.'

He took them from her, put them on. The focused world was no more real.

When he spoke, his voice was shaky.

'It's happening again,' he said.

'TOMORROW?' HE asked.

Amy shook her head 'Daddy has guests—all day.' She rolled her eyes. 'I'm on duty.'

'Business?'

'Uh-huh. Potential investors from Lyon. He invited them for the weekend, but thank God they could only make it for Sunday. They fly back Monday afternoon, after they've visited the company. He's disappointed— he wanted to show off the island as well.'

Paul Sebire, Amy's father, was chief executive of Jacarte International, a powerful financial investment company based in the offshore island, itself a low-tax haven for those on the Continent as well as on the mainland. Although predominantly British, the island was physically closer to France.

'Pity,' Childes said.

'I'm sorry, Jon.' She leaned back into the car to kiss him, her hair, now tied back into a tail, twisting around her neck to brush against his chest.

He returned her kiss, relishing the smell of sea on her, tasting the salt on her lips.

'Doesn't he ever relax?' he asked.

'It is relaxation for him. I'd have swung you an invite, but I didn't think you'd enjoy yourself.'

'You know me so well.' He prepared to drive away. 'Give your father my love.'

She mock-scowled. 'I doubt he'll reciprocate. Jon, about earlier . . .'

'Thanks again for dragging me out.'

'I didn't mean that.'

'What I saw?'

She nodded. 'It's been so long.'

He looked straight ahead, but his gaze was inward. After a while, he replied, 'I never really thought it was over.'

'But almost three years. Why should it start again now?'

Childes shrugged. 'Maybe it's a freak. Could be it won't happen again. It may just have been my own imagination playing tricks.' He closed his eyes momentarily, knowing it wasn't, but unwilling to discuss it just then. Leaning across the steering wheel, he touched her neck. 'Hey, c'mon, stop looking so anxious. You have a good time tomorrow and I'll see you in school Monday. We'll talk more then.'

Amy took her hold-all from the back seat, Childes helping her lift it over. 'Will you call me tonight?'

'I thought you'd planned to mark papers.'

'I don't have much choice, with Sunday so busy. I'll have earned a few minutes break, though.'

He forced a light tone. 'Okay, Teach. Don't be too hard on the kids.'

'Depends on what they've written. I'm not sure which is more difficult: teaching them French or decent English. At least with computers your own machines can correct their mistakes.'

He huffed, smiling. 'I wish it were that simple.' He kissed her cheek once more before she straightened. The first raindrops stippled the windscreen.

'Take care, Jon,' she said, wanting to say more, needing to, but sensing his resistance. Getting to know Childes had taken a long, long time and even now she was aware there were places—dark places—inside him she would never reach. She wondered if his ex-wife had ever tried.

Amy watched the little black Mini pull away, frowning as she gave a single wave. She turned and hurried through the open iron gates, running down the short drive to the house before the rain began in earnest.

Childes soon turned off the main highway, steering into the narrow lanes which spread through the island like veins from primary arteries, occasionally slowing and squeezing close to hedges and walls to ease past oncoming vehicles, whose drivers adopted the same tactics. He clutched the wheel too tightly, his knuckles white ridges, driving by reflex rather than consideration; his mind, now that he was alone, was preoccupied with other thoughts. By the time he reached the cottage he was trembling once more and the sour taste of bile was back in his throat.

He swung the Mini into the narrow opening before the old stone cottage, a patch he had cleared of weeds and brambles when he had first arrived, and switched off the engine. He left the bag containing his swimming gear in the car, jumping out and fumbling for the front-door key. The key resisted his first attempts to insert it in the lock. At last successful, he thrust open the door and rushed down the short corridor, just making it to the tiny bathroom as the bottom of his stomach rose like an express elevator. He retched over the toilet bowl, shedding, it seemed, only a small portion of the substance clogging his insides. He blew his nose on tissue, flushing the toilet and watching the soft paper swirl round until it was gulped away. Removing his brown-rimmed glasses, he washed his face in cold water, keeping his hands over his eyes for several moments, cooling them.

Childes regarded himself in the cabinet mirror as he dried his face and his reflection was pallid; he wasn't sure if his own imagination was creating the shadows under his eyes. Stretching his fingers before him, he tried to keep them still; he couldn't.

Childes replaced his glasses and went through to the sitting room, ducking his head slightly as he entered the door; he wasn't especially tall, but the building was old, the ceilings low, the door frames lower. The room lacked space, but then Childes had not packed too much into it: a faded and lumpy sofa, portable TV, square coffee table; low bookcases flanked the brick fireplace on either side, their shelves crammed. On top of one, by a lamp, was a small cluster of bottles and glasses. He went over and poured himself a stiff measure of Scotch.

Outside, the rain had become a steady downpour and he stood by the window overlooking his diminutive rear garden, broodingly watching. The cottage, among a row of others, all detached, but only just, backed on to open fields. At one time the houses had all been field-hands' tied homes, but the estate had been divided up long since, land and properties sold off. Childes had been fortunate to rent one when he had come to the island over two, almost three, years before, for empty property was scarce here, and it was the school's principal, Estelle Piprelly, eager for his computer skills, who had directed him towards the place. Her considerable influence had also helped him obtain the lease.

In the far distance, on the peninsula, he could just make out the college itself, an odd assortment of buildings, expanding over the years in various, unbalanced styles. The predominant structure, with its tower, was white. From that far away, it was no more than a rain-blurred greyish projection, the sky behind gloomed with rolling clouds.

When Childes had fled the mainland, away from pernicious publicity, the curious stares, not just of friends and colleagues, but of complete strangers who had seen his face on TV or in the newspapers, the island had provided a halcyon refuge. Here was a tight community existing within itself, the mainland and its complexities held at arm's length. Yet, close-knit though their society was, it had proved relatively easy for him to be absorbed into the population of over fifty thou-

sand. Morbid interest and—he clenched the glass hard—
and *accusations* had been left behind. He wanted it to
stay that way.

Childes drained the Scotch and poured another; like
the brandy earlier, it helped purge the foul taste that
lingered in his mouth. He returned to the window and
this time saw only the ghost of his own reflection. The
day outside had considerably darkened.

Was it the same? Had the images his mind had seen
beneath the sea anything to do with those terrible,
nightmare, visions which had haunted him so long
ago? He couldn't tell: nearly drowning had altered the
sensation. For a moment, though, during and shortly
after, when he had lain gasping on the beach, he had
been *sure,* certain the sightings had returned.

Dread filled him.

He was cold, yet perspiration dampened his brow.
Apprehension gripped him, and then a fresh anxiety
homed in.

He went out into the hallway and picked up the
phone, dialled.

After a while, a breathless voice answered.

'Fran?' he said, eyes on the wall but seeing her face.

'Who else? That you, Jon?'

'Yeah.'

A long pause then his ex-wife said, 'You called me.
Did you have something to say?'

'Where's, uh, how's Gabby?'

'She's fine, considering. She's next door with Annabel
playing at who can create most havoc. I think Melanie
planned to banish them to the garden for the afternoon, but the weather won't allow. How's it over
there?—it's piddling here.'

'Yeah, the same. I think it's working its way up to a
storm.'

Another silence.

'I'm kinda busy, Jonathan. I have to be in town by
four.'

'You working on a Saturday?'

'Sort of. A new author's arriving in London today and the publisher wants me to cosy him, give him a prelim on his tour next week.'

'Couldn't Ashby have handled it?'

Her tone was sharp. 'We run the agency on a partnership basis—I carry my load. Anyway, what do you expect of a born-again career woman?'

The barely veiled accusation stung and, not for the first time, he wondered if she would ever come to terms with his walking out. Walking out is how she would have put it.

'Who's taking care of Gabby?'

'She'll have dinner at Melanie's and Janet'll collect her later.' Janet was the young girl his former wife had hired as a daily nanny. 'She'll stay with Gabby until I get home. Is that good enough for you?'

'Fran, I didn't mean—'

'You didn't have to go, Jon. Nobody pushed you out.'

'You didn't have to stay there,' he replied quietly.

'You wanted me to give up too much.'

'The agency was only part-time then.'

'But it was *important* to me. Now it's even more so—it has to be. And there were other reasons. Our life here.'

'It'd become unbearable.'

'Whose fault was that?' Her voice softened, as though she regretted her words. 'All right, I know things happened, ran out of control; I tried to understand, to cope. But you were the one who wanted to run.'

'There was more to it, you know that.'

'I know it would have all died down eventually. *Everything.*' They both knew what she meant.

'You can't be sure.'

'Look, I don't have time for this now, I have to get moving. I'll give your kisses to Gabby and maybe she'll call you tomorrow.'

'I'd like to see her soon.'

'I . . . I don't know. Perhaps at half-term. We'll see.'

'Do me one thing, Fran.'

She sighed, anger gone. 'Ask me.'

'Check on Gabby before you leave. Just pop in, say hello. Make sure she's okay.'

'What is this, Jon? I'd have done that anyway, but what are you saying?'

'It's nothing. I guess this empty house is getting to me. You worry, y'know?'

'You sound . . . funny. Are you really that down?'

'It'll pass. Sorry I held you up.'

'I'll get there. Do you need anything, Jon, can I send anything over?'

Gabby. You can send over my daughter. 'No, I don't need anything, everything's fine. Thanks anyway.'

'Okay. Gotta run now.'

'Good luck with your author.'

'With business the way it is, we take anything we can get. He'll get a good promo. See you.'

The connection was broken.

Childes returned to the sitting room and slumped onto the sofa, deciding he didn't want another drink. He removed his spectacles and rubbed his eyes with stiffened fingers, his daughter's image swimming before him. Gabriel had been four when he'd left them. He hoped one day she would understand.

He rested there for a long time, head against the sofa back, legs stretched out onto the small patterned rug on the polished wood floor, glasses propped in one hand on his chest, sometimes staring at the ceiling, sometimes closing his eyes, trying to remember what he had seen.

For some reason, all he could visualise was the colour red. A thick, glutinous red. He thought he could even scent the blood.

THE FIRST nightmare visited him that night.

He awoke afraid and rigid. Alone.

The after-vision of the dream was still with him, yet it resisted focus. He could sense only a white, shimmering thing, a taunting spectre. It faded, gradually overwhelmed by the moonlight flooding the room.

Childes pushed himself upright in the bed, resting his back against the cool wall behind. He was frozen, fear caressing him with wintry touches. And he did not know why, could find no reason.

Outside, in the bleak stillness of the silver night, a solitary gull wailed a haunted cry.

'NO, JEANETTE, you'll have to go back and check. Remember, the computer hasn't got a mind of its own—it relies totally on yours. One wrong instruction from you and it doesn't just get confused—it sulks. It won't give you what you want.'

Childes smiled down at the girl, a little weary of her regular basic errors, but well aware that not *every* youngster's brain was tuned into the rapidly advancing technological era, despite what the newspapers and Sunday colour supps informed their parents. No longer in the commercial world of computers, he had had to adjust himself to slow-down, to pace himself with the children he taught. Some had the knack, others didn't, and he had to ease the latter through their frustration.

'Okay, back to RETURN and go through each stage slowly this time, step by step. You can't go wrong if you think about each move.'

Her frown told him she wasn't convinced. Neither was he.

He left Jeanette biting her lower lip and pressing each key with exaggerated deliberation as though it was a battle of wills between girl and machine.

'Hey, Kelly, that's good.'

The fourteen-year-old glanced at him and beamed, her eyes touching his just a little too deeply. He peered at the screen, impressed.

'Is that your own spreadsheet?' he asked.

She nodded, her gaze now back on the visual display.

'Looks like you won't get through the year on those expenses.'

'I will when I send the printout home. Dad'll pay up when he sees the evidence.'

Childes laughed: Kelly had soon discovered the potential of microelectronics. There were seven such machines on benches around the classroom, itself an annexe to the science department, and it seemed all were in constant demand even when he was not there to supervise. He had been fortunate when he had come—*fled*—to the island, for the colleges there, so many of them private concerns, were keen to embrace the computer age, well aware that fee-paying parents regarded such knowledge as an essential part of their children's education. Until his arrival, Childes had been employed on a freelance basis by a company specialising in aiding commercial enterprises, both large and small, to set up computer systems tailored to their particular needs, advising on layout and suitable software, devising appropriate programs, often installing the machinery itself and running crash courses on their functions. One of his usual tasks was to smooth out kinks in the system, to solve problems that invariably arose in initial operation, and his flair—*intuition,* some called it—for cutting through the intricacies of any system to find a specific fault was uncanny. He had been highly skilled, highly paid, and highly respected by his colleagues; yet his departure had come as a relief to many of them.

Kelly was smiling at him. 'I need a new program to work on,' she said.

Childes checked his watch. 'Bit late to start one now. I'll set you something more difficult next time.'

'I could stay.'

One of the other girls giggled and, despite himself, Childes felt a sudden, ridiculous flush. Fourteen years old, for Chrissake!

'Maybe you could. Not me, though. Just tidy your

bench until the bell goes. Better still, run through Jeanette's program with her—she seems to be having difficulties.'

A mild irritation flickered in her eyes, but the smile did not change. 'Yes, sir.' A little too brisk.

She sidled rather than walked over to Jeanette's monitor and he mentally shook his head at her poise, her body movement too knowing for her years. Even her close-cropped sandy hair and pert nose failed to assert her true age, and eagerly budding breasts easily defeated any youthful image presented by the school uniform of blue skirt, plain white shirt and striped tie. By comparison, Jeanette appeared every inch the young schoolgirl, with womanhood not yet even peeking over the horizon. It seemed aptitude was not confined just to learning.

He shifted along the benches, leaning forward here and there to give instructions to the other girls, some of whom were sharing machines, soon enthused by their enthusiasm, helping them spot their own 'bugs', showing them the correct procedures. The bell surprised him even though he knew it was imminent.

He straightened, noticing Kelly and Jeanette were not enjoying each other's company. 'Switch off your machines,' he told the class. 'Let's see, when do I take you again . . . ?'

'Thursday,' they replied in unison.

'All right, I think we'll cover the various types of computers then, and future developments. Hope you'll have some good questions for me.'

Someone groaned.

'Problem?'

'When do we get on to graphics, sir?' the girl asked. Her plump, almost cherubic, face was puckered with disappointment.

'Soonish, Isobel. When you're ready. Off you go and don't leave anything behind; I'm locking up when I leave.'

The concerted break for the door was not as orderly

as the principal of La Roche Ladies College would have wished for, but Childes considered himself neither teacher nor disciplinarian, merely a computer consultant to this school and to two others on the island. So long as the kids did not get out of hand and appeared to absorb much of what he showed them, he liked to keep a relaxed atmosphere in the classroom; he didn't want them wary of the machines and an informal atmosphere helped in that respect. In fact, he found the pupils in all three schools remarkably well-behaved, even those in the boys college.

His eyes itched, irritated by the soft contact lenses he wore. He considered changing them for his glasses lying ready for emergencies at the bottom of his briefcase, but decided it was too much trouble. The irritation would pass.

'Knock, knock.'

He looked around to see Amy standing in the open doorway.

'Is sir coming out to play?' she asked.

'You asking me to?'

'Who am I to be proud?' Amy strolled into the classroom, her hair tied back into a tight bun in an attempt to render her schoolmarmish. To Childes, it only heightened her sensuality, as did her light-green, high-buttoned dress, for he knew beyond the disguise. 'Your eyes look sore,' she remarked, quickly looking back at the open doorway, then pecking his cheek when she saw it was clear.

He resisted the urge to pull her tight. 'How was your day?'

'Don't ask. I took drama.' She shuddered. 'D'you know what play they want to put on for end-of-term?'

He dropped papers into his briefcase and snapped it shut. 'Tell me.'

'Dracula. Can you imagine Miss Piprelly allowing it? I'm frightened even to put forward the suggestion.'

He chuckled. 'Sounds like a good idea. Beats the hell out of Nicholas Nickleby again.'

'Fine, I'll tell her Dracula has your support.'

'I'm just an outsider, not a full member of staff. My opinion doesn't count.'

'You think mine does? Our headmistress may not be the Ayatollah in person, but I'm certain there's a family connection somewhere.'

He shook his head, smiling. 'She's not so bad. A little over-anxious about the school's image, maybe, but it's understandable. For such a small island, you're kind of heavy on private schools.'

'That comes with being a tax haven. You're right, though: competition is fierce, and the college's governing body never lets us forget it. I do have some sympathy for her, even though . . .'

They were suddenly aware of a figure in the doorway.

'Did you forget something, Jeanette?' Childes asked, wondering how long she had been standing there.

The girl looked shyly at him. 'Sorry, sir. I think I left my fountain pen on the bench.'

'All right, go ahead and look.'

Head bowed, Jeanette walked into the room with short, quick steps. A sallow-complexioned girl with dark eyes, who one day might be pretty, Jeanette was petite for her age; her hair was straggly long, not yet teased into any semblance of style. The jacket of her blue uniform was one size too large, shrinking her body within even more, and there was a timidity about her that Childes found disarming and sometimes faintly exasperating.

She searched around the computer she had been using, Amy watching with a trace of a smile, while Childes set about unplugging the machines from the mains. Jeanette appeared to be having no luck and finally stared forlornly at the computer as though it had mysteriously swallowed up the missing article.

'No joy?' Childes asked, approaching her section of the bench and stooping to reach the plug beneath.

'No, sir.'

'Ah, I'm not surprised. It's on the floor here.' Kneeling, he offered up the wayward pen.

Solemnly, and avoiding his eyes, Jeanette took it from him. 'Thank you,' she said, and Childes was surprised to see her blush. She hurried from the room.

He pulled the plug and stood. 'What are you smiling about?' he asked Amy.

'The poor girl's got a crush on you.'

'Jeanette? She's just a kid.'

'In a girls-only school, many of them fulltime boarders, any halfway decent-looking male is bound to receive some attention. You haven't noticed?'

He shrugged. 'Maybe one or two have given me some funny looks, but I—what d'you mean *halfway* decent-looking?'

Smiling, Amy grabbed his arm and led him towards the door. 'Come on, school's out and I could use some relaxation. A short drive and a long gin and tonic with lots of ice before I go home for dinner.'

'More guests?'

'No, just family for a change. Which reminds me: you're invited to dinner this weekend.'

He raised his eyebrows. 'Daddy had a change of heart?'

'Uh-uh, he still despises you. Let's call it Mother's influence.'

'That's pretty heartwarming.'

She looked up at him and pulled a face, squeezing his arm before releasing it as they went out into the corridor. On the stairway to the lower floor she was aware of surreptitious appraisal by several pupils, a few nudged elbows here and there. She and Jon were strictly formal with each other in the presence of others on school grounds, but a shared car was enough to set tongues wagging.

They reached the large glass entrance doors of the building, a comparatively new extension housing the science laboratories, music and language rooms, and separated from the main college by a circular driveway with a lawned centre. In the middle, a statue of La Roche's founder stared stoically at the principal white building as if counting every head that entered its portals. Girls hurried across the open space, either towards the carpark at the rear of the college where parents waited, or to dormitories and rest-rooms in the south wing, their chatter unleashed after such long restraint. The salt tang of sea air breezing over the clifftops was a welcome relief from the shared atmosphere of the classroom and Childes inhaled deeply as he and Amy descended the short flight of concrete steps leading from the annexe.

'Mr Childes! Can you spare a moment?'

They both groaned inwardly when they saw the headmistress waving at them from across the driveway.

'I'll catch you up,' he murmured to Amy, acknowledging Miss Piprelly with a barely-raised hand.

'I'll wait by the tennis courts. Remember, you're bigger than her.'

'Oh yeah, who says?'

They parted, Childes taking a direct path over the round lawn towards the waiting headmistress, her frown informing him that he really should have walked around. Childes could only describe Miss Piprelly as a literally 'straight' woman: she stood *erect,* rarely relaxed, and her features were peculiarly angular, softening curves hardly in evidence. Even her short, greying hair was rigidly swept back in perfect parallel to the ground, and her lips had a thinness to them that wasn't exactly mean, but looked as if all humour had been ironed from them long ago. The square frames of her spectacles were in resolute harmony with her physical linearity. Even her breasts refused to rebel against the general pattern and Childes had sometimes wondered if they were battened down by artificial means. In darker moments, the thought crossed his mind that there were none.

It hadn't taken long, in fact, to find that Estelle Piprelly, MA (Cantab), MEd, ABPsS, was not as severe as the caricature suggested, although she had her moments.

'What can I do for you, Miss Piprelly?' he asked, standing beside her on the entrance step.

"I know it may seem premature to you, Mr. Childes, but I'm trying to organise next term's curriculum. I'm afraid it's necessary for parents of prospective pupils, and our governing body insists that it's finalised well before the summer break. Now, I wondered if you could spare us more of your time in the autumn term. It appears that computer studies—mistakenly, to my way of thinking—have become something of a priority nowadays.'

'That could be a little awkward. You know I have the other colleges, Kingsley and de Montfort.'

'Yes, but I also know you still have a certain amount of free time available. Surely you could fit in just a few more hours a week for us?'

How did you explain to someone like Miss Piprelly, who lived and breathed her chosen profession, that the work ethic was not high on his priorities? Not any more. Things had changed within him. Life had changed.

'An extra afternoon, Mr Childes. Could we say Tuesdays?' Her stern gaze defied refusal.

'Let me give it some thought,' he replied, and sensed her inner bristling.

'Very well, but I really must have the first draft curriculum completed by the end of the week.'

'I'll let you know on Thursday.' He tried a smile, but was annoyed at the apology in his own voice.

Her short sigh was one of exasperation and sounded like a huff. 'On Thursday then.'

He was dismissed. No more words, no 'Good day'. He just wasn't there any more. Miss Piprelly was calling to a group of girls who had made the mistake of following his route across the hallowed lawn. He turned away, feeling somehow that he was sloping off, and had to make an effort to put some briskness into his stride.

Estelle Piprelly, having reproved the errant girls (a

task that for her needed very few words and a barely-raised voice), returned her attention to the retreating figure of the peripatetic teacher. He walked with shoulders slightly hunched forward, studying the ground before him as if planning each footfall, a youngish man who sometimes seemed unusually wearied. No, wearied was the wrong word. There was sometimes a shadow behind his eyes that was haunted, an occasional glimpse of some latent anxiety.

Her brow furrowed—more parallel lines—and her fingers plucked unconsciously at a loose thread on her sleeve.

Childes disturbed her and she could not reason why. His work was excellent, meticulous, and he appeared to be popular with the pupils, if not a trace *too* popular with some. His specialist knowledge was a useful addition to the prospectus and without doubt he relieved a partial burden from her overloaded science teachers. Yet, although she had requested extra lessons of him because of the governing body's dictum, something in his presence made her uneasy.

A long, *long* time ago, when she herself had been no more than a child and the German forces had occupied the island as a spearhead for their attack on the mainland of England, she had felt a pervading air of destruction around her. Not uncommon in those tragic warring times, but years later she realised that she possessed a higher degree of awareness than most. Nothing dramatic, nothing mediumistic or clairvoyant, just an acute sensing. It had become subdued yet never relinquished with the passing of time, the pragmatism of her chosen career, but in those early days she had seen death in the faces of many of those German soldiers, an unnatural foreboding in their countenance, in their mood.

In a more confusing way, she sensed it in Childes. Although he was now gone from view, Miss Piprelly shivered.

As HE returned from the hotel bar with the drinks, weaving his way round the garden tables and chairs, Amy was releasing her hair at the back so that it fell into a ponytail, an old style transformed through her into something chic. There was a subtle elegance to Amy that was inborn rather than studied and, not for the first time, Childes thought she looked anything *but* a schoolteacher—at least not the type who had ever taught him.

Her skin appeared almost golden in the shadow of the table's canopy, her pale green eyes and lighter wisps of hair curling over her ears heightening the effect. As usual, she wore the minimum of make-up, a proclivity that often made her resemble some of the girls she instructed, her small breasts, just delicate swellings, hardly spoiling the illusion. Yet at twenty-three, eleven years younger than himself, she possessed a quiet maturity that he was in just a little wonder of; it was not always evident, for there was also a tantalising innocence about her that enhanced the pubescent impression even more. The combination was often confusing, for she was unaware of her own qualities and the moods could quickly change.

Amy's slender and mockingly desperate fingers reached for the glass as he approached and early-evening sunlight struck her hand, making it glow a lighter gold.

'If only Miss Piprelly knew she had a lush on her staff,' he remarked, passing the gin and tonic to her.

She allowed the glass to tremble in her grasp as she brought it to her lips. 'If only Pip knew half her staff were inebriates. And she's the cause.'

Childes sat opposite so that he could watch her, sacrificing closeness for the pleasure of eye contact. 'Our headmistress wants me to put in more time at the school,' he said, and Amy's sudden smile warmed him.

'Jon, that would be lovely.'

'I'm not so sure. I mean, yes, great to see more of you, but when I came here I was opting out of the rat race, remember?'

'It's hardly that. This is a different civilisation to the one you were used to.'

'Yeah, another planet. But I've got used to the easy pace, afternoons when I can go walking, or diving, or just plain snoozing on the beach. At last I've found time to think.'

'Sometimes you do too much thinking.'

The mood change.

He looked away. 'I said I'd let her know.'

Humour came back to Amy's voice. 'Coward.'

Childes shook his head. 'She makes me feel like a ten-year-old.'

'Her bark isn't as bad as her bite. I'd do as she asks.'

'Some help you are.'

She placed her glass between them. 'I'd like to think I am. I know you spend too much time on your own and perhaps a bigger commitment to the college might be what you need.'

'You know how I feel about commitments.'

A look passed between them.

'You have one to your daughter.'

He sipped his beer.

'Let's lighten up,' he said, after a while. 'It's been a long day.'

Amy smiled, but her eyes were still troubled. She reached for his hand and stroked his fingers, masking more serious thoughts with bright banter. 'I think Pip would consider it quite a coup to have you on the staff full-time.'

'She only wants me for an extra afternoon.'

'Two and a half days of your time now, tomorrow your soul.'

'You were supposed to be encouraging me.'

Her expression was mischievous. 'Just letting you know it's useless to resist. Others have tried,' she added, her voice deepening ominously, making him grin.

'Strangely enough, she has been giving me some peculiar looks lately.'

'Working her voodoo.'

He relaxed back in the chair. A few more people were wandering out into the hotel's beer garden, drinks in hand, taking advantage of a welcome relief from the preceding weeks of cold drizzle. A huge, furry bee hovered over nearby azaleas, its drone giving notice of the warmer months to come. Until recently, he had felt close to finding his peace on the island. The easy-going lifestyle, the pleasant nature of the island itself, Amy—beautiful Amy—, his own self-imposed occasional solitude, had brought a balance to his existence, a steadiness far removed from the frenetic pace of the constantly changing microchip world, a career in and around the madding city, a wife who had once loved him, but who had later been in fear of . . . of what? Something neither of them understood.

Psychic power. An inconsistent curse.

'Who's serious now?'

He stared blankly at Amy, her question breaking into his thoughts.

'You had that faraway look, the kind I should be

getting used to by now,' she said. 'You weren't just day-dreaming.'

'No, just thinking back.'

'It's in the past and best kept that way, Jon.'

He nodded, unable to explain it to himself. Unsure of the creeping uneasiness he had felt since the nightmare two weeks ago.

She rested her folded arms on the table. 'Hey, you haven't given me an answer yet.' She frowned at his puzzled expression. 'My dinner invitation: you haven't said you'll come.'

'Do I have a choice?' For the moment the bad thoughts had retreated, vanquished by Amy's wickedly innocent smile.

'Of course. You can either accept or be deported. Daddy hates bad manners.'

'And we all know his influence in the States' affairs.'

'Precisely.'

'Then I'll come.'

'How sensible.'

'How much coaxing did your mother have to do?'

'Not much. She relied on threats.'

'Hard to imagine your father being afraid of anybody.'

'You don't know Mother. She may seem all sweetness and light on the surface, but there's a hidden streak of steel underneath it all that frightens even me sometimes.'

'At least it's nice to know *she* likes me.'

'Oh, I wouldn't go that far. Let's just say she's not totally against you.'

He laughed quietly. 'I'm really looking forward to the evening.'

'You know, I think she's quite intrigued by you. A darkly attractive man with a shady past, and all that.'

For a moment, Childes looked down into his beer. 'Is that how she sees my past?' he asked.

'She thinks you're mysterious and she likes that.'

'And dear Daddy?'

'You're not good enough for his daughter, that's all.'

'You sure?'

'No, but it's not important. He respects my feelings, though, and I haven't disguised how I feel about you. Pig-headed as he is sometimes, he would never hurt me by going against you.'

Childes wished he could be sure. The financier's hostility on the few occasions they had met was barely masked. Perhaps he didn't like divorcés; or perhaps he distrusted anyone who did not conform to his own standards, his perception of 'normality'.

In danger of becoming too serious again, Childes asked with a grin, 'Do I need a dinner suit?'

'Well, one or two of his business associates have been invited—and that includes a member of La Roche's governing body and his wife, incidentally—so nothing too informal. A tie would be nice.'

'And I thought the *soirée* was for my benefit.'

'Your being there is for *my* benefit.' She looked intently at him. 'It may seem a trivial thing, but it means a lot to have you with me. I don't know why there's this antagonism between you and my father, Jon, but it's unnecessary and destructive.'

'There's no animosity from me, Amy.'

'I know that. And I'm not asking you to bend his way. I just want him to see us together at a normal gathering, to let him see how well we go together.'

He could not help chuckling and she gave him a reproving look. 'I know what you're thinking and I didn't mean that. I'm still his little girl, remember.'

'He'd never understand how much of a woman you are.'

'He doesn't have to. I'm sure he doesn't imagine I'm still as pure as driven snow, though.'

'I wouldn't be too sure. Such things are hard enough for any doting father to face.' The intimacy of their conversation charged his body with a flush of pleasure and he felt good with her, warm in her presence. It was the same for Amy, for her smile was different, not secretive but knowing, and her pale green eyes were lit with an inner sharing. She looked away and gently whirled the melting ice in her glass, watching the clear, rounded cubes as if they held some meaning. Conversations from other tables drifted in the air, occasionally punctuated by soft laughter. An aircraft banked around the western tip of the island, already over the sea just seconds after take-off from the tiny airport, its wings catching the reddening sun. A slight evening breeze stirred a lock of hair against Amy's cheek.

'I should be going,' she said after a while.

Both were aware of what they really wanted.

Childes said, 'I'll take you back to La Roche for your car.'

They finished their drinks and stood together. As they walked through the garden towards the white gate leading to the carpark, she slipped her hand into his. He squeezed her fingers and she returned the pressure.

Inside the car, Amy leaned across and kissed his lips, and his desire was tempered and yet inflamed by her tenderness. The sensation for them was as paradoxical as the kiss: both weakening and strengthening at the same time. When they parted, breathless, wanting, his fingertips gently touched a trail along her cheek, brushing her lips and becoming moist from them. He realised that recently their relationship had unexpectedly, and bewilderingly, reached a new peak. It had been slow in developing, gradual in its emergence, each always slightly wary of the other, he afraid to give too much, she cautious of him as a stranger, unlike any other man she had known. It now seemed that they had just passed a point from which there could only be a lingeringly painful return, and both recognised the inexorable yet purely sensory truth of it.

He turned away, unprepared for this new, plunging shift of emotions, unsure of why, *how,* it had happened so swiftly. Turning on the ignition and engaging gear, Childes drove into the lane leading away from the hotel.

Childes pushed open the front door of the cottage and briefly stood in the small hallway, collecting his thoughts, catching his breath. He closed the door.

Amy's presence was still with him, floating intangibly in the air, and again he wondered at the startling new pace of their feelings for one another. He had held his emotions in check for so long, enjoying her company, taking pleasure in all her aspects, her maturity, her innocence, not least her physical beauty, aware that their relationship was more than friendship, but always in control, unwilling to let go, to succumb to anything deeper. Wounds from his broken marriage were not yet entirely healed, a bitterness still lingered.

He could not help but smile wryly. He felt as if he had been zapped by some invisible force.

The ringing phone made him start. Childes moved away from the door and picked up the receiver.

'Jon?' She sounded breathless.

'Yes, Amy.'

'What happened?'

He paused before answering. 'You too?'

'I feel wonderful and terrible at the same time. It's like an exciting ache.'

He laughed at her description, realising its aptness. 'I should say the feeling will pass, but I don't want it to.'

'It's scary. And I love it.'

He could sense her uncertainty and her voice was quiet when she added: 'I don't want to be hurt.'

Closing his eyes and leaning back against the wall, Childes struggled with his own emotions. 'Let's give each other time to think.'

'I don't want to.'

'It might be better for us both.'

'Why? Is there anything more to know about each other? I mean, anything important? We've talked, you've told me about yourself, your past, how you feel: is there any more that I should know?'

'No, no dark secrets, Amy. You know all that's happened to me. More, much more, than anyone else.'

'Then why are you afraid of what's happening to us?'

'I thought *you* were.'

'Not in that way. I'm only scared of being so vulnerable.'

'That's the answer don't you see?'

'You think I would do anything to hurt you?'

'Things can happen that we have no control over.'

'I thought they already had.'

'I didn't mean that. Events can somehow interfere, can change feelings. It's happened to me before.'

'You told me your marriage was shaky before those dreadful things happened, that they just widened the gulf between you and Fran. Don't run away, Jon, not like . . .'

She stopped and Childes finished for her. 'Not like before.'

'I'm sorry, I didn't mean it that way. I know circumstances had become intolerable.' Amy sighed miserably. 'Oh, Jon, why has this conversation turned out like this? I was so happy, I needed to talk to you. I *missed* you.'

His tenseness loosened. Yet a gnawing, subconscious disquiet remained. How could he explain his own almost subliminal unrest? 'Amy, I'm sorry too. I'm being stupid. I suppose I'm still masochistically licking ancient wounds.'

'Bad past experiences can sometimes distort the new.'

'Very profound.'

She was relieved the humour was back in his voice, yet could not help but feel a little deflated. 'I'll try to keep a tighter grip on myself,' she said.

'Hey, c'mon. Don't mind an old man's self-pity. So you missed me? I only left you ten minutes ago.'

'I got home from school and felt so . . . so, I don't know—flushed. Happy. Mixed-up. Sick. I wanted you here.'

'Sounds like a bad case.'

'It is, God help me.'

'I've got it too.'

'But you—'

'I told you: pay no attention. I get moody sometimes.'

'Don't I know it. Can I buy you lunch tomorrow?'

'Creep.'

'I don't care.' The warmth was quickly returning.

'Tell you what,' he said. 'If you can stand it, I'll cook you lunch here.'

'We'll only have an hour.'

'I'll prepare it tonight. Nothing fancy; freezer stuff.'

'I love freezer stuff.'

'I love you.' He'd finally said the words.

'Jon . . .'

'I'll see you in school, Amy.'

Her voice was hushed. 'Yes.'

He said goodbye and barely heard her response. The line clicked dead. Cradling the receiver, his hand still resting on the smooth plastic, Childes stared thoughtfully at the wall. He hadn't meant to let the words slip out, hadn't wanted to breach the final barrier with an admission he knew they both felt. Why did it matter when it was the truth? Just what was he afraid of? It wasn't hard to reason.

The bizarre vision followed by the nightmare a fortnight before had left him with a dispiriting and familiar apprehension, a rekindling of the dread that had once nearly broken him. It had ruined his life with Fran and Gabby; he didn't want it to hurt Amy. He prayed that he was wrong, that it wasn't happening all over again, that his imagination was running loose.

Childes rubbed a hand over his eyes, aware of how sore they had become. Drawing in a deep breath, then releasing the air as if ridding himself of festering notions, he went into the tiny, ground-floor bathroom and opened the medicine cabinet. After taking out a small plastic bottle and his lens case, he closed the cabinet door to be confronted by his own image, reflected in the mirror. His eyes were bloodshot and he thought there was an unnatural pallor to his skin.

Imagination again, he told himself. He was foolishly allowing the morbid introspection to build, to become something other than it was. Which was a throwback, a long-delayed reaction to something past, and that was all. When he had nearly drowned it was probably because he had stayed too long beneath the water, not noticing his lungs had used up precious air, lack of oxygen bringing on the confused images. The nightmare later was ... was just a nightmare, with no particular significance. He was attributing too much to an unpleasant but unimportant experience, and perhaps it was understandable with past memories to goad his thoughts. Forget it. Things had changed, his life was different.

Peering close to the mirror, Childes gently squeezed the soft lens from his right eye, cleansed it in the palm of his hand with the fluid, and dropped it into its liquid-filled container. He repeated the procedure with the left lens.

Outside in the hallway, he dipped into his briefease and withdrew his spectacles, his eyes already feeling relief from the irritation. He was about to go through into the kitchen to discover what he could come up with for lunch the following day when a soft thud from upstairs stopped him. He held his breath and gazed up the narrow stairway, seeing only as far as the bend. He waited, going through that peculiar middle-of-the-night sensation of not wanting to hear again a mysterious, intrusive noise, yet seeking confirmation that one had been heard. There was no further sound.

Childes mounted the creaky, wooden stairs, unreasonably nervous. He rounded the bend and saw that his bedroom door was open. Nothing wrong in that: he had left it open that morning—he always did. Climbing the rest of the stairway, he walked the few feet along the landing and pushed the bedroom door open wider.

The room was empty and he admonished himself for behaving like a timorous maiden-aunt. Two windows faced each other across the room and something small and delicate was clinging to the outside of one. He went over, feeling the bare, wooden floorboards giving slightly beneath his weight, and clucked his tongue when he saw the shivering flotsam was no more than a feather stuck to the glass, either a gull's or a pigeon's, he couldn't be sure which. It had happened before: the birds saw sky in the window on the other side of the room and tried to fly through, striking the windowpane on that side but rarely doing more damage than giving themselves a shock and probably a severe headache, leaving a plume or two on the glass. Even as he watched, the breeze caught the feather and whisked it away.

Childes was about to turn around when he caught sight of the distant school. His heart stopped momentarily and his hands gripped the sill when he saw the fiery glow. His relief was instant when he quickly realised the white building was merely reflecting the setting sun's rubescent rays.

But the image remained in his mind, and when he sat down on the bed his hands were trembling.

It watched from beneath a tree, the cheerfully sunny day giving the lie to the misery witnessed in the cemetery.

The mourners were grouped around the open grave, dark clothes struck grey by the sunlight. Stained white crosses, slabs, and smiling cracked angels were dispassionate observers in the field of sunken bones. The mushy cadence of traffic could be heard in the distance; somewhere a radio was snapped off, the graveyard worker realising a ceremony was in progress. The priest's voice carried as a muffled intonation to the low knoll where the figure waited in the yew's shadow.

When the tiny coffin was lowered, a woman staggered forward as if to forbid the final violation of her dead child. A man at her side held the woman firm, supporting her weight as she sagged. Others in the group bowed their heads or looked away, the mother's agony as unbearable as the untimely death itself. Hands were raised to faces, tissues dampened against cheeks. The features of the men were frozen, pale plastic moulds.

It watched from the hiding place and smiled secretly.

The little casket disappeared from view, swallowed by the dank soil, green-edged lips eagerly wide. The father threw something in after the coffin, a bright-coloured object—a toy, a doll, something that had once been precious to the child—before earth was scattered into the grave.

Reluctantly, yet with private relief, the bereaved group began to drift away. The mother had to be gently led, supported between two others, her head constantly turning as if the dead infant were calling her back, pleading with her not to leave it there, lonely and cold and corrupting. The grief overwhelmed and the mother had to be half-carried to the waiting funeral cars.

The figure beneath the tree stayed while the grave was filled.

To return again later that night.

'THANK YOU, Helen, I think you can clear away now.'
Vivienne Sebire noted with manifest satisfaction that
the meal she had so carefully and lovingly prepared
earlier that afternoon, salmon mousse followed by ap-
ple and cherry duckling, served with *mangetouts* and
broccoli, had been devoured with relish and much
voiced praise. She observed, however, that Jonathan
Childes had not eaten as heartily as the rest of their
guests.

Grace Duxbury, sitting close to the host, Paul Sebire,
who was at the head of the table, trilled, 'Marvellous,
Vivienne. Now I want to know the secret of that
mousse before I leave this house tonight.'

'Yes,' agreed her husband. 'Excellent first course.
Why is it, Grace, that yours rarely venture beyond
avocado with prawns unless we've got the caterers in?'

A remark that would be paid for later if she knew
Grace, thought Vivienne, smiling at them both. 'Ah,
the secret's in just how much anchovy essence you
add. A little more than is recommended, but not too
much.'

'Delicious,' reaffirmed George Duxbury.

Helen, a short, stoutish woman with a cheerful smile
and eyebrows that tended to converge to a point above
her nose, and who was the Sebires' housekeeper-cum-
maid, began collecting dishes while her mistress preened

herself on more praise. Amy, sitting opposite and slightly to the right of Childes, rose from her seat. 'I'll give you a hand,' she said to Helen, making eye-contact with Childes, a covert smile passing between them.

'What I'd like to know, Paul, is how a reprobate like you manages to have a beautiful and brilliant cook for a wife and an absolute charmer for a daughter?' The good-humoured jibe was delivered by Victor Platnauer, a *conseiller* of the island and a member of La Roche Ladies College's governing board. His wife, Tilly, seated next to Childes, tutted reproachfully, although allowing herself to join in the chuckles of her fellow-guests.

'Quite simple, Victor,' Sebire riposted in his usual crisp manner. 'It was my darling wife's culinary expertise that coaxed me to marry her and my genes that produced our beautiful Aimée.' He always insisted on calling his daughter by her correct name.

'No, no,' Platnauer insisted. 'Amy inherits her looks from her mother, not her father. Isn't that correct, Mr Childes—er, Jonathan?'

'She has both her parents' finer points,' Childes managed to say diplomatically, dabbing his lips with a napkin.

Score one, thought Amy, halfway through the door to the kitchen, as someone clapped and proclaimed, 'Bravo!' So far, so good. She had observed her father discreetly studying Jon throughout the evening, knowing so well that calculating appraisal usually reserved for prospective clients, colleagues or rivals. Nevertheless, he had played the perfect host, courteous and suitably inquisitive of his guest, allowing Jon as much attention as any of the others, including a business associate from Marseilles. Amy suspected that Edouard Vigiers had been invited not just because he happened to be on the island that week to discuss certain financial arrangements, but because he was young, successful, yet still thrusting, and *very* eligible. An ideal

son-in-law in Paul Sebire's eyes. She was beginning to
wonder if her father's sole motive in inviting Jon was
so that she, Amy, would be presented with a direct
comparison between the two, Edouard and Jon, the
contrast undeniable.

She had to admit that the Frenchman was attractive
as well as bright and amusing, but her father was
wrong, as usual, in judging by such obvious and superficial standards. She knew Paul Sebire to be a kind
man with a generous heart, despite his cutting ruthlessness in business affairs and thorniness over certain
matters, and she loved him as much as any daughter
could love a father; unfortunately, his self-concealed
possessiveness dictated that if he were to surrender his
daughter to another, then it would be someone in his
own image, of his own kind, if not a younger version of
himself. It was a transparently clumsy ploy, although
her father probably deemed it subtle, as usual under-
estimating others, particularly his only child.

Amy thought dreamily of her lunch with Jon earlier
that week, their first confrontation alone in his cottage
after having realised just how far their relationship
had journeyed, how much more deeply they cared for
each other than either had understood before. There
had been little time for intimacies that day, but touching, holding, caressing had been filled with a new
potency, a new tenderness.

'I'd like those plates, Miss Amy, when you've finished listening at the door.' Helen's amused voice had
broken into the reverie. She stood, one hand on the
sink, the other clenched on her hip.

'Oh.' Amy smiled sheepishly. She carried the dishes
over to the draining board. 'I wasn't eavesdropping,
Helen, only daydreaming. Just lost somewhere.'

Victor Platnauer was leaning forward over the table,
looking directly at Childes. In his early sixties, Platnauer
was still a well-proportioned man, with a hard ruddi-
ness to his features and large hands that was common
to many of the native islanders; there was a gravelly

tone to his voice, a bluffness in his manner. By contrast, his wife Tilly was soft-spoken, almost demure, similar in appearance and demeanour to Vivienne Sebire.

'I'm pleased to hear you're to give La Roche a little more of your time,' Platnauer said.

'Only an extra afternoon,' Childes replied. 'I agreed earlier this week.'

'Yes, so Miss Piprelly informed me. Well, that's good news, but perhaps we can persuade you to spend even more time at the college. I'm aware that you also teach at Kingsley and de Montfort, but it's important to us that we extend this particular area of our curriculum. It isn't only a parental demand—I'm told the pupils have shown great keenness for computer sciences.'

'That's not true of all of them, unfortunately,' said Childes. 'The children, I mean. I think we're fooling ourselves if we imagine every kid has a natural aptitude for electronic calculation and compilation.'

Tilly Platnauer looked surprised. 'I thought we were well into the Star Wars era, with every boy and girl a microchip genius compared to their elders.'

Childes smiled. 'We're just at the beginning. And electronic games are not quite the same as the practical application of computers, although I'll admit they're a start. You see, the computer process is totally logical, but not every child has total logic.'

'Neither do many of us grown-ups,' Victor Platnauer commented drily.

'It's a double-edged sword, in a way,' Childes went on. 'The leisure industry has encouraged the consumer to think that computers are fun, and that's okay, it creates interest; it's when the public, or the kids in our case, discover hard work is involved before enjoyment through understanding begins, that the big turn-off comes.'

'Surely then, the answer is to begin the teaching at the earliest age, so it will become an everyday part of the child's life.' It was Edouard Vigiers who had spoken, his accent softening rather than distorting his words.

'Yep, you're right. But you're talking of an ideal situation where the computer is a normal household item, a regular piece of furniture like the TV or stereo unit. We're a long way off from that situation.'

'All the more reason for schools to introduce our children to the technology while their minds are still young and pliable, wouldn't you say?' asked Platnauer.

'Ideally, yes,' agreed Childes. 'But you have to understand it isn't a science that's within everybody's grasp. The unfortunate side is that microtechnology *will* become a way of life within the next couple of decades and a hell of a lot of companies and individuals are going to feel left behind.'

'Then we must ensure that the children of this island don't fall by the wayside,' stated Paul Sebire to Platnauer's nodded approval.

Childes hid his exasperation that his point had been missed, or at least gone unheeded: technical knowledge could be spoon- or force-fed, but it was not so easily digested if the inclination was not there.

Vigiers changed the conversation's direction. 'Do you also teach science at La Roche and these other schools, Jon?'

Sebire unexpectedly answered for him. 'Not at all. Mr Childes is a computer specialist, Edouard, something of a technical wizard, I gather.'

Childes looked sharply at Sebire and wondered how he had 'gathered'. Amy?

'Ah,' said Vigiers. 'Then I am curious to know what made you turn to the teaching of children. Isn't this a, let me see, er . . . a slow down? Is that correct? I am sorry if my question appears impertinent, but an abrupt change of lifestyle—*un brusque changement de vie* we would say—is always interesting, do you not agree?' He smiled charmingly and Childes was suddenly wary.

'Sometimes you discover running on a constant treadmill isn't all it's cracked up to be,' he replied.

Vivienne Sebire enjoyed the response and added, 'Well who could resist the peacefulness of the island, despite how much you money-men try to disrupt it?' She looked meaningfully at her husband.

The door leading to the kitchen opened and Amy and Helen came through carrying the dessert on silver trays.

'More delights!' enthused George Duxbury. 'What are you tempting us with now, Vivienne?'

'There's a choice,' she told them as the sweets were placed in the centre of the table. 'The apricot and chocolate dessert is mine and the raspberry soufflé omelet is a speciality of Amy's. You can, of course, have both if you've room.'

'I'll make room,' Duxbury assured her.

'My nutritionist would throw a fit if she could see me now.' His wife was already offering up her plate to the amusement of all. 'Apricot and chocolate, please, but *don't* ask me if I want cream.'

Amy sat while Helen served. Vigiers, seated next to her, leaned close and spoke confidentially. 'I shall most certainly try the soufflé; it looks delicious.'

She smiled to herself. Edouard had the kind of low voice that could sell liqueurs on television. 'Oh, Mother is a far superior chef. I only dabble, I'm afraid.'

'I am sure that whatever you do, it is well. Your father tells me you also teach at La Roche.'

'Yes, French and English. I also help out with Speech and Drama.'

'So you are fluent in my language? Your name implies that you are of French descent, yes? And if I may be permitted to say, you have a certain ambience that has an affinity with the women of my country.'

'Your own Victor Hugo once wrote that these islands were fragments of France picked up by England. And as we were once part of the Duchy of Normandy, many of us have French forebears. The *patois* is still spoken by a few of our older residents here, and I'm sure you've noticed we retain many of the ancient placenames.'

Grace Duxbury had overheard their conversation. 'We've always been a prized possession, Monsieur Vigiers, for more than one nation.'

'I hope my country has never caused you distress,' he responded, humour in his eyes.

'Distress?' laughed Paul Sebire. 'You've tried to invade us more than once, and your pirates never left us alone in the old days. Even Napoleon had a crack at us in later times, but I'm afraid he got a bloody nose.'

Vigiers sipped his wine, obviously amused.

'We've always appreciated our French origins, though,' Sebire continued, 'and I'm pleased to say our associations have never been relinquished.'

'I gather you do not have the same warm feelings towards the Germans.'

'Ah, different thing entirely,' Platnauer voiced gruffly. 'Their wartime occupation is recent history and with their pill-boxes and damn coastal fortresses all over the place, it's hard to forget. Having said that, there's no real animosity between us now; in fact, many veterans of the occupying forces return as tourists nowadays.'

'It's rather strange how attractive this island has been to man from far, far back,' said Sebire, indicating his preference for the soufflé, too. 'In Neolothic times, he made his way here to bury his dead and worship the gods. Massive granite tombs still survive and the land is practically littered with megaliths and menhirs, those standing stones they paid homage to. Aimée, why don't you show Edouard around the island tomorrow? He returns to Marseilles on Monday and hasn't had a chance to take a really good look at the place since he's been here. What do you think, Edouard?'

'I should like that very much,' replied the Frenchman. 'Unfortunately Jon and I have made plans for tomorrow.' Amy smiled, but there was a coolness in the look she flashed her father.

'Nonsense,' Sebire persisted, conscious of her annoyance, but undeterred. 'You see each other all the time at the college, and most evenings, it seems nowadays. I'm sure Jonathan wouldn't mind releasing you for a few hours considering how little time our guest has left.' He looked amiably along the table at Childes, who had been engaged in conversation with Vivienne Sebire, but whose attention had been drawn at the mention of his name.

'I, uh, I guess it's up to Amy,' he said uncertainly.

'There you are,' Sebire said, smiling at his daughter. 'No problem.'

Embarrassed, Vigiers started to say, 'It really does not matter. If—'

'That's quite all right, Edouard,' Sebire cut in. 'Aimée is well-used to helping entertain my business visitors. I often wish she had chosen my profession rather than teaching; she would have been a remarkable asset to the company, I'm sure of that.'

'You know I have no interest in corporate finance,' said Amy, disguising her chagrin at having little choice but to accept her imposed role as tourist guide. Jon, why didn't you help me? 'I enjoy children, I enjoy doing something useful. I'm not criticising, but your way of making money wouldn't be fulfilling enough for me. I need to see some tangible evidence of success for my efforts, not just figures on balance sheets.'

'And you find this with your students?' asked Vigiers.

'Why, yes, with many.'

'I'm sure with most, with you as their tutor,' Sebire put forward.

'Daddy, you're being patronising,' she warned menacingly.

The two men laughed together and Grace Duxbury said, 'Pay them no mind, Amy dear. They're both obviously of that near-extinct breed who imagine that men still rule the world. Tell me, Monsieur Vigiers, have you tried many of our restaurants during your stay? Tell me how you found them compared to some of the excellent cuisines of your own country.'

While the conversation went on, Amy glanced over at Childes. She tried to convey apology for the next day in her expression and he understood, shaking his head imperceptibly. He raised his wine glass, tilting it slightly in her direction before drinking; lifting her own glass, Amy returned the toast.

Helen had returned to the kitchen and was already loading the dishwasher with plates and cutlery from the sink. She was pleased for her mistress that the dinner party appeared to be going so well. Miss Amy was lucky to have two men in attendance and Helen wondered how she could resist the smooth, cultured Frenchman, with his French ways and his French looks and his French voice . . . irresistible.

She shivered and reached over the work surface near the sink to close the window. The night had turned chilly. And it was black out there, the moon but a thin sliver. Helen pulled the window shut.

There was laughter around the dining table as Duxbury who, as well as being a commodity importer to the island, supplying local companies with office furniture, equipment and generally whatever else they needed, also arranged sales conferences for outside organisations, regaled his fellow-guests with one of his long-winded but generally funny conference-mishap stories.

Childes took a spoonful of the soufflé and made an appreciative face at Amy. She mouthed a discreet kiss in return. He had felt on edge at the beginning of the evening, unsure of Paul Sebire, aware that he would be put through some devious kind of test by him, a judgement of character and perhaps of his worth now that it was evident Amy was becoming emotionally tied. Yet the financier had been more than cordial throughout, the curtness of previous meetings gone or at least held in check. Still Childes had not relaxed, gradually becoming aware that the younger Frenchman was not just another dinner guest, but introduced by Sebire as a potential rival; the Sebire-inspired outing for Amy and Vigiers the following day had confirmed his suspicions. It was both obvious and disingenuous, but Childes had to admit he did look a little shabby against Vigiers.

On the other hand, Vivienne Sebire had been gracious and attentive, genuinely welcoming him and, like the perfect hostess, making him feel a valued guest. She was the ideal counter to her husband's general brusqueness.

He joined in the laughter as Duxbury reached the climax of his story, the importer barely giving them all time to recover before launching into another. Childes reached for his wine, and as he brought it towards him, he thought he caught a glimmering in the glass. He blinked, then peered into the light liquid. He had been mistaken: it must have been a reflection. Childes sipped and was about to place the wine glass back on the table when something seemed to stir within it. He looked again, bemused rather than concerned.

No, just wine inside, nothing else, nothing that could . . . nothing that . . .

An image. But not in the glass. In his mind.

Suppressed chuckling as Duxbury continued his yarn.

The image was unreal, unfocused, *like the nightmare,* a shimmering blur. Childes set the wine glass down, aware that his hand was shaking. A peculiar sensation had gripped the back of his neck, like a hand, a frigid hand, clasped there. He stared into the liquid.

Amy giggled, suspecting Duxbury's story was building to a somewhat risqué ending.

The image had become images. They were slowly swimming into focus. The warmth of the room had become suffocating. Childes' other hand unconsciously went to his shirt collar as if to loosen it.

Grace Duxbury, having heard her husband's story on numerous other occasions in different company, and knowing the punchline, was already twittering with embarrassment.

Childes' vision had shifted inwards; he viewed a scenario inside his mind, an event that was beyond the confines of the room, yet within himself. He seemed to be moving closer to the ethereal activity, becoming integrated with it, a participant; but still he was only watching. Soft earth was being disturbed.

Victor Platnauer's rasping chuckle, a low rumble about to erupt, was infectious, and Vivienne Sebire found herself laughing even before the story was concluded.

Blunt, stubby fingers, covered in damp soil. Scraping against wood. The effort renewed, frantic. The wood cleared of earth so that its shape was revealed. Narrow. Rectangular. Small. Childes shuddered, spilling wine.

Vigiers had noticed, was staring across the table at Childes.

The coffin lid was smashed, splinters bursting outwards under the axe blows. Jagged segments were ripped away, the hole enlarged. The tiny body was exposed, its features unclear in the dismal light. Childes' hand tightened on the glass. The room was shifting; he could barely breathe. The invisible pressure on the nape of his neck increased, squeezing like a vice.

For a moment, the hands, seen by Childes almost as his own, paused as if the defiler had sensed something, had become aware of being observed. Sensed Childes, himself. Something deep inside his mind was coldly touched. The moment passed.

Tilly Platnauer knew she should not be enjoying the tale, but Duxbury's bluff rendition was compelling. Her shoulders were already beginning to judder with mirth.

The little corpse was torn free from the silk-lined casket and now Childes could see the tiny open eyes that had no depth, no life-force. The boy was laid on the grass beside the pit, where the night breeze ruffled his hair, blowing wisps across his pale, unlined fore-head, giving an illusion of vitality. His clothes were cut free and pulled aside so that the body was naked to the night, white marble in colour and stillness.

Metal glinted in the thin moonlight. Plunging down-ward. Entering.

Slicing.

The glass shattered, wine mixed with blood spilling on the lace tablecloth. Someone screamed. Childes had risen, knocking over his chair, was standing over them, swaying, his eyes staring towards the ceiling, a glistening wetness to his lips, a light sheen moistening his skin.

His body shook, went rigid, even his hair appeared brittle. With a desolate cry he fell forward onto the table.

Gloatingly, it bit into the heart of the dead child.

AMY CLENCHED her fists and closed her eyes against the reflection of her father.

They were in her bedroom, she white-faced with eyes tear-puffed and red, sitting miserably at her dressing-table, Paul Sebire agitated, angrily pacing the room behind her. She could not clear from her mind the sight of Jon when he had been led away from the house by Platnauer, the *conseiller* helping him into his own car, refusing to allow him to drive himself home, despite his protests: Jon's face had been so taut, so stricken.

He had refused a doctor, had insisted that he was okay, that he had just suffered a blackout, that the heat of the dining room had overcome him. They knew that the night was cool, that the house was merely warm, not too hot, but hadn't argued. He would be fine as soon as he could lie down, he had told them, as soon as he could rest; he strenuously declined Amy's and Vivienne's offer of a bed for the night, saying he just needed to be on his own for a while. His distant gaze had frightened her as much as his ashen face, but it was useless to argue.

She had held him before he left, feeling his inner trembling, wishing she could soothe it away. His cut hand had been treated and bandaged, and Amy had brought it to her lips before letting him go, kissing the fingertips, careful not to hold on too tightly. Childes hadn't allowed her to go with him.

Paul Sebire stopped pacing. 'Aimée,' he said, putting a hand on her shoulder. 'I don't want you to be angry, I just want you to listen to me and to be rational.'

He stroked her hair, then let his hand fall back onto her shoulder. 'I'd like you to end this relationship with Childes.' He waited for the outburst, which never came. Amy was merely staring coldly at his reflection in the mirror and, in a way, that was more unsettling. He went on, his tone cautious: 'I believe the man is unstable. At first I thought tonight he was suffering from an epileptic fit of some kind, but soon realised the symptoms were not the same. Aimée, I think the man is heading for a mental breakdown.'

'He's not unstable,' Amy said calmly. 'He's not neurotic and he's not heading for a breakdown. You don't know him, Daddy, you don't know what he's been through.'

'But I do, Aimée. I just wonder if you're fully aware of his background.'

'What do you mean?' She had turned towards Sebire, his hand sliding from her shoulder with the movement.

'Something rang a bell for me a long time ago when you first started mentioning his name; I couldn't put my finger on it, although I was bothered for quite some time. More recently, when I began to suspect you were becoming seriously involved with him, I did some checking.' He raised a defensive hand. 'Now don't look at me like that, Aimée. You're my only daughter, and I care more about you than anything in the world, so do you really think I wouldn't pursue a troublesome matter which concerned you?'

'Wouldn't it have been possible to ask me about Jon?'

'Ask you what? I had a feeling, that was all, a nagging doubt. And I couldn't be sure of how much you yourself knew about Childes.'

'And what did you discover?' she asked caustically.

'Well, I knew roughly when he had come over from the mainland and that he had a career in the computer industry before. I asked Victor Platnauer, as a member of the Island Police Committee, to make a discreet—I promise you it was discreet—investigation into Childes' background, whether he had had any dealings with the police in the past, that sort of thing.'

'Do you imagine he would have been employed by any of the colleges if he had some kind of criminal record?'

'Of course not. I was looking for something else. I told you, his name was somehow familiar to me and I didn't know why.'

'So you found out what drove him away from England, why he was forced to leave his family.'

'You made no secret of his divorce, so that didn't come as a surprise. But what did was the fact that he had been under suspicion for murder.'

'Daddy, if you had him thoroughly investigated you must be aware of all the facts. Jon helped *solve* those crimes. The penalty he paid was false accusations and relentless hounding by the media, even for long afterwards.'

'Officially, the murders were never solved.'

She groaned aloud, half in despair, half in anger.

Sebire was undaunted. 'There was a series of three murders and the evidence indicated the killer was the same person. All the victims were children.'

'And Jon was able to give the police vital clues.'

'He led them to where the last two were buried, that's true enough. But everyone wanted to know *how*, Aimée, that's what caused the outcry.'

'He told them, he explained.'

'He said he witnessed the killings. Not physically, he hadn't actually been there when the crimes had been committed, but he had "seen" them happen. Can you blame the police, the public, for wondering?'

'He has . . . had a . . . a kind of second-sight. It's

not unusual, Daddy, it's happened to others. Police have often used psychics to help them solve crimes.'

'Whenever a particularly gruesome series of murders is reported, any number of crackpots always contact the police saying the spirits have told them what the murderer looks like or where he'll strike next. It's common and pathetic, and a total waste of police time.'

'Not always, it isn't always. Crimes have been solved by such people many times in the past.'

'And you're telling me Childes is one of these gifted persons.' Sebire made the word 'gifted' sound like a sneer. 'That's what the newspapers reported at the time.'

'That's just the point: he isn't. He's not clairvoyant, he's not psychic in the usual sense. Jon had never experienced such an insight before, not in that way. He was just as mystified and confused as anyone else. And frightened.'

'The police held him on suspicion.'

'They were staggered by what he knew. Of course they suspected him at first, but he had too many witnesses testifying he was elsewhere at the time of the murders.'

'It was still felt he was involved in some way. He was too accurate with his information.'

'They eventually traced the murderer and proved that Jon had no connection with him.'

'I'm sorry, but that's not on record. The killings were never solved.'

'Check with your sources, Daddy. You'll find they were—unofficially. The madman cut his own throat. The case was never officially closed because he left no suicide note, nothing to admit he had murdered the children. All the authorities had was very strong circumstantial—no, conclusive—evidence against him. They hinted as much at the time, and so did the newspapers, but no one could officially announce the fact; the law, itself, prevented them from doing so.

But the murderer killed himself because he knew they were closing in; Jon had given the police enough information for them to pinpoint their man, someone who was known to them as a child-molester, who had spent time in prison because of it. The killings stopped when he took his own life.'

'Then why did Childes run away?' Sebire was pacing the room again, determined not to leave until he had made his daughter see sense. 'He deserted his wife and child to come here. What could make him do such a thing?'

'He didn't desert them, not in the way you're suggesting.' Amy's voice had risen in pitch. 'Jon begged his wife to come with him, but she refused. The pressure had been too much for her as well. She didn't want either herself or Gabriel, their daughter, to be subjected to any more innuendo, phone calls from cranks, the media at first pointing the finger of suspicion and later trying to build Jon into some kind of super-freak! She knew there'd be no peace for them . . .'

'Even so, to leave them . . .'

'Their marriage was in trouble before that. Jon's wife was a career woman when they were first married. When their daughter came along she took up all her time; Fran became sick of being a housewife, always living in his shadow. She wanted her own life before these incidents took place.'

'And the child? How could—?'

Amy's voice lowered. 'He loves Gabriel. It nearly broke him to leave her, but he knew if he stayed the tension would destroy them all. There was nothing he could offer his daughter on his own; he didn't know at that stage how he would live, what he would do. My God, he'd thrown away a brilliant career, was leaving his wife everything they possessed and almost all their savings. How could he take care of a four-year-old daughter?'

'Why here of all places? Why did he come to this

island?' Sebire had once more stopped his pacing and was now hovering over Amy, his own anger building.

'Because it's close to home, don't you see? It's far enough away for him to have been a stranger when he arrived, yet easy for him to return, to keep in touch with his family. Jon hasn't walked out, he hasn't turned his back on them. He was devastated when he discovered his wife had sued for divorce—perhaps he imagined one day they'd patch things up for the sake of Gabriel, that they'd come to live with him here, I don't know. He may even have had plans for returning to England in a few years time when he would be long forgotten by the public. All that changed when he received the divorce papers.'

'Okay, Aimée, given all that, accepting there was no complicity on his part in those brutal killings and that he was not totally to blame for the break-up of his marriage—'

Amy opened her mouth to speak, her pale eyes blazing, but Sebire stopped her.

'Hear me out.' His manner was firm, allowing no dissension. 'The fact remains that the man is *not* normal. How do you explain these—I don't know what you'd call them, I'm not familiar with psychic mumbo-jumbo—let's just say "intuitions"? Why on earth did they happen to him?'

'Nobody knows, least of all Jon himself. No one can explain them. Why are you blaming him?'

'I am not blaming him for anything. I'm merely pointing out that there's something odd about the man. Can you tell me exactly what happened here tonight, what caused his so-called blackout? Has this sort of thing ever occurred before? Good God, Aimée, what if he'd been driving a car, perhaps with you in it?'

'I don't *know* what happened to him, and neither does he. And as far as I know, he's never suffered anything similar.'

'But he refuses to even consult a doctor.'

'He will; I'll make him.'

'You will stay away from him.'

Amy smiled disbelievingly. 'Do you really think I'm still a child to be told what I can and cannot do? Do you honestly imagine you can forbid me to see him again?' She laughed, but the sound was brittle, without humour. 'Wake up to the twentieth century, Daddy.'

'I shouldn't think Victor Platnauer is too keen on having a tutor in his school who is susceptible to fainting spells.'

Her breath escaped her. 'Are you serious?'

'Absolutely.'

She shook her head and stared at him with a simmering anger. 'He wasn't well, it could have happened to anybody.'

'Perhaps. With anyone else it would soon be forgotten though.'

'And you won't forget this?'

'That's hardly the point.'

'Tell me what is.'

'He worries me. I'm afraid for you.'

'He's a kind, gentle man.'

'I don't want you involved with him.'

'I already am. Very.'

Sebire visibly flinched. He strode to the door and stopped, looking back at her. She knew her father so well, knew his ruthlessness when opposed. His words were controlled, but there was seething intensity in his eyes.

'I think it's time others were made aware of Childes' dubious past,' he said, before leaving the room and firmly closing the door behind him.

Perspiration flowed from him, literally trickling in smooth rivulets onto the sheets of the bed. He turned onto his side, damp bedclothes clinging, his own dank smell unpleasant.

The vision, the sighting, was still fresh in Childes' mind, for it had been so real, its horror so tangible, so palpable. It filled him now. Potent. Vigorous.

His presence had been in the graveyard, so close to the little corpse, almost *feeling* its cold, clammy touch. For a few brief moments he had existed *inside* the other being, this thing that had defiled the dead child. Had felt its obscene glory.

Yet had been apart from it, an observer with no influence, a watcher of no power.

Still the thoughts persisted and with them, sneaking through like an insidious informant, came a new dread, an unspeakable notion that caused him to moan aloud. The thought was too distressing to contemplate, yet would not go away. Surely he would have known, would have been aware in some way, no matter how deeply hidden his conscious mind had kept the secret? But hadn't he felt at one stage, when those monstrous hands had raised the lifeless body from the grave, that they were his own, that those hands belonged to him?

Was the vision merely a released memory? Was he, himself, the desecrator? No, that couldn't be, it couldn't be!

Childes stared at the closed window and listened to the night.

It sat in the shadows watching the slender crescent of light that was the moon through the grimy window, and it grinned, thoughts dwelling on the ceremony it had carried out in the burial ground earlier that night.

It relived the exquisite moment of opening the body, of scattering the contents, and relished the memory.

A tongue slid across parted lips. The silent heart had tasted good.

But now a frown changed its countenance.

In the cemetery, for one brief moment as it had drawn out the dead child, a sensation had stayed the movement, a feeling of being watched. The graveyard had been deserted, though, that was certain, only head-stones and frozen angels the nocturnal spectators.

Yet there had been contact with something, with some-one. A touching of spirits.

Who?

And how was it possible?

The figure stirred in the chair as a cloud engulfed the moon; its breathing was shallow and harsh until the feeble light returned. It considered the possibility that someone was aware of its existence, and stretched its mind, seeking the interloper, searching but not finding. Not yet.

But in time. In time.

'YOU LOOK a little pale,' Estelle Piprelly remarked as Childes entered the study and took a chair facing her on the other side of the broad desk.

'I'm fine,' he responded.

'You've hurt yourself.'

He raised the bandaged hand in a deprecative gesture. 'I broke a glass. Nothing serious, just a few minor cuts.'

The ceiling was high, the walls half-panelled in light oak, the upper portions a restful pastel green, except one wall which was covered from floor to ceiling with crowded bookshelves. A portrait of La Roche's founder dominated the wall to Childes' right, undoubtedly an accurate facsimile but one that revealed little of the sitter's true character, so typical of many Victorian studies. Beside the door, an ancient clock loudly ticked away the seconds as if each one was an announcement in itself. Childes looked past La Roche's principal, bright sunlight from the huge windows behind her blazing her grey hair silver. Outside were the school gardens, green lawns bordered with awakening flowers and shrubs, the slanted roof of a white-framed summerhouse dazzlingly mirroring the sun's rays. Beyond were the clifftops, rugged and decaying, slowly eroding bastions against the sea. The darker blue of the horizon indicated the clear divide between sea and sky, a distinct edge to the calm affinity between both elements. Although the room itself was spacious and its tones soothing, Childes suddenly felt confined, as if the walls were restraining an energy emanating from within himself, a force that the bounds of his own physical body could not contain. He knew that the sensation was simple claustrophobia, nothing more, and much of it was due to the impending confrontation with the headmistress.

'I had a call from Victor Platnauer this morning,' Miss Piprelly began, confirming his expectation. 'I believe you met on a social basis last Saturday evening.'

Childes nodded.

'He told me of your, er, unfortunate accident,' the principal went on. 'He said that you had fainted during dinner.'

'No, dinner was just about over.'

She eyed him coolly. 'He was concerned over your state of health. There is, after all, a huge responsibility on your shoulders when teaching youngsters, and such an occurrence in the classroom could cause some distress among the girls. As one of our governors, *Conseiller* Platnauer was seeking some assurance that you were not prone to such collapses. I think that's reasonable, don't you?'

'It's the first time ever for me. Really.'

'Any idea as to why it happened? Have you consulted a doctor yet?'

He hesitated before answering. 'No to both questions. I'm okay now, I don't need a doctor.'

'Nonsense. If you fainted, there must be a reason for it.'

'Maybe I was a little tensed up on Saturday. A personal thing.'

'Enough to make you black out?' she scoffed mildly.

'I can only tell you it's not a regular occurrence with me. I feel healthy nowadays, probably healthier than I've felt in a long time. Life on the island has meant a big change for me, a different style of living, away from the pressure of my last job, out of a rat-race profession. And I don't mind admitting there was a considerable strain on my marriage for several years. Things have changed since I came here: I'm more relaxed, I'd even say more content.'

'Yes, I can believe that. But as I said when you came in, you look a trifle peaky.'

'What happened shook me as well as the other dinner guests,' he said testily.

He felt uncomfortable under her gaze and looked away, brushing an imaginary speck of dust from his cords. For a moment it had seemed she had looked into the very core of him.

'All right, Mr Childes, I don't intend to pursue that particular matter any further. However, I do suggest you consult a doctor at the earliest opportunity; your fainting spell may well be a symptom of some hidden illness.'

He was relieved, but said nothing.

Miss Piprelly lightly tapped the blunt end of a fountain pen on the desktop as if it were a gavel. 'Victor Platnauer also brought something else to my attention, something, I'm afraid, to do with your past history, Mr Childes, and of which you have omitted to inform me.'

He straightened in his seat, body tensed, hands clasping his knees, knowing what was coming.

'I refer, of course, to the unhappy dealings you had with the police before you came to the island.'

He should have realised it would not be forgotten so easily, that England was too close, too accessible, for such news not to have travelled, and to have been remembered by some. Had Platnauer always known? No, it would have been mentioned long before. Someone had told him very recently, and Childes smiled to himself, for it was so obvious: Paul Sebire had 'looked into' his background—either that, or Amy had told her father—and passed on the interesting information to the school governor. In a funny way, he was glad the secret was out, even though he considered it to be nobody's business but his own. Suppression leads to depression, right? he told himself.

'Right,' he answered.

'I beg your pardon?' The headmistress looked surprised.

'My "dealings with the police" as you put it, were purely as a source of information. I helped, in the true sense, with their investigations.'

'So I gather. Although your method was rather peculiar, wouldn't you say that?'

'Yes, I would say that. In fact, the idea still astounds me. As to my not having informed you when you hired me, I hardly thought it necessary. I wasn't criminally involved.'

'Quite so. And I'm not making an issue of it now.'

It was Childes' turn to be surprised. 'My, uh, standing here isn't affected in any way?'

The ticking clock timed the pause. Six seconds.

'I think it only fair that I tell you I've asked our police department to supply me with more information on the matter. You should appreciate my reasons for doing so.'

'You're not going to fire me?'

She didn't smile and her manner had its usual brusqueness, but he regarded her with new interest when she said: 'I see no reason for doing so; not at this stage, at any rate. Unless you have anything further to tell me right now, anything that I'll probably find out anyway?'

He shook his head. 'I've got nothing to hide, Miss Piprelly, I promise you that.'

'Very well. We have a particular need for your special abilities, otherwise I wouldn't have asked you to spare La Roche more of your time, and that I've explained to Victor Platnauer. I must admit he was reluctant to see my point of view at first, but he's a fair-minded man. He will, however, be keeping a close eye on you, Mr Childes, as I shall. We've agreed to keep the whole affair strictly to ourselves: La Roche would find any such publicity regarding yourself totally unacceptable. We have a long-established reputation to protect.'

Estelle Piprelly sat back in her chair and, even though her body was still ramrod straight, the position seemed almost relaxed for her. She continued to study Childes with that unsettling, penetrating gaze and the fountain pen stood stiffly between her fingers, base resting on the desktop, like a tiny immovable post. He wondered about her, wondered about her sudden frown, what she was reading in his expression. Was there just a hint of alarm behind the thick lenses of her spectacles?

She quickly recovered, leaving him unsure that he had seen any change at all in her demeanour.

'I won't keep you any longer,' Miss Piprelly said curtly. 'I'm sure we both have lots to do.'

I want him out of the room, she thought, I want him out *now*. It wasn't his fault, he wasn't to blame for this outrageous extra sense he possessed, just as she was not responsible for her own strange faculty. She could not get rid of the man on that basis; it would have been too hypocritical, too cruel. *But she wanted his presence away from her, now, that instant.* For a moment she had thought he'd seen through her own rigid mask, had sensed the ability in her, an unwelcome gift that was as unacceptable to her as adverse publicity was unacceptable to the school. Her secret, her *affliction,* was not to be shared; it had been too closely guarded for too many years. She would take the chance of keeping him on—he was owed that much—but she would keep away from him, avoid unnecessary contact. Miss Piprelly would not give Childes the opportunity to recognise their similarity. That would be too foolhardy, too much to give after so long. Dangerous even, for someone in her position.

'I'm sorry, Mr Childes, is there something you wanted to say?' She deliberately quelled her impatience, years of self-discipline coming to her aid.

'Only thanks. I appreciate your trust.'

'That has nothing whatsoever to do with it. If I thought you untrustworthy I wouldn't have employed you in the first place. Let's just say I value your expertise.'

He rose, managed to smile. Estelle Piprelly was an enigma to him. He started to say something, then thought better of it. He left the room.

The principal closed her eyes and let her head rest against the high-backed chair, the sun on her shoulders unable to dispense the chill.

Outside in the corridor, Childes began to shake. Earlier that morning he had assumed he was in control, that much of the anguish had been purged the day before, literally walked from his system, so exhausting him that when he returned home sleep would overwhelm him. And it had. There had been no dreams, no restless turning in the bed, no sweat-soaked sheets; just several hours of oblivion. That morning he had awoken feeling refreshed, the sighted images of Saturday evening a contained memory, still disturbing but at least uneasily settled in a compartment of his mind. Subconscious reflex, self-protecting mental conditioning; there had to be a legitimate medical term with which to label the reaction.

The morning newspaper had easily shattered that temporary defence.

Still he had gone through the motions of everyday living, unnerved but determined to get through the day. Halfway there and then his meeting with Miss Piprelly. Now he was shaking.

'Jon?'

He turned startled, and Amy saw his fear. She hurried to him.

'Jon, what's wrong? You look awful.'

Childes clung to her briefly. 'Let's get out of here,' he said. 'Can you get away for a while?'

'It's still lunchbreak. I've got at least half an hour before my next lesson.'

'A short drive then, to somewhere quiet.'

They parted when footsteps echoed along the corridor, and turned towards the stairs leading to the main entrance, saying nothing until they were outside, the sun warming them after the coolness of the school's interior.

'Where were you yesterday?' Amy asked. 'I tried to reach you throughout the day.'

'I thought you were showing Edouard Vigiers around the island.' There was no criticism in his response.

'I did for an hour or so. He understood my concern for you, though, and suggested we cut it short. I wasn't terribly good company, I'm afraid.' They walked towards the carpark. 'I came by the cottage, but there was no sign of you. I was so worried.'

'I'm sorry, Amy, I should have realised. I just had to get away, I couldn't stay inside.'

'Because of what happened at dinner?'

He nodded. 'I hardly ingratiated myself with your father.'

'That's not important. I want to know the cause, Jon.' She took his arm.

'It's starting all over again, Amy. I knew it that time on the beach; the feeling was the same, like being somewhere else, watching, seeing an action taking place and having no control over it.'

They had reached his car and she noticed his hands were trembling as he fumbled with the keys. 'It might be a good idea if I did the driving,' she suggested.

He opened the car door and handed Amy the keys without argument. They headed away from the school, taking a nearby winding lane that led to the coast. She occasionally glanced at him while she drove and his tenseness was soon passed on to her. They parked in a clearing overlooking a small bay, the sea below a sparkling blue, hued green in parts, lighter in the shallows. Through the open windows of the car they could hear the surf softly lapping at the shingle beach. In the far distance, a ferry trundled through the calm waters towards the main harbour on the eastern side of the island.

Childes watched its slow progress, his mind elsewhere, and Amy had to reach out and turn his face towards her. 'We're here to talk, remember,' she said. 'Please tell me what was wrong with you on Saturday.' She leaned forward to kiss him and was relieved that his trembling had lessened.

'I can do better than that,' he told her. 'I can show you.' He reached over to the back seat and unfolded the newspaper before her. 'Take a look,' he said, pointing a finger.

' "INFANT'S GRAVE DESECRATED",' she said aloud, but the rest was read silently, disbelievingly. 'Oh, Jon, this is horrible. Who could do such a thing? To dismember a child's corpse, to . . .' She shuddered and jerked her head away from the open page. 'It's so vile.'

'It's what I saw, Amy.'

She stared incredulously at him, her yellow hair curling softly over one shoulder.

'I was there, at the grave-side. I saw the body being torn open. I was part of it somehow.'

'No, you couldn't have . . .'

He gripped her arm. 'I saw it all. I touched the mind of the person who did this.'

'How?' The question was left hanging in the air.

'Like before. Just like before. A feeling of being inside the person, seeing everything through their eyes. But I'm not involved, I've got no control. I can't stop what's happening!'

Amy was shocked by his sudden abject terror. She clung to him, speaking soothingly. 'It's all right, Jon, you can't be harmed. You're *not* part of it, what's happened has nothing to do with you.'

'I had my doubts on that score the other night,' he said, drawing away. 'I wondered if I were only recalling violence I'd committed myself, certain acts my own mind had blanked out.' He indicated the newspaper. 'This occurred on the mainland on the night I was at your home. At least that fact came as a relief.'

'If only I could have been with you yesterday to knock that silly idea out of your head.'

'No, I needed to be alone. Talking wouldn't have helped.'

'Sharing the problem would have.'

He tapped his forehead. 'The problem's inside here.'

'You're not mad.'

He smiled grimly. 'I know that. But will I stay sane if the visions keep coming at me? You have to know what it's like, Amy, to understand how scary it becomes. I'm left ragged when it's over, as if a portion of my brain has been eaten away.'

'Is that how you felt last time? In England, I mean.'

'Yeah. Maybe it was worse then; it was a totally new experience for me.'

'When they found the man responsible for those killings, what then?'

'Relief. Incredible relief. It was as though a huge black awareness had been released, something like, I'd imagine, when someone suffering from over-sensitive hearing suddenly finds the overload has been blocked out, that their ear-drums have finally managed the correct balance. But strangely, the release came before they tracked the man down; you see, somehow I knew the exact moment he committed suicide, because that was when my mind was set free. His death let me go.'

'Why him; why that particular murderer, and why only him? Have you ever wondered about that?'

'I've wondered, and I've never reached a satisfactory conclusion. I've sensed things before, but nothing startling, nothing you could describe as precognition or ESP, anything like that. They've always been mundane, ordinary stuff that I suppose most people sense: when the phone rings you guess who's at the other end even before you pick it up, or when you're lost, guessing the right turn to make. Simple, everyday matters, nothing dramatic.' He shifted in the car seat, eyes watching a swooping gull. 'Psychics say our minds are like radio receivers, tuning into other wavelengths all the time, picking up different frequencies: well, maybe he was transmitting on a particular frequency that only I could receive, the excitement he felt at the kill boosting the output, making it powerful enough to reach me.' The gull was soaring upwards once more, its wings brilliant in the sun's rays.

Childes twisted round to face Amy. 'It's a stupid theory, I know, but I can't think of any other explanation,' he said.

'It isn't stupid at all; it makes a weird kind of sense. Strong emotions, a sudden shock, can induce a strong telepathic connection between certain people, and that's well known. But why now? What's triggered off these psychic messages this time?'

Childes folded the newspaper and tossed it onto the back seat. 'The same as before. I've picked up another frequency.'

'You have to go to the police.'

'You've got to be kidding! That kind of publicity finished off my marriage and sent me scuttling for cover last time. Do you really imagine I'd bring it all down on myself again?'

'There's no alternative.'

'Sure there is. I can keep quiet and pray that it'll go away.'

'It didn't last time.'

'As far as I know, nobody's been murdered yet.'

'As far as you know. What happened the other week, when you saw something that shook you so much you nearly drowned?'

'Just a confused jumble, impossible to tell what was going on.'

'Perhaps it was a killing.'

'I can't ruin everything again by going to the law.

What chance would I have at La Roche or the other schools if word got around that there was some kind of psychic freak teaching kids on the island? Victor Platnauer's already gunning for me and I'd hate to gift-wrap more ammunition for him.'

'Platnauer?'

He quickly summarised his meeting with Estelle Piprelly.

'I think Daddy had a hand in this,' she said when he had concluded.

'And did you tell your father about me? I'm sorry, I didn't mean that harshly—there's no reason for you to keep secrets from your family, so I wouldn't blame you if you had.'

'He got the local police to look into your history. I had nothing to do with it.'

Childes sighed. 'I should have known. Anything to break us up, right?'

'No, Jon, he's just concerned about who I get involved with,' she half-lied.

'I can't blame him for getting upset.'

'Acting a wimp doesn't suit you.' She touched his lapel, her fingers running along its edge, a frown hardening her expression. 'I still think you should inform the police. You proved last time you weren't a crank.'

He held her moving fingers. 'Let's give it a bit more time, huh? These . . . these visions might just amount to nothing, might fade away.'

Amy turned from him and switched on the ignition. 'We have to get back,' she said. Then: 'What if they don't? What if they get worse? Jon, what if someone is murdered?'

He found he had nothing to say.

CHILDES ASSUMED his mock-official voice when he heard Gabby's squeaky 'Hello?'

'To whom am I speaking to?' he asked, for the moment pushing aside troubled thoughts.

'*Daddy,*' she warned lowly, used to the game. 'Guess what happened in school today, Daddy.'

'Let me see.' He pondered. 'You shot the teacher?'

'No!'

'The teacher shot you lot.'

'Be *serious*!'

He grinned at her frustration, imagining her standing by the phone, receiver pressed to her ear as if glued, her glasses slipped to the end of her nose in their usual fashion.

'Okay, you tell me, Squirt,' he said.

'Well, first we brought our projects in and Miss Hart held mine up to the class and told everyone it was really good.'

'Was that the one on wild flowers?'

'Yes, I told you last week,' she replied indignantly.

'Oh yeah, it slipped my mind. Hey, that's great. She really liked it, eh?'

'Yes. Annabel's was nearly as good, but I think she copied me a little bit. I got a gold star for mine and Annabel got a yellow one, which is very good really.'

He chuckled. 'I think it's marvellous.'

'Then Miss Hart told us we were all going to Friends Park next Tuesday on a big coach where they've got monkeys in cages, and a big lake with boats, and slides and things.'

'They've got monkeys on a coach?'

'No, at Friends Park, silly! Mummy said she'd give me some money to spend and make me up a picnic.'

'That sounds lovely. Isn't she going with you?'

'No, it's just school. Do you think the weather will be sunny?'

'I should think so, it's pretty warm now.'

'I hope it will, so does Annabel. Are you coming to see me soon?'

As usual, she threw in the question with innocent abandon, not knowing the tiny stab wound it caused.

'I'll try, darling. Maybe at half-term. Mummy might let you come over here to see me.'

'On a plane? I don't like the boat, it's too long. It makes my tummy feel sick.'

'Yes, on a plane. You could stay with me for a few days until term begins again.'

'Can I bring Miss Puddles? She'd be very lonely without me.' Miss Puddles was Gabby's pet, a black cat bought for her on her third birthday. The cat's development had easily out-paced his daughter's, kittenish behaviour giving way to imperious coolness long before Childes had left the household.

'No, that wouldn't be a good idea. Mummy will need someone to keep her company, won't she?' He hadn't seen his daughter for almost six months and he wondered how tall she'd grown. Gabby seemed to grow in sudden leaps, taking him by surprise each time he saw her.

'I suppose so,' she said. 'Did you want to speak to Mummy?'

'Yes please.'

'She isn't here. Janet's looking after me.'

'Oh. All right, let me have a word with Janet.'

'I'll go and fetch her. Oh, Daddy, I sprinkled

glitterdust all over Miss Puddles yesterday to make her sparkly.'

'I bet she liked that,' he said, shaking his head and grinning.

'She didn't. She got really sulky. Mummy says we'll never get it out and Miss Puddles keeps sneezing.'

'Get Janet to run the vacuum attachment over her. That should shift some of it if you can keep the cat still for long enough.'

Gabby giggled. 'She's going to get cross. I'll tell Janet you want to speak to her, all right?'

'Good girl.'

'Love you, Daddy, 'bye.' As abrupt as that.

'I love you,' he returned, hearing the phone clunk down before he'd completed the sentence. Running footsteps echoed away; her squeaky little voice called in the distance.

More footsteps along the hall, heavier, and the receiver was picked up.

'Mr Childes?'

'How're things, Janet?'

'Okay, I guess. Fran's working late at the office this evening, so I'm staying until she gets home. I brought Gabby home from school as usual.'

'Any luck with a job yet?'

'Not yet. I've got a couple of interviews next week so I'm keeping my fingers crossed. Neither are really what I wanted, but anything's better than nothing.'

He sympathised. Janet was a bright teenager, although with few qualifications: with fulltime employment so difficult to come by for the young and inexperienced, she had quite a struggle on her hands.

'Did you want to leave a message, Mr Childes?' Janet asked.

'Uh, no, it's okay, I'll probably call again tomorrow. I just wanted to chat with Gabby.'

'I'll tell Fran you rang.'

'Thanks. Good luck for next week.'

'I'll need it. 'Bye for now, Mr Childes.'

The link was severed and he was alone again in his cottage. At such times there was a brutal finality in the replacing of a receiver. His injured hand throbbed dully and there was an unnatural dryness at the back of his throat. He stood by the telephone for some time, his thoughts slowly drifting away from his daughter and settling on the memory of the police detective who had been involved in the child-slaying case years before, someone whom he'd helped to track down the maniac killer. His fingers rested on the still-warm plastic, but he could not make them grip the receiver. Amy was wrong: there was no point in going to the police. What could he tell them? He couldn't identify the person who had dug up the dead boy, could give them no clues as to the desecrator's whereabouts. Until he had seen the morning paper, he'd had no idea even that the offence had taken place in England; he had assumed, if the sighting was a true one and not merely a fantasised image, that it had happened closer, somewhere on the island. There was nothing to say to the police, nothing at all. He took his hand away from the phone.

Gabby's birth had been difficult, a breech.

She had come from the womb feet first and a purplish shade of blue, almost causing Childes, who had stayed by Fran's side throughout, to collapse with fear. He had felt that nothing looking like that, so shrivelled and frail, so darkly-coloured, could possibly live. The obstetrician had tilted the baby, drawing mucus from her mouth, having no time to reassure the parents, anxious only for the life of the child. He had cleared the blockage and blown hard against her slippery little chest to encourage breathing. The first cry, no more than a quietly-pitched whimper and hardly heard, sent relief surging through them all, doctor, nurse and parents alike. She had been wrapped and placed on Fran's breast, the umbilical cord deftly cut and Childes, as exhausted mentally as Fran was physically, had viewed them both with a spreading glow which transformed his weariness into a relaxed tiredness.

Fran, her features wan and aged after the ordeal; the baby, still wet and bloodied, her face screwed up and wrinkled like an ancient's; both so peaceful in the struggle's aftermath. He had leaned over them, careful not to crush, yet needing to be as close as possible, the sterile hospital smell mixing with the sweat odour of battle, and had thought then that nothing could ever disrupt their unity, nothing could make them part.

In the ensuing weeks it was as though Gabby was slowly emerging from a deep and terrible trauma, as indeed she was—the transition between mere existence and dawning awareness. He had begun to understand the shock creation brought with it.

Sleep laid claim to most of her life in those early days, releasing her in gentle episodes to absorb and learn, to sustain herself, and the transformation was fascinating to see. Her growing was a marvel to him and he spent hours just observing, watching her develop, become a little girl who toddled on unsteady legs and who had a great affection for her own thumb and a ragged piece of material that had once been her blanket. Her first word had delighted him, even though it hadn't been 'Dadda', and her unbounded reliance on him and Fran and her uncomplicated love had drawn from him a new tenderness that was reflected in other areas of his life. Gabby had made him understand the vulnerability of every living person and creature; a time-consuming career involved in machines and abstractions had tended to blunt that perception.

The newfound compassion had nearly destroyed him when he had mind-witnessed the indecent destruction of the children.

Three years later the thoughts still haunted him and, just lately, their power to do so was greater than ever.

Childes had spent the evening preparing exercises

for the next day's lessons, the Tuesday afternoon he had promised to Miss Piprelly and which had already come into practice. Examinations for the girls would soon be upon them and Computer Studies would be one. He was irritated that his thoughts had kept wandering throughout the evening, thinking of Gabby, the years of happiness they had shared as a family, even though Fran had never completely laid to rest the ghost of her PR career. So much had happened to spoil that in such a short time, and the intervening years could not quite dispel the anguish of it all.

He stared unseeingly at the papers spread before him, the shielded desk-lamp casting deep shadows around the small living room. Was Gabby asleep by now, glasses folded next to her pillow for security? He glanced at his watch: nearly half-past nine. She had better be. Did Fran still read her a bedtime story, or was she too busy nowadays, too exhausted when she got home? Childes shuffled the papers together, dismayed that some of the girls he had tested today with quick-fire questions still did not know the difference between analog and digital computers, or that they could be combined in a hybrid. Simple, basic stuff that shouldn't have been a problem. He dreaded the exam results, hoping practice would prove more fruitful than theory.

He ran a hand across weary eyes, his contact lenses feeling like soft grit against his pupils. Food, he thought. Ought to eat, they say it's good for you. So tired, though. Maybe a sandwich, a glass of milk. A stiff drink might be more beneficial.

He was about to rise when something cold, numbing, stabbed at his mind.

Childes put both hands to his temples, confused by the unexpected sensation. Blinking his eyes, he tried to rid himself of the coldness. It persisted.

Outside he could hear the night breeze stirring the trees. A floorboard cracked somewhere inside the house, a timber settling after the warmth of the day.

The numbness faded and he shook his head as if dizzy. Too much paperwork, he told himself, too much concentration far into the night. Concentration disturbed by thoughts of Gabby. And other things.

That drink might relax him. He rose, pressing down on the desk top to heave himself up. The icicle touched nerves once more and he swayed, hands gripping the sides of the desk to steady himself.

His thoughts were jumbled, tumbling over each other in his head, the iciness now like probing fingers pushing through those thoughts, taking them and somehow . . . somehow . . . feeding upon them. His shoulders hunched and his head bowed. His lips drew back as though he were in pain, yet there was no hurt, just the spreading numbness and the mental chaos. A groan escaped him.

And then his mind began to clear. He remained standing, leaning over the desk, breathing heavily, allowing the sensation to subside. It seemed to take a long while, but Childes knew it was no more than seconds. He waited until his quivering nerves had settled before crossing the room and pouring himself a drink. Strangely, the whisky was almost tasteless.

He choked on the next swallow as the burning flavour came back at him at full strength. Spluttering, he wiped the back of his arm against his lips. What the hell was happening to him? He tasted the drink again, this time more carefully, sipping slowly. He was warmed.

Childes looked around the room uneasily, not sure of what he was searching for, merely feeling another presence. Foolish. Apart from him, the room was empty, nobody had crept in while he had been hunched over paperwork.

The shadows thrown by the metal desk-lamp made him uncomfortable and he went to the switch by the door, bandaged hand outstretched to turn on the overhead light. He stopped before touching the switch and

stared at his fingers, surprised by the sudden tingling
in them, as if they had received a mild electric shock.
They had not touched the light-switch. He glanced
down when the peculiar tingling began in the hand
clutching the whisky glass and it seemed as though the
glass itself was vibrating.

The unseen, insidious fingers probed again.

His body sagged and he quickly sank onto the nearby
sofa, pushing into its softness as if trying to evade a
pressing weight. The glass fell to the floor, the rug
soaking up its spilled contents. Childes' eyes closed as
the sense of intrusion became intense. Images whirled
inside his head, computer matrixes, faces, the room he
was in now, numbers, symbols, floating in and out,
something white, shimmering, past events, his own
face, his own self, his fears, dreams long-forgotten
recalled and pried into.

He moaned, pushing away the delving ice tentacles,
forcing a calmness in his mind, willing the confusion to
stop.

Childes' muscles relaxed a little when the cold probing faded once again, his chest rising and falling in
exaggerated motion. He stared blankly at the shadows
cast against the opposite wall. Something was attempting to reach him, something—*somebody*— was trying
to *know* him.

With scarcely any relief, the creeping sensation came
back, tautening his body, infiltrating his consciousness. No! his mind screamed. And '*No!*' he cried aloud.
But it was there, inside, searching, sucking at his
thoughts. He could feel its existence, delving into him
like some psychic thief. It invaded him and dwelt on
thoughts of the island, the schools he taught in, thoughts
of Amy, of Fran, of . . . Gabby. Of GABBY! It
seemed to linger.

Childes forced himself off the sofa, struggling against
the extraneous consciousness, painfully dislodging each
numbing tentacle as though they were physical enti-

ties. He felt their grip loosen and the effort sent him to his knees. He made himself think only of a white mist, nothing else, nothing to distract him nor give sustenance to the intruder, and soon his head began to clear.

But before relief came fully, leaving him crouched and shivering on the floor, he heard a sound so real it caused him to twist his head and search the dark corners of the room.

He was alone. But the low snickering seemed close.

JEANETTE WAS late. The other girls from her dormitory had already gone down and she was still in her dressing gown, furiously brushing her teeth.

Today of all days! Exams! Maths! *Aargh, maths!* Jeanette sometimes wondered if she were a bonehead as far as figures were concerned.

Morning sunlight poured into the washroom, reflecting off the rows of porcelain basins, making them gleam; water gathered in small pools on the tiled floor, liquid debris from the girls' washing rituals. She was alone and preferred to be: the others often embarrassed her by comparing breast sizes and shapes, all of them eager competitors in the development race. Jeanette was a long way behind most of the other thirteen- and fourteen-year-olds in her class and did not care much for the comparisons. To add to her feelings of inadequacy, her periods had not even started yet.

Jeanette rinsed her mouth, spat into the basin, dabbed her lips with a face-cloth, and dumped her toiletries into her pink plastic washbag. She padded to the door, bare feet nearly slipping on the wet tiles, then hurried along the gloomy corridor, leaving damp footprints on the polished floorboards in her wake. Bare feet were forbidden inside the school, but she had not had time to rummage beneath her bed for skulking slippers, and besides, everyone, staff included, would be downstairs by now tucking into breakfast.

It was shivery in the dormitory she shared with five other girls, despite the bright sun outside, and Jeanette quickly laid out her underwear, plain regulation navy-blue panties and white vest, on the narrow, rumpled bed. Shrugging off her quilted dressing gown, she pulled her pyjama top off over her head without undoing the buttons and threw it onto the bed alongside the underwear. She briskly rubbed at the sudden goosepimples on her arms as if to brush them off, then reached for the vest. Before pulling on the garment, she paused to examine her chest and sighed at its complacency. The nipples were longish, erect now because of the chill, but the tiny mounds they thrust from were, as usual, a disappointment. She tweaked the nipples to make them harder and tugged at the soft bumps to encourage growth. A delicate flush of pleasure warmed her and she imagined her breasts had swelled a little more. She sat on the bed, still in her pyjama bottoms, and cupped a mound in each hand. It felt pleasant and she wondered what it would be like if . . . No, no time for that—she was late enough already!

She stripped off the pyjama legs and swiftly donned vest, panties, and white socks retrieved from the bottom drawer of her bedside locker. Since the weather had changed for the better, La Roche girls were allowed their light blue, short-sleeved summer dresses and Jeanette shrugged on hers, shoes, badly in need of a polish, following. She tidied the bed, hiding her nightwear beneath the sheets, then grabbed a brush and attacked her long, tangled hair, wincing at her efforts. The small blue-rimmed mirror, a china butterfly frozen on one top corner, standing on top of the locker, reflected the results, which were not pleasing. In spite of her haste Jeanette leaned close and examined her face for overnight blemishes. She had almost entirely cut out chocolate and did her utmost, pukemaking though it was, to finish off all the green vegetables on her dinner plate, but the spots came up with predictable regularity, and nearly always on special occasions. But there—today wasn't special, only rotten exams, and her skin was clear! She bet that on her wedding day there would be at least five zits to every square inch of flesh on her face and she'd have to wear a veil all through the ceremony and she'd be afraid to lift it afterwards for her husband's kiss and when she eventually did she would look like an ice-cream topped with raspberry pips.

Jeanette moved even closer to the blue-rimmed mirror, looking deep into her own dark eyes, dreamily wondering if she could see the future there. She had been scolded enough by her parents and tutors alike for spending too much time day-dreaming and not enough time *thinking,* and she had tried to concentrate on more serious things, but after a few minutes her mind always drifted inwards and became lost in her own fantasies. She tried, she *tried,* but it seemed her thoughts had a separate will. To look through a window at the sky meant seeing herself soar over tree tops, swooping down into valleys, skimming over white-crested oceans, not as a bird but as her own free spirit. The sun warming her face would evoke fiery deserts, golden beaches, sultry days spent with—a keen-edged excitement with the word—her future *lover.* To catch a flower's fragrance initiated thoughts on the existence of all things, large or small, animate or inanimate, and her part in such order. To see the moon—

A shadow passed behind her.

She turned and there was no one there; save for her, the dormitory was empty.

Posters and cut-outs of pop stars, movie stars, tennis stars, hair styles, fashion styles, *crazee* styles, covered the walls in carefully assembled groups. One or two raggedy teddy-bears and dolls, kept now as mascots rather than the cuddly, loved companions they once were, watched with dead eyes. Colourful mobiles over beds stirred gently as if touched by a breeze.

There was no one there; yet Jeanette felt there was.

The goose-bumps had returned to tickle her bare arms. The sun did not seem as bright. She moved away from the locker, treading warily into the centre aisle between two equal rows of beds, examining the shadows beneath each one before passing, almost as if she expected a hand to emerge and snatch her ankle. Her pace increased as she neared the doorway.

Then, with a rush, she was through, looking back and seeing only an empty dormitory, bright with posters, motionless mobiles and coloured quilts, the sun streaming in to warm and to disperse shadows.

There was no one else there. Nonetheless she hurried away.

SHE STOOD over him and vigorously shook her head, showering him with sea-water. He opened one eye, shielding it from the sun's rays which were still strong even though it was late afternoon, appreciating the cool droplets on his chest.

'How is it?' Childes asked.

'Cold,' Amy replied, dropping to her knees beside him and briskly rubbing her hair with a thick towel, 'but lovely. Why don't you come in for a while?'

He closed his eye again and answered lazily, 'Too much trouble to take out my lenses.' He did not mention he hadn't swum since his unfortunate experience of nearly a month before, when they had been snorkling; the near-drowning had left him feeling just a little too vulnerable in deep water.

'Ah, come on, it'll refresh you.' She placed a flat, damp hand on his tummy and giggled as the muscles there quickly retracted.

He pulled her down to him, enjoying her wetness, her salty, sea smell. 'I need rest,' he told her, 'not exertion.'

'Rest? This is exam week; you've never had it so easy.'

'That's right, and I intend to keep it that way for as long as possible.'

Amy draped the towel around her head and shoulders, creating a shade over both of them. She crossed her hands on his chest, supporting herself, and pecked at his lips with her own.

'Nice taste,' Childes remarked. 'Like kissing an oyster.'

'I'm not sure if that's a compliment or not, so I'll let it go.' Her damp, tangled hair trailed across his cheek and he raised his head slightly to lick moisture from her chin.

There were few people on the beach at that time of day, tourists from the mainland and the Continent not yet having descended upon the island in force, and most of the island's working inhabitants being still trapped inside places of employment. The cove held a wide stretch of sand, one end guarded by a triple-level German bunker, a huge granite monolith facing the sea, and a grim reminder of recent history. Jagged rocks, as if freshly tumbled from the cliffs, blocked the opposite end.

'You made it up with Daddy yet?' asked Childes.

Amy knew his use of the word 'Daddy' was only slightly mocking, a faint jibe that she was still her father's little girl and still using the word herself, and she had long since given up taking offence. 'Oh, he's still huffy with me and I'm still huffy with him, but I think he'll eventually come to accept the situation.'

'I don't think I quite believe that.'

'He's not an ogre, Jon, he doesn't wish you any harm.'

'That wasn't the case a couple of weeks ago when he primed Victor Platnauer to complain to Miss Piprelly about me.'

'Pip's nobody's stooge; she makes up her own mind about things. In fairness to Daddy, though—and I don't condone for a minute what he did—your past is a tiny bit disconcerting.'

He could not help but smile as he curled clogged strands of her hair around his finger. 'Does it still bother you?'

'How can it not, Jon? Especially after recent events. You know how much I care for you, so how can you expect me to put aside everything that's happened?'

'Nothing's happened since, Amy, not after the dinner party. I don't feel so uneasy any more, I'm not jumping at shadows. I can't explain it, but I feel as though a huge pressure has been lifted from me. At least for the moment.' He hadn't told her of the night alone in his cottage when the strange tension in his mind had brought him to his knees. In the following days, the sense of foreboding had slowly dissipated as though he were being released from an outside force, a debilitating spell lifted. He felt the threat had somehow passed him by. And yet that malignant snicker of laughter still echoed inside his head.

'I hope so, Jon,' Amy said, her soft voice dismissing the final dregs of doubt. 'I like the old you better, the one I first met. Quiet, easy-going, sometimes amusing . . .' he tugged her hair '. . . sometimes sexy . . .'

He drew her hair down so that her lips pressed against his. Their kiss, at first soft, soon hardened, became almost fierce, their tongues tasting each other's warm moistness. Her body pushed firmly against his, one slim leg parting his knees.

'Hey, take it easy,' he said breathlessly after a few moments. 'I'm only wearing swimming trunks, remember, and this is a public place.'

'Nobody's watching.' She nuzzled his neck and her thigh was strong against his.

'This is no way for a schoolmarm to behave.'

'School's out.'

'And so will I be if you carry on.'

'Oh, is it peeping over the top?'

'Amy,' he warned.

She chuckled and drew away. 'What a prude,' she said, sitting up and continuing to dry her hair.

He sat up too, drawing up his legs and resting his arms over his knees for the sake of modesty.

'Shame,' she mocked.

'I've got an idea,' he said brightly.

'Oh yeah?' she replied, still mocking, but her voice deeper, a huskiness to it.

'Why don't you dry off properly back at my place. Unless you've got to get home for some reason?'

'As a matter of fact, I said I wouldn't be home for dinner tonight.'

'Is that right? You had plans, huh?'

'No, but I thought you might.'

'Some ideas are coming to mind . . .'

They drove to the cottage, not bothering to change back into their clothes, semi-nude figures driving cars being a common feature of the island when the weather was warm, and they were soon inside the small, grey-stone house.

Amy shivered as Childes closed the front door. 'It's cooler in here,' she said.

'I'll get you my robe and fix you a drink.'

'I'd like to soak off this salt.'

'I'll get you my robe, fix you a drink, and run the bath.'

Her arms went around his neck and she kissed his nose. 'You just do the drinks.'

He gripped her waist, hugging her close, his lips seeking hers.

Amy returned his kiss with equal fervour, feeling him hard against her stomach, but she pulled away when things began to get out of control. 'Let me get cleaned up first,' she said, slightly out of breath.

'You've just come out of the sea—you're clean enough.'

She broke free. 'Do the drinks and read your mail. I won't be long.' She disappeared into the bathroom before he could protest further, leaving him to retrieve the letters lying on the doormat. The pink envelope with Snoopy in one corner caught his eye and he grinned, recognising the childish scrawl. Pulling on his shirt which had been tossed over the stair banister with his other clothing, Childes strolled into the sitting room, throwing the other two brown envelopes which were bills onto the desk. He crossed the room, opening the pink envelope as he went. Gabby wrote to him at least once a week, sometimes the letters long and informative, other times, like today's, only a few scribbled lines, her way of keeping open the link despite the miles between them. Miss Puddles still had glittering hi-lites, Annabel had CHICKEN SPOKS, and Mummy had promised to show her how to make fairy cakes next weekend. Childes touched his lips to the row of XXXXXXs, his and Gabby's shared secret that all written kisses were sealed by a real one.

The sound of running water came from the bathroom and he returned the letter to its envelope, placing it on one side. He poured a Scotch for himself and a dry Martini for Amy, then went through to the kitchen for ice. She was just stepping into the bath, the water still running, when he brought the Martini in to her. He watched from the doorway, admiring her lightly browned skin, the slimness of her legs and body, the long, delicate fingers gripping the edge of the tub. Her hair, still darkly wet from the sea, hung in tangled strands around her face and over her shoulders. Her pale green eyes closed as she sank further into the water and she sighed, a quiet moan of pleasure, as the warmth flooded her. The nipples of her small breasts rose above the waterline.

Childes turned off the taps and handed her the drink. Her eyes opened as she took the glass and the smile in them was his thank-you. They clinked glasses and sipped, Childes trailing one hand in the water, brushing the smoothness of her skin, running his fingers down so that they entwined in the fine hair between her legs.

Amy drew in a short breath and her teeth pressed gently against her lower lip. 'Feels good,' she murmured as his hand lingered. He leaned over and kissed an erect nipple as she lightly stroked his hair, sliding her fingers into its dark thickness, following the flow to where it lapped over his shirt collar, sinking her hand beneath the material so that she touched his spine. She kneaded the flesh there, soothingly, without hurry, and it was his turn to murmur pleasure. His lips moved to her shoulder and he nipped the skin, not enough to hurt, before moving on, his mouth finding certain nerves in her neck where it loitered, drawing softly on them so that her head twisted to one side in sensuous delight.

He relaxed, not wanting to take the love-making too far, not yet. She turned her head back to look at him, and there was a shine in her eyes. 'I love you,' she said simply.

He kissed her again, just lightly, and his hand brushed lank hair from her cheek. 'There's a comfortable bed waiting upstairs,' he whispered.

Amy lowered her eyes, as if suddenly timid. 'And I love being with you.' She sipped her Martini, content in the soothing liquid warmth. He helped her massage shampoo into her hair, rinsing it with his own empty whisky glass, using a cloth on her back, all movement slow, languid, no vigour and no haste used. Eventually he drew her from the water and she stood before him, a golden, lissom figure, so sensually innocent in her nakedness, so knowing in her smile. Childes towelled her dry, using a restrained, patting movement as though her her skin would break if touched too hard. He reached her legs and they parted a little as he dabbed at them; he paused to kiss her tummy, her hips, the top of her thighs. She was very damp there and it was not just water.

'Jon,' she said, and there was a mild urgency in her tone. 'Can we go upstairs now?'

He rose and reached for the dark blue bathrobe hanging behind the door, wrapping it around her shoulders and tying the belt at the front for her, her arms trapped inside. 'You go ahead, I'll pour us another drink.'

Back in the sitting room, he heard her bare foot-

steps overhead, the bed creaking as she lay down. He
quickly replenished their glasses and climbed the short
stairway, forgetting about ice. Amy, still in the bathrobe, was lying on top of the bedclothes, waiting. One
leg was provocatively exposed to the thigh, while the
robe was loose enough around her neck to reveal the
delicate curves of her breasts.

Childes took in the sight before moving into the
room. He put their drinks on a bedside cabinet and sat
on the bed close to her. Neither of them spoke, but
they watched each other, enjoying what they saw,
both relishing the waiting.

Finally, Amy drew him down, easing off his shirt as
he sank. His hands went inside the robe, reaching
round to her back, pressing her flesh, pulling her
close. They kissed and there was no control, their
mouths open to each other's, their lips crushing. Her
relentless hands caressed his sides, his back, his hips,
squeezing, scratching, inciting. He fondled her breasts
and they were soft and malleable, only their centres
resisting, the hardened tips thrusting themselves at the
moving palms of his hands.

She kissed his chest, causing pleasurable tension
there, her tongue heightening that sensation.

His hand slid towards her thigh, delving beneath the
rough material of the robe to feel the roundness of her
buttocks, pressing them in a circular motion, his fingers probing the end of her spine. Amy moaned aloud
and collapsed onto her back, one leg raised over his.
His searching hand came back to find her warm moistness and a small cry welcomed its approach. He
touched, lingered, entered when her risen hips urged
him. She opened to him and his fingers pierced, his
thumb caressing her sensitive outer regions, using soft,
smooth friction to make her gasp, to clutch him tightly,
to grip his body with all her limbs.

Amy's breath was fast, shallow, and she groaned in
disappointment when he released her, craving more,
more touching, more feeling, but he needed her, wanted

to be engulfed by her. She realised his intent and helped him free himself from his remaining clothing, reaching for him when the swimming trunks were gone and guiding him down to her.

He entered and there was no hindrance, the journey into her liquid-smooth, and the motion causing them both to murmur. Childes forced himself to stop, wishing to see her face, her love, to show his. They kissed once more and the tenderness was soon overtaken by driving need.

He felt the hot, pliant softness of her thigh around his own and he ducked low to kiss her breasts, their taste a bitter stimulant; he supported himself on his elbows so that their stomachs parted while their bodies remained locked together, with no intention of separating. The sight of her beneath him was exquisite and his thrusting became hurried, Amy soon matching him. He collapsed onto her, his chin pressing into the side of her neck, and she revelled in his strength, holding him to her, their bodies moving against each other's, their gasps filling the room, her appreciative whimpers driving him on, their final cries resounding off the walls, their slow, sinking sighs whispering their contentment.

After a while, they drew apart, kissing as they did so. They lay on their backs, both allowing the excitement to ebb away, each catching their breath. Childes' chest heaved with the exertion and there was a faint shine to his dampened skin. Amy recovered more quickly and turned to him, a hand draping loosely over his waist. She studied his profile, loving the roughness of his chin, the slight bump on the bridge of his nose. She traced a finger across his open lips and he bit softly, his breathing slowing down.

'Seconds?' she asked mischievously.

He groaned and slid an arm beneath her shoulders. Amy settled against his chest.

'Sometimes, you know,' he said, 'you look about fifteen.'

'Now?'

He nodded. 'And a few minutes ago.'

'Does it put you off?'

'Far from it, because I know different. I know the woman inside.'

'The whore in me?'

'No, the *woman*.'

She nipped his skin. 'I'm glad it pleases you.'

'You've made an old man very happy.'

'Thirty-four isn't exactly ancient.'

'I've got eleven years on you.'

'H'mn, on consideration maybe that is a little old. I may have to rethink my plans.'

'You've made plans?'

'Let's say I have intentions.'

'Care to tell me what they are?'

'Not at the moment. You're not ready to hear them.'

'I wonder if your father would approve.'

'Why does he always have to come into it?'

'He's an important element in your life and I don't think you enjoy his disapproval.'

'Of course I don't, but I have my own life to live, my own mind to make up.'

'Your own mistakes to make?'

'Those too. But why are you such a pessimist? Do you think we're a mistake?'

Childes propped himself up on one elbow and looked down at her. 'Oh no, Amy, I don't think that at all. It's so good between us lately that sometimes it frightens me—I get scared I'm going to lose you.'

Her arm tightened around him. 'You were the one who put up barriers that had to be broken down.'

'We both held back part of ourselves for a long time.'

'You were a married man when I first met you at the school, even though you were separated from your wife and daughter. And you were something of a mystery, but maybe that aspect attracted me initially.'

'It took me a year to ask you out,' he said.

'I asked you, don't you remember? The beach barbecue one Sunday? You said maybe you'd turn up.'

He smiled. 'Oh, yeah. I was keeping pretty much to
myself those days.'

'You still are.'

'Not as far as you're concerned.'

She frowned. 'I'm not so sure. There's a corner of
you I've never managed to reach.'

'Amy, without sounding too self-absorbed, I often
feel there's a point inside me that even *I* can't reach.
There's an element in me—I don't know what the hell
it is—that I can't explain, a factor that's tucked away
in the shadows, something dormant, sleeping. Sometimes it feels like a monster waiting to pounce. It's a
weird and uncomfortable sensation, and it makes me
wonder if I'm not just a little crazy.'

'We all have areas inside that we're not certain of.
That's what makes humans so unpredictable.'

'No, this is different. This is like . . . like . . .' His
body, having become tensed, seemed to deflate. 'I can't
explain,' he said at last. 'The nearest I can get is to say
it's like some eerie, hidden power—maybe that's too
strong a word, too definite. It's so insubstantial, so
unreal, it could be my imagination. I just sense there's
something there that's never been explored. Perhaps
that's common to all of us, though.'

She was watching him intently. 'In some ways, yes.
But has the feeling got anything to do with these
"sightings", as you call them?'

He thought for a few moments before answering.
'The awareness seems stronger then, I must admit.'

'Haven't you ever looked into it further?'

'How? Who do I go to? A doctor, a shrink?'

'A parapsychologist?'

'Oh no, no way would I jump on that particular
roundabout.'

'Jon, you're obviously psychic, so why not contact
someone who knows about these things?'

'If you had any idea of the crank calls and letters

from so-called "psychics", not to mention those who turned up on the doorstep to torment my family three years ago, you wouldn't say that.'

'I didn't mean those kind of people. I meant a genuine parapsychologist, someone who makes a serious study of such phenomena.'

'No.'

She was surprised by the firmness in his voice.

He lay back looking at the ceiling. 'I don't want to be investigated, I don't want to probe any deeper. I want it left alone, Amy, so maybe the feelings will fade, die away.'

'Why are you so afraid?'

His tone was sombre and his eyes closed when he replied. 'Because I've got a peculiar dread—call it a sense of foreboding, if you like—that if this unknown . . . power . . . really is discovered in me, is aroused, then something terrible will happen.' His eyes opened once more, but he did not look at her. 'Something terrible and unthinkable,' he added.

Amy silently stared at him.

Later that evening, Amy cooked supper while Childes restlessly mooched around from sitting room to kitchen. The mood had changed with their earlier talk although the closeness between them remained. She was both puzzled and anxious over his remarks, but decided not to press him further. Jonathan had his problems, but Amy was confident enough in their relationship to know that when the time was right, he would unburden himself to her. In a way, she was sorry the conversation had taken place, for he had become introspective, pensive even. When they ate supper, it was she who did most of the chatting.

They made love again before she left, this time downstairs on the sofa, and with more ease, less hurriedly, both prolonging their release, savouring every moment of their shared pleasure. The bond between them had become strong and there was no element of doubt in their feelings for each other. He was tender and caring, his mood eventually reverting to its earlier relaxed state, and he loved her in a way that made her quietly weep. She told him it was joy, not sadness, that caused the tears, and he held her so tightly, so firmly, that she feared her bones might break.

When he finally drove Amy home it was in the late hours and both felt as if a warm mantle of euphoria had been drawn over them, joining, combining their spirits.

She lingeringly kissed him goodnight in the car, then left him sitting there, having to wrench herself away. He waited until she reached the front door before turning out from the drive; only when the red tail-lights disappeared did she insert the doorkey.

Before entering the house, Amy took one last look at the night, the landscape somehow magical under the flooding light of the full moon.

The old man heard the door open, but kept his eyes closed tight, pretending to be asleep. Footsteps came into the room, that curiously lumbering shuffle he had come to hate, causing him to stiffen against the restraining straps of the narrow cot. The odious smell confirmed his suspicions and he gave the game away, unable to keep his tongue still.

'Come to torment me again, have you?' he rasped. 'Can't leave me alone, can you? Can't leave me in peace.'

There was no reply.

The old man strained his neck to get a clear view. The overhead bulb, protected by a tough wire covering, burned low and was no more than a dimmed nightlight, but he could see the dark form waiting by the door.

'Ha! I knew it was you!' cried the recumbent man. 'What d'you want this time, heh? Couldn't you sleep? No, you couldn't, that's what they say about you, did you know that? Never sleeps, prowls all night. They don't like you, you know, none of them do. I don't. As a matter of fact, I detest you. But then, you've always known that!' The old man's laugh was a dry cackle.

'Why are you standing there? I don't like being stared at. That's right, close the door so no one can hear you torment me. Wouldn't want to wake the other loonies, would we? I've informed the doctors, you can be sure

103

of that. I've told them what you do to me when we're alone. They said they'd have words with you.' He sniggered. 'No doubt you'll be got rid of, and pretty soon, I should think.'

The figure moved away from the door, towards the cot.

'Bet you thought they wouldn't listen to me,' the old man prattled. 'But they know all the lunatics aren't locked away at night. There's them that roam the corridors when others sleep, them that pretend sweetness and kindness in the day. Them whose brains are as crazy as the maniacs they guard.'

It stood over him, blocking out the dim light. It carried a bag in one hand.

'Brought me something, have you?' said the old man, squinting his eyes in an attempt to discern features in the blackness hovering over him. 'More of your nasty little tricks. You left marks on me last time. The doctors saw them.' He chuckled triumphantly. 'They believe me now! Couldn't say I hurt myself this time!' Spittle crept from the edge of his mouth, slithering down the cracked parchment of his cheek. He felt the weight of the bag on his frail chest, heard the metal clasp snapped open. Large hands delved inside.

'What's that you've got there?' the old man demanded. 'It's shiny. I like shiny things. I like them sharp. Is that sharp? Yes, it is, I can see it is. I didn't really tell the doctors, you know. I only pretended just now to upset you. I wouldn't, no, I really wouldn't tell them about you. I don't mind you . . .' the words came out like short gasps 'hurting . . . me. We . . . have . . . fun. . .'

He twisted against the stout straps, his wasted muscles having no effect. Strangely, the terror in his eyes gave him an expression of clarity, of saneness.

'Tell me what that is you're holding.' His words were fast now, almost strung together, rising in a whine. His shoulders and chest heaved painfully against the binding leather. The figure bent low and he could see its features. 'Please, please don't look at me like that. I

hate it when you smile at me that way. No . . . don't put that across my . . . across my . . . forehead. Don't. It's . . . it's hurting. I know if I scream no one will hear me, but I'm . . . going to scream . . . any . . . anyway. Is that blood? It's in my eyes. Please, I can't see . . . please don't do that . . . it's hurting . . . it's cutting . . . I'm . . . going . . . to . . . scream . . . now . . . it's going . . . too . . . deep . . .'

The scream was just a gurgling retch, for one of the old man's bedsocks, lying close by, had been stuffed into his open mouth.

The figure crouched over the cot, its patient sawing motion regular and smooth, while both inmates and staff of the asylum slept on undisturbed.

THE NIGHTMARE came to Childes that night, but he was not sleeping. It hit him as he drove towards home.

A feeling of cloying heat gripped him at first, the atmosphere becoming heavy as if thick with unpleasant fumes. His hands tightened on the steering wheel and, although clammy with dampness, the fingertips seemed to tingle. He concentrated on the moonlit road ahead, trying to ignore the building pressure inside his head. The pressure increased, a cloudy substance expanding in his brain, and his neck muscles stiffened, his arms became leaden.

The first vision flashed before him, dispersing the pressure for an instant. He could not be certain of what he had seen, the moment too soon gone, the dark heaviness quickly crowding back, causing him to swerve the car, bushes and brambles on the roadside tearing and scratching at the windows as if attempting to break in. Childes slowed down but did not stop.

He thought the vision had been of hands. Large hands. Strong.

His head now felt as if it were filled with twisting cotton wool that was steadily pushing aside his own consciousness as it grew in ill-defined shape. There was not far to go to reach home and Childes forced himself to keep a constant though reduced speed, using the centre of the narrow road, knowing there would be little other traffic that late at night. His mind saw the sharp instrument wielded by the big hands, a brilliant vision that struck like lightning and excluded all else.

He fought to keep the car straight as the manifestation just as abruptly vanished. The heaviness was less dense when it returned, although the tingling sensation in his fingers had travelled along his arms.

Not far to go now, the road leading to the cottages was just ahead. Childes eased his foot from the accelerator and began to brake. A sweat droplet from his soaked forehead trickled down to the corner of one eye and he used the back of his hand to clear his sight. The movement was slow and deliberate, almost difficult. He turned the wheel, the Mini's headlights revealing the row of small houses in the near-distance. He was aware of what was happening to him and dreaded what images were to be further unveiled. He experienced a desperate need to be safe inside his home, feeling terribly exposed, vulnerable to the luminescent night, the moon's stark glare causing the surroundings to appear frozen, the trees oddly flat as if cut from cardboard, the shadows deep and clear-edged.

Nearly there, a few more yards. Keep it steady. The car pulled up in the space before the cottage and Childes cut the engine, sagging forward, his wrists resting over the steering wheel. He drew in deep breaths, the pressure at his temples immense. Pulling the keys from the ignition, he staggered from the Mini, moonlight bathing his head and shoulders silvery white. He fumbled with the lock, finally managed to turn the key and push open the door, falling to his knees in the hallway when the full force of the vision poured into his mind.

The old man's terror-stricken features were vivid, the horror clear in his eyes. His thin, cracked lips babbled words that Childes could not hear, and spittle dribbled from the corner of his mouth as he struggled against the straps that restrained him on the narrow bed. The tendons of his scrawny neck stretched loose skin taut as he twisted his head, and the exaggerated bump of his thyroid cartilage constantly moved up and down as if it were swallowing air. His pupils were large against their aged, creamy surrounds, and Childes saw a reflection in them, an indefinable shape that grew in size as someone moved closer to the old man.

Childes slumped back against the wall as a metal object was placed across the frightened man's forehead, and he cried out when the sawing motion began, bringing his hands up to his own eyes as if to block out the vision. Blood oozed from the wound, flowing thickly down the victim's head, washing his sparse white hair red, blinding his eyes against the horror.

Movement stopped for a moment, save for the quivering of the old man's frail body, the surgeon's small saw fixed firmly into the bone. Recognition streamed through Childes, a touching of minds; but it was the perpetrator who identified *him*.

And welcomed him.

'Overoy?'

'Detective Inspector Overoy, yes.'

'It's Jonathan Childes here.'

'Childes?' A few moments pause. 'Oh yes, Jonathan Childes. It's been a long time.'

'Three years.'

'Is it? Yes, of course. What can I do for you, Mr Childes?'

'It's . . . it's difficult. I don't quite know how to begin.'

Overoy pushed his chair back, propping a foot up against the edge of his desk. With one hand he shook a cigarette free of its pack and grasped it with his lips. He flicked a cheap lighter and lit up, giving Childes time to find the words.

'You remember the murders?' Childes said finally.

Overoy exhaled a long stream of smoke. 'You mean the kids? How could I forget? You were a great help to us then.'

And I paid the price, Childes thought but did not say. 'I think it's happening to me again.'

'Sorry?'

Overoy was not making matters any easier for him. 'I said I think it's happening to me again. The sightings, the precognitions.'

'Wait a minute. Are you saying you've discovered more bodies?'

'No. This time I seem to be witnessing the crimes themselves.'

Overoy's foot left the desk and he pulled himself forward, reaching for a pen. If it had been anyone else on the end of the line, the policeman would have dismissed him as a crank, but he had come to take Childes' statements seriously, despite a hard-bitten reluctance to do so in earlier times. 'Tell me exactly what it is you've, er, "seen", Mr Childes.'

'First I want an understanding between us.'

Overoy looked at the receiver as if it were Childes himself. 'I'm listening,' he said.

'I want whatever I tell you kept strictly between ourselves, no leaks to the media. Nothing like last time.'

'Look, that wasn't entirely my fault. The Press have a nose for anything unusual, always will have. I tried to keep them off you, but once they caught the scent it was impossible.'

'I want your guarantee, Overoy. I can't take the chance of being hounded again—it did enough damage last time. Besides, what I have to tell you may mean nothing at all.'

'I can only say I'll do my best.'

'Not good enough.'

'What d'you expect from me?'

'An assurance, for the moment at least, that you'll keep whatever I tell you between ourselves. Only if you find some verification will you take matters further, and then only to your superiors or whoever's directly involved in the particular cases.'

'Which cases are you talking about?'

'Just one for now. Another's possible.'

'I'd like to hear more.'

'Do I have your word?'

Overoy scribbled Childes' name on a piece of paper,

underlining it twice. 'Since I don't have any idea of what you're talking about, fine, you've got my word.'

Still the other man hesitated, as if not trusting the detective. Overoy waited patiently.

'The boy whose grave was torn open, his body mutilated: have your investigations come up with anything yet?'

Overoy's eyebrows rose in surprise. 'As far as I know, not a thing. Do you have information?'

'I saw it happen.'

'You mean, like before? You dreamt it?'

'I wasn't physically there, but I didn't dream it, either.'

'Sorry, wrong word. You saw what happened in your mind.'

'The coffin was smashed open by a small axe of some kind, the body laid on the grass beside the grave.'

There was another silence at the end of the line. 'Go on,' Overoy said eventually.

'The corpse was split open with a knife and the organs torn out.'

'Mr Childes, I'm not saying I don't believe you, but those details were in most of the nationals. I know you had a difficult job convincing me before—I admit I thought you were just another nutter at first—but you managed to in the end. Even I couldn't dispute the facts when you showed us where the second body was. But, I need a little more to go on, you understand?'

Childes' tone was flat, without expression. 'One thing the newspapers didn't mention—certainly not the one I read anyway. The boy's heart was eaten.'

The pen Overoy had been restlessly twirling in his fingers came to a stop.

'Overoy? Did you hear me?'

'Yes, I heard. The heart wasn't actually eaten, but it had been torn open; the pathologist found teethmarks. There were other bites on the body also.'

'What manner of creature . . . ?'

'We'd like to find out. What else can you tell me, Mr Childes?'

'About that—nothing. I saw what happened, but I can't describe the person who did it. It was as if I were seeing the mutilation through the eyes of whoever was responsible.'

Overoy cleared his throat. 'I understand you went to the Channel Islands after the last, er, business. Is that where you're calling from now?'

'Yes.'

'Could you let me have your address and phone number?'

'You mean you don't have it on file?'

'You'll save me time looking it up.'

Childes gave the information and then asked, 'So you're taking what I've told you seriously?'

'I did last time, didn't I?'

'Yeah, eventually.'

'Just one routine question, Mr Childes, and I think you'll appreciate my reason for asking. Can I take it you were still in the Channel Islands on the night the boy's grave was desecrated?'

There was a weariness to the reply. 'Yes, I was here and I'll give you the names of witnesses who'll verify.'

Overoy's pen scribbled on paper again. 'Sorry about that,' the policeman apologised, 'but it's better to get these things out of the way right at the outset.'

'I should be used to it after last time.'

'The circumstances were somewhat unusual, I think you'd admit. Now are you sure there's nothing more you can tell me about this particular incident?'

'I'm afraid not.'

The detective dropped the pen and retrieved his cigarette from the ashtray. Ash fell onto his notes. 'This happened a couple of weeks ago, so I'm surprised you didn't call earlier.'

'At the time I thought it might have been a one-off, an isolated sighting, and in any case, there wasn't much I could tell you.'

'What's changed your mind since?'

Childes' voice faltered. 'I . . . I had another vision last night.'

The pen was picked up once again.

'It's all a bit confused now, like . . . like a dream remembered. I was driving home quite late when an image jumped into my mind, a sensing so strong I nearly crashed my car. I barely made it to my house and when I did manage to get inside, I collapsed. It felt like my mind had gone to another place.'

'Tell me what you saw.' Overoy was tensed, expectant.

'I was in a room—I couldn't see too much of the place, but it seemed stark somehow, bare—and I was looking down at an old man. He was afraid, terribly afraid, and trying to avoid something that was approaching him. That something—that *someone*—was me, and yet it wasn't. I was seeing everything from someone else's point of view. There was something abhorrent about this . . . this monster—'

'Monster?'

'That's how I felt. It was sick, depraved; I know because I was inside that mind for a while.'

'Any clue as to identity?'

'No, no, it was like before, three years ago. Wait—I remember large hands. Yes, it had large, brutal hands. And they carried a bag . . . there were instruments inside.'

'Cutting instruments,' said Overoy, not as a question.

'I didn't see them all, but I *felt* that's what they were.'

'Did the old man call out anything, perhaps the other person's name?'

'I couldn't hear, everything was silent to me.'

'Was the old man trying to get away?'

'He couldn't. He was struggling, trying to escape, but he couldn't move from the bed. That was another thing that was so strange: he was lying on a narrow bed, like a bunk, and he was held there by straps of some kind, I think. He fought, but he was pinned to the bed. He couldn't get away!'

'Okay, take it easy, Mr Childes. Just tell me what happened.'

'The hands, those big hands, took a small saw from the bag, began to cut into the old man's head . . .'

Overoy could sense the anguish in the silence that followed. He waited several seconds before asking, 'Do you have any idea where this took place, any clue at all?'

'I'm sorry, but no. Not much help, is it? But you see, the reason I decided to call you was because I'm sure the person who did this to the old man is the same one who mutilated the boy's corpse.'

Overoy swore under his breath. 'How can you be so certain? You said yourself that you didn't see whoever committed these acts.'

'I . . . I just know. You have to take my word. For a few moments I was inside this creature's mind, sharing its thoughts. I *know* it's the same person.'

'Did you say this happened last night?'

'Yes. It was late, after eleven, maybe around twelve, I'm not sure. I looked through this morning's newspapers and thought perhaps the story was too late to catch the early editions. There was no mention on the radio, either.'

'As far as I know, nothing like that has happened within the last twenty-four hours. I can check with Central, but cases like this tend to get circulated pretty fast.' Cigarette replaced pen once more and the detective inhaled deeply. 'Tell me,' he said through a cloud of smoke, 'are these the only two incidents you've seen recently?' Such a question would never have been asked so naturally a few years before.

'Why do you ask?'

'Well . . .' the word was drawn out as if the policeman were reluctant to divulge too much. He came to a decision. 'A prostitute was murdered a month or so ago and we believe there's a connection with that crime and the opening of the kid's grave.'

'The same person?'

'There are more than strong indications. The same kind of mutilations, the body torn open, insides removed, indents in the flesh that proved to be teethmarks, certain—'

'A month ago?'

The sharpness in Childes' question brought Overoy to a halt. 'Roughly, yes. Does that mean something to you?'

'The first sighting . . . I was swimming . . . I saw blood . . . organs . . .'

'Round about that time?' the detective interrupted.

'Yes. But nothing was clear, I didn't realise what I'd seen. You're certain it was the same person?'

'Very certain. We matched saliva left on both bodies as well as wax dental impressions: there's little doubt. As for motive, well, the insane need no such thing. The prostitute was sexually abused and we believe that took place *after* her death—no living woman, no matter how far down the road she was, would have allowed such abuse. As far as forensic could tell, no penetration took place—there were no semen traces— but objects had been forced into the vagina, so maybe the killer was frustrated by his own inadequacy. We know he had to be immensely powerful, because the prostitute had been strangled with bare hands, and she was no lightweight. Far from it, in fact: she had a record for violence herself, particularly against men.'

Overoy drew on the cigarette. 'There was one other thing that makes the connection conclusive. I want you to think, though: did you "see" anything else, anything unusual, something you could identify?'

'I told you, there was nothing.'

'Just take time to think.' Overoy stared down at his notepad and waited. After a while, he heard Childes' voice again.

'I'm sorry, there's nothing more. When I concentrate, it only becomes more hazy. Can you tell me what you had in mind?'

'Not right now. I'll tell you what I'm going to do, Mr Childes. First I'll check out this old-man business, see if anything's come in yet. Then I'll contact the officer in charge of the prostitute murder and the violation of the dead boy's corpse. I'll try and get back to you after that, okay?'

'And you'll keep this strictly between you and me?'

'For the moment, yes. There really isn't much for me to tell anybody, is there? And despite getting a result last time, I'm still the butt of a few jokes around this department for involving myself with you in the first place, so I've got precious little inclination to revive the whole matter again. Sorry to be so frank, but that's how things are.'

'That's all right, I feel the same way.'

'I'll call you if I learn anything definite, then. It may be a while.'

When Overoy replaced the receiver he stared down at his notepad for some time. Childes was sincere, he was sure of that. A bit weird, perhaps, but that was hardly surprising with the extra sense he possessed. And then again, it was really the gift that was strange, not Childes himself.

The policeman stubbed out his cigarette and examined his fingers, frowning at the nicotine stains between them. He lit another cigarette, then reached for the pumice stone which doubled as a paperweight and began rubbing it vigorously against the stained skin. Childes had been right about the dead boy, yet had needed prompting over the prostitute, and even then had been vague. So what was he, a so-called hard-bitten, cynical police detective, to make of it? Maybe nothing. Maybe something. He scanned his notes again. This grisly business of the old man—what the hell was that all about? Overoy dropped the pumice stone and circled one word with the pen.

Straps. Childes had said the old man had been

strapped to a narrow bed. And the room had been sparsely furnished—how had he put it? Stark, that was it. What kind of place . . . ?

Overoy stared hard at the circled word, then looked blankly at the wall opposite. He could see movement in the outer office through the frosted glass, hear typewriters, telephones ringing, voices, but none of that registered. There *was* something, a tragic incident the previous night. Could there possibly be a connection?

Uncertain, but more than curious, Overoy picked up the phone.

THE POLICEMAN waited by the arrivals gate, conspicuous in his uniform of light-blue epauletted shirt and dark trousers. His height made him even more noticeable, and one or two of the passengers who had just alighted from the Shorts SD330 from Gatwick and were approaching the Customs desk eyed him nervously.

The small airport was crowded with seasonal tourists and businessmen. Outside, the sun blazed with a summer intensity, any lingering chill in the air fiercely shrugged off by now. A constant stream of vehicles prowled the non-parking zone, spilling passengers and their luggage, swallowing up arrivals. Inside, the rows of seats were full with travellers, bored, scampering children tripping over stretched legs, weary mothers pretending not to notice, groups of healthy-looking holidaymakers laughing and joking, determined to enjoy even the last few minutes of their vacations.

Inspector Robillard grinned when he spotted the familiar figure striding along the arrivals corridor. At first glance, Ken Overoy didn't appear to have changed much over the years, but as he drew closer, the thinning, sandy-coloured hair and the slight bulge of his waistline became more apparent.

'Hello, Geoff,' said Overoy, switching his overnight bag to his left hand and extending his right. He ignored two Customs officers waiting by their desk. 'Good of you to meet me.'

'No problem,' said Robillard. 'You're looking well, Ken.'

'Yeah, who you kidding? Island life looks good on you though.'

'Put it down to weekend sailing. It's great to see you after all this time.' The two police officers had met while Robillard was on a CID training course at New Scotland Yard and later when both were attending an Inspectors course in West Yorkshire. Robillard had kept in contact with Overoy through the years, always seeking him out whenever excursions took him to England, enjoying the stories of intrigues that inevitably went with policing the nation's capital, so different from law enforcement on the island—although Robillard had to admit they had their share of skulduggery. On this occasion, he took pleasure in being of assistance to the London detective.

He led Overoy from the air terminal to the waiting vehicle outside, a white Ford, the island's crest on its sides, a blue light mounted on the roof.

'How's crime here?' asked Overoy as he tossed his bag onto the back seat.

'Increasing rapidly with the start of the tourist season. Wish you'd keep your tearaways over there where they belong.'

The other man laughed. 'Even villains need a break.'

Robillard switched on the ignition and turned to face his companion who was settling into the passenger seat and lighting a cigarette. 'Where to first?' he enquired.

Overoy consulted his watch. 'It's just after three, so where's he likely to be at this time of day? In school?'

The inspector nodded. 'Let's see, it's Tuesday, so he'll be at La Roche.'

'La Roche it is then—I'll catch him when he comes out.'

'You'll have a wait.'

'Doesn't matter, I've got plenty of time. Maybe I could check into a hotel first, though.'

'No way. Wendy would never forgive me if I didn't insist you stay with us overnight.'

'I don't want to put—'

'You won't. We'd be glad of your company, Ken, and you can fill us in on crime in the wicked city. Wendy'll love it.'

Already beginning to relax, Overoy smiled. 'Okay. Let's talk on the way to the school, shall we?'

Robillard soon forsook the busy main road for the quieter shaded lanes leading to the coast. The brilliant colours of the hedgerows and the sea-freshness of the air served to relax Overoy even more. He dropped the half-smoked cigarette from the moving car and took in a deep breath through the open window.

'What d'you know of Jonathan Childes?' he asked, keeping an eye on the narrow road ahead.

Robillard slowed the car, to allow an oncoming vehicle to squeeze past. 'Not too much, only what we sent you in our report. He's lived here alone for nearly three years, appears to take life fairly easy even though he's employed by more than one college. Keeps a low profile, generally. Funny enough, we asked the Met. for information on him ourselves just a few weeks back.'

Overoy regarded him with curiosity. 'Oh? Why was that?'

'A *conseiller* here who happens to be a member of our Police Committee asked us to look into Childes' background. Name of Platnauer. He also serves on the governing board for La Roche, so presumably that's why he was checking.'

'But why now? Childes has taught at the school for some time, hasn't he?'

'Couple of years or so. I have to admit to being puzzled myself by the sudden interest in the chap. What's he been up to, Ken?'

'Don't worry, he's clean. Certain incidents have occurred that he may be able to give us a lead on, that's all.'

'Now I'm really curious. The information, such as it was, was given to *Conseiller* Platnauer who passed it on to Miss Piprelly, headmistress of La Roche, and we've heard nothing since. Childes' assistance in police investigations three years ago on the mainland was documented well enough, but that was his only involvement with the law. As you were on that case, I'm surprised you weren't contacted personally.'

'There wouldn't be any need; it's all on record.'

'So come on, tell me what this is about.'

'Sorry, Geoff, can't at the moment. It could amount to nothing and I'd hate to cause Childes any further embarrassment—I caused him enough last time.' Overoy took out another cigarette. 'I blew too much to the Press and they were on him like vultures on a fresh carcase.'

'What is he, this feller? Some kind of clairvoyant?'

'Not exactly. He's psychic, that much we know. But he doesn't have premonitions, or hear spirits of the dead—that sort of thing. He mentally saw where the bodies of those kids were buried three years ago and gave us enough clues about the killer for us to find him. Unfortunately, we were too late—already topped himself by the time we reached him.'

'But how—?'

'I've no idea; I don't even pretend to understand these things. Call it telepathy, if you like. All I know is that Childes isn't a kook of any kind—in fact, he seems to be more upset by what he can do than anyone else.'

Overoy saw the girls college before his companion pointed it out to him. The main building, white and imposing, loomed up before them over the treetops as the police car rounded a bend, the sun striking its walls to dazzling effect. They drew up before the gates and the detective whistled as he looked down the long drive.

'That's some setting,' he commented. Behind the tall building and its various annexes was the sea, a sparkling cobalt blue that challenged the sky itself for dominance. The lush greenery of the clifftops and surrounding woodlands provided a pleasing variation in tones, the colours of sky, sea and land blending rather than contrasting. Close to where they were parked were tennis courts fringed by lawns and flowerbeds; even the mechanical colours in the nearby carpark failed to intrude.

'I could happily go back to learning if it were in this place,' said Overoy, waving cigarette smoke from his face.

'You'd have to change sex first,' Robillard replied.

'I'd even do that.'

The inspector chuckled. 'D'you want me to take you right up to the school itself?'

Overoy shook his head. 'I'll wait for Childes on the bench over there by the courts; no need to draw attention.'

'Up to you. His car's a black Mini.' He withdrew a slip of paper from his shirt pocket. 'Registration 27292—I checked before I picked you up. Let's just make sure he's there before I leave you.' He smoothly eased the police car through the iron gates and drew up near the carpark. 'There she is,' he said, pointing, 'so he's still inside the school.'

Overoy pushed open the passenger door and reached for his overnight bag lying on the back seat.

'You can leave that there, if you like,' Robillard told him. 'I'll have to pick you up later, anyway.'

'Just need something,' replied the detective, unzipping a side-pocket and delving in. He took out a plain brown envelope. 'No need to collect me, Geoff. Hopefully Childes will invite me back to his place so we can talk and I'll call a cab from there.'

'You know our address.'

'Yeah, got it.' Overoy stood outside the car, squinting against the sunshine. He leaned back through the open window for a moment. 'Oh, and Geoff,' he said, 'I'd appreciate it if you kept quiet about all this back at the station. I promised Childes I'd play it low-key.'

'What would I tell anyone?' Robillard returned, smiling. 'Catch you later.'

He reversed the Ford through the main gates and gave Overoy a wave as he drove off. The detective stretched his back, then tucked the envelope into the inside pocket of his jacket. He wandered towards a bench, bemoaning both the fact that he had neglected to bring sunglasses and that none of the older girls were playing tennis.

Cars were pulling into a road on the other side of the courts and Overoy assumed the drivers were parents arriving to collect their day-girl daughters from a separate carpark near the rear of the buildings. He glanced at his watch: Childes would be out soon.

The detective's jacket lay on the seat beside him and his shirtsleeves were rolled up to his elbows, tie loosened around his neck. It had been peaceful to sit there in the sun with time to think for a change, and in many ways he envied his friend Robillard for the congenial atmosphere he operated in. Overoy knew, however, that attractive though the conditions appeared, they would soon frustrate someone too used to city life with all its corruption, seediness and villainy. Someone like him, who, at thirty-eight, revelled in the faster pace of city policing. Josie would love it, though, he thought, picturing his wife glorying in the relaxed way of life, the beaches, the barbecues, the freshness of the air—the fewer late-night calls for himself and less overtime. How bleak was it here in winter, though? There was the rub.

A distant bell sounded within the college and soon girls began drifting from the various buildings, their chatter disturbing the previous quiet. It was still some time before he noticed Childes strolling towards him accompanied by a slim blonde girl in a yellow summer dress. As they walked, the girl reached around and did something at the back of her head, releasing her hair so that it swung loose in a tail. Overoy studied her as

they approached: young, lightly tanned, and *very* pretty.
He wondered if there was a relationship between her
and Childes and the briefest touch of her fingers to the
man's arm confirmed that indeed there was. Overoy
stood as they drew near, swinging his jacket over one
shoulder and sliding his other hand into his trouser
pocket.

Childes was about to enter the carpark when he
caught sight of the detective. He became still and the
girl looked up at him in surprise. She followed his gaze
and saw Overoy as the policeman started forward.

'Hello, Mr Childes,' he said. 'You recognise me?'

'You're hard to forget,' came the reply and Overoy
understood the rancour behind it. The two men shook
hands, Childes reluctantly.

'Sorry to surprise you like this,' apologised the detective, 'but I've been looking into the, uh, situation
we discussed over the phone a week or so ago and
thought it might be appropriate to see you in person.'
He nodded at the girl, noticing her pale green eyes;
close up, she was more than just *very* pretty.

'Amy, this is Detective Inspector Overoy,' Childes
said. 'He's the policeman I told you about.'

Amy shook Overoy's hand and now there was suspicion in those eyes.

'Can we talk privately?' the detective asked, switching his attention to Childes.

Amy immediately said, 'I'll call you later, Jon,' and
turned to walk away.

'There's no need—'

'It's all right,' she assured him. 'I've got things to
do, so let's talk later. Goodbye, Inspector.' She hesitated before moving off, as if to say more, but changed
her mind. She went to a red MG and glanced back at
Childes with apparent concern before getting in. Childes
waited until she had driven through the gates before
rounding on the detective.

'Surely you could have taken care of this by phone?'
he said, unable to disguise his anger.

'Not really,' Overoy replied easily. 'You'll understand after we've spoken. Could we go to your home?'

Childes shrugged. 'All right. Have you been assigned to this case?' he asked as the policeman followed him to his car.

'Not entirely. Let's just say I happen to be dealing with one particular aspect of it because I'm acquainted with you.'

'Then there is a connection.'

'Maybe.'

'But a man was murdered in the circumstances I described to you?'

'We'll talk back at your place.'

They drove from La Roche and Overoy was surprised how quickly they reached the narrow lane in which Childes' house stood; but then, he reasoned, the island was not many miles in length and width. The house, no more than a cottage, stood at the end of a row, and he appreciated even more Childes' resentment at the intrusion on his domicile. The cottages had great old-world charm, the type the wealthy on the mainland paid an arm and a leg for as a second-home country retreat.

The air was cool inside, much to Overoy's relief, and he settled into a sofa as Childes removed his own jacket and hung it in the small hallway.

'Can I get you something to drink?' Childes asked, his tone less hostile. 'Tea, coffee?'

'Uh, a beer would be great.'

'Beer it is.'

Childes disappeared into the kitchen and soon returned carrying a six-pack and two glasses. He broke off a can and passed it and a glass to Overoy, who relished its chill after the heat of the day. He poured the beer and raised his glass to Childes in a gesture of friendliness. Childes sat in a chair opposite without acknowledging the gesture.

'What do you have to tell me?' he asked, pouring his own beer, the cans placed on a low coffee table between them as if in a neutral zone.

'You may have been right about the old man,' Overoy said, and Childes leaned forward in his seat.

'You found the body?'

The detective took a long swallow of beer, then shook his head. 'When you told me he was strapped down to a bed—a narrow bed, if I remember correctly—and the room itself was bare of other furniture, it rang a bell with me. A report had come in that morning concerning the burning down of part of a psychiatric hospital.'

Childes was staring across the room at him, glass poised halfway to his lips. 'That's it,' he said quietly.

'Well, we can't be sure. Twenty-five people were killed in the fire, staff among them, and several were elderly male patients, mostly senile, others more seriously disturbed. One of them could have been your man, but nearly all the bodies had been so badly burned it was impossible to tell if any had been mutilated beforehand.'

'How did the fire—'

'It was no accident, because the experts are certain it was started in two places, somewhere on the upper floors *and* in the basement. Empty petrol cans were found in both locations. We've no idea who the arsonist was, though, but it's generally considered that one of the inmates had been wandering around loose in the night and had discovered the cans of petrol in the basement. Those in charge of the investigation suspect the arsonist might also have perished in the blaze.'

'How can they be so sure?'

'They can't. But patients and staff who survived have been questioned all this week and there's no reason to believe any are responsible. Of course, as quite a few of the patients are total lunatics, it's impossible to be a hundred per cent certain. Then again, it could just as easily have been an outsider.'

Childes rested back in his chair and drank the beer, thoughts directed inwards. Overoy waited, in no rush. The distant drone of an aeroplane could be heard passing overhead.

'What happens now?' Childes said after a time.

'Obviously, if there is a connection between all these crimes, then we'll need any scrap of information we can gather to build up a picture of the madman involved. At the moment, I should tell you, nobody's seriously considering a tie-in with the arson attack—nobody except me, that is—but there is evidence regarding the other two suggesting a link. D'you mind if I smoke?'

Childes shook his head and Overoy took cigarettes from his jacket and lit one, using the empty beer can as an ashtray.

'What kind of evidence do you have?' asked Childes.

'The similar mutilation of the prostitute and the boy's corpse, for a start. They had all the hallmarks of a ritual defilement: organs severed and removed, the heart torn out, foreign objects placed inside the open body—in the case of the woman, junk from the room she lived in; for the boy it was mostly dirt and grass, dead flowers even. The wound itself stitched up again. Acts of a lunatic, of course, but with some crazy method.'

'Then maybe it was more than one person, a sect of some kind.'

'Fingerprints of only one person were found at both scenes of crime: on the boy's coffin and on objects taken from inside the prostitute, and whoever it was didn't give a damn about leaving prints. Naturally, with the near-gutting of the mental home no evidence was left.'

'No fingerprints on the petrol cans?'

'Too badly charred themselves. Tell me about the incident with the old man: what more did you see?'

Childes looked pale. 'I'm afraid I blacked out fairly quickly. The image was so intense, the torture . . . I couldn't take too much.'

'That's understandable. But you're convinced the other person was the same as before?'

'Absolutely, but it's difficult to explain why. When

you're in someone else's mind the recognition is as easy as seeing them physically, maybe even easier—there can be no disguising.'

'You mentioned you saw a large pair of hands.'

'Yes, I was looking down at them as if they belonged to the person whose mind I'd reached. They were big, rough like a workman's. Strong hands.'

'Was there jewellery of any kind? Rings, a chain, a watch?'

'No, nothing like that.'

Overoy had been appraising the other man while they were talking, noting the weariness in his face, the tension in his movements. If he had found his peace in his years on the island, it was no longer in evidence. Overoy felt pity for Childes, but he also knew he had no choice but to press him further. The detective spoke almost soothingly. 'Do you remember last time, how we finally traced the killer?'

'He left something at the scene of the last murder.'

'That's right, a note. A note saying he would murder another child, he couldn't help himself. A psychiatrist said at the time that the man wanted to be caught, to be stopped from committing those acts, that he'd written begging us to do just that. When we showed you that note you were able to describe the killer and give us a general idea of where he lived, how he was employed. All we had to do was check our records for known sex offenders in that area who matched the description.'

'I still don't understand how I knew.'

'That's because you ran away from it.'

'Plenty of people contacted me to explain what had happened and they couldn't understand why I wasn't interested. The Institute for Psychical Research wanted to publish a paper on me; one or two American universities invited me to give lectures, and God knows how many people wanted me to find missing relatives for them. I didn't know what the hell was going on inside my head and truthfully I had no desire to know.

All I wanted was to be left in peace, but unfortunately that wasn't meant to be. Have you any idea what I felt like?'

'Yeah, the Elephant Man. I think you let yourself take things too seriously.'

'You may be right, but I was shaken, scared. You can't imagine what I had to witness because of this freak in me.'

'But you contacted me last week, despite all that attention before.'

Childes opened another can of beer, his glass still half-full. He filled it to the brim and drank. 'I had to,' he said at last. 'Whoever is doing this now has to be stopped. I'm praying the fire did just that.'

'Apart from waiting for another incident, there may be a way of finding out.'

Childes eyed him suspiciously. 'How?'

The detective placed his glass on the coffee table and reached for his jacket, taking the brown envelope from the inside pocket. 'I told you we have evidence of a connection between the first two and that there was something almost ritualistic in both.' He held the envelope up to Childes and said, 'Inside is an object, identical to another which is still with forensic. Both were taken from the scenes of crime, one from inside the body of the prostitute, the other from inside the boy. It took some doing, but I managed to get permission to bring one to show you.'

Childes stared at the envelope, unwilling to touch it.

'Take it,' urged the detective.

Childes' hand was unsteady as he reached forward. He let the hand drop. 'I don't think I want to do this,' he said.

Overoy rose and carried the package to him. 'This mental torment only stopped for you last time when we found the killer.'

'No, when he killed himself. I knew it had ended at that precise moment.'

'What do you feel now? Did this maniac die in the fire?'

'I . . . I don't think so.'

'Then take the envelope, hold what's inside.'

Tentatively, Childes took the brown envelope from Overoy.

He flinched as if touched by a low charge of electricity. There was hardly any weight to the object.

He opened the envelope and probed inside with thumb and forefinger. He felt something smooth, round. Something small.

Childes withdrew the clear, oval stone. And as he held it in the palm of his hand, he saw the iridescent flash of blue inside its silvery shape, a blue fire contained within the stone's own shimmering body.

Childes swayed and Overoy grabbed his shoulder, immediately letting go as if he had received a shock. The detective took a step backwards and saw movement in Childes' hair, ripples, as if static were running through.

The tingling swept through Childes, clenching his body tight, yet seeming to expand his nerve cells. He felt his body quivering and had no control. A stab of cold lightning touched his mind. He felt surprise, not just his, but from another. Something putrid seemed to crawl inside his head. Eyes watched him, but from within. His hand closed around the stone, fingernails piercing his own skin.

He sensed It . . .

. . . It sensed him . . .

'IT WAS a moonstone,' Childes told Amy. 'A tiny moon-stone that had been left inside the body of the prosti-tute. Overoy said their pathologist had discovered another inside the boy's corpse.'

Amy sat on the floor at Childes' feet, one arm resting over his knee, her face staring anxiously into his. He leaned back on the sofa, whisky glass in his lap. He had continued drinking after the policeman's departure two hours before, the alcohol having little effect, causing him to wonder if his brain was already too numbed by his experience earlier.

'But one wasn't found at the hospital after the fire?' asked Amy.

'There was too much damage to find anything so small.'

'Yet this man Overoy believed you when you told him the same person had done all this.'

'He learned to trust me before, difficult though it was for him.' Childes sipped the whisky, the taste bitter in his mouth, but the fiery liquid helping to drive out some of the coldness he felt inside. 'It's the image I've been catching glimpses of all along, Amy, a shimmering whiteness, like the moon seen through thin clouds. It was even there in a nightmare I had.'

'You've no idea of its meaning?'

'None at all.'

'The moonstone caused a strong reaction in you.'

His smile held no humour. 'I scared the hell out of Overoy. And myself. This creature, whoever, whatever, it is, knows me. It was here, in this room, *inside* my head, Amy, feeding off my mind like some crawling parasite. I tried to resist, to keep my mind clear, but it was too strong. The same thing happened once before, but not so overwhelmingly.'

'You didn't tell me.'

'What could I say? I thought maybe I was going crazy, and then it eased off for a while, I felt okay, not threatened. Today it came back with a vengeance.'

'I still don't understand why *you*, Jon. You don't claim to be psychic except on these few occasions, and you're not even interested in the subject—quite the reverse, in fact. You shun the subject of the paranormal as if it's taboo.'

'We've discussed what happened to me before.'

'I didn't mean that. I meant in general terms, the occult, the supernatural, the kind of things people like to talk openly about nowadays. You've always shied away whenever I've happened to mention anything to do with spiritualism or ghosts or vampires.'

'That's all kids' stuff.'

'There you are, dismissing the subject out of hand. Almost as if you're scared to talk about it.'

'That's nonsense.'

'Is it? Jon, why have you never really spoken to me about your parents?'

'What kind of question is that?'

'Answer me.'

'They're both dead, you know that.'

'Yes, but why don't you ever tell me about them?'

'I hardly remember my mother. She died when I was very young.'

'When you were seven years old, and she died of cancer. What of your father? Why don't you ever speak of him?'

Childes' lips tightened. 'Amy, I've been through

enough for one day without an inquisition from you. What are you getting at? You think I'm the seventh son of a seventh son, some kind of mystic? You know how ridiculous that is?'

'Of course! I'm only trying to make you open up, Jon, to delve a bit deeper into yourself. Ever since I've known you I've sensed you've been holding something back, not just from me, but more importantly, from yourself!' Amy was angry and it was his blind stubbornness that caused the feeling. And she could tell by his eyes that she had hit a nerve, that there was truth in what she told him.

'All right, you're so eager to hear, I'll tell you. My father was a rational, pragmatic man who worked for twenty-six years as a wages clerk for the same company and who was a lay preacher in his spare time—'

'You've told me that much.'

'—and who died of alcoholism.'

She stopped, taken aback, but anger still rising in her. 'There's more, I know there's more to it.'

'For God's sake, Amy, what do you want from me?'

'Just the truth.'

'My past has got nothing to do with what's happening now.'

'How do you know?'

'He hated anything to do with mysticism or the supernatural. After my mother died he wouldn't mention the dead. I couldn't even visit her grave!'

'And he was a lay preacher?' she said disbelievingly.

'*He was a drunkard.* He choked on his own vomit when I was seventeen! And d'you know something? I was relieved. I was glad to be rid of him! Now what do you think of me?'

She knelt and her arms went around his shoulders. She felt him stiffen, try to pull away, but she held him there. Gradually the tension seemed to drain from him.

'You're spilling my drink,' he said quietly. Amy squeezed him harder until he said, 'Hey.'

She eased off and sat beside him, her body at an angle so that she could see his face. 'Were you so guilt-ridden all this time that you couldn't tell me? Didn't you know it wouldn't have made any difference to us?'

'Amy, let me tell you something. I don't feel guilty at all over my father. Saddened, maybe, but not guilty. He killed himself.'

'He missed your mother.'

'Yes he did. But he had another obligation, a son to look after. He did that to some degree, but there were other things I could never forgive him for.'

'Was he cruel?'

'Not to his way of thinking.'

'He beat you.'

A shadow passed across Childes' face. 'He raised me after his own fashion. Let's drop the subject now, Amy, I don't have any more energy.' He noticed her eyes were moist and leaned forward to kiss her. He said, 'You wanted to help me, but this hasn't really got us anywhere, has it?'

'Who can tell? At least I know you a little more.'

'Some achievement!'

'It helps me understand.'

'What?'

'Some of your reserve. Why you keep certain things to yourself. I think your emotions were repressed after your mother died. You didn't have a father you could fully love and a moment ago you called him rational, a pragmatist, strange words for the only person you had to turn to.'

'That's how he was.'

'And some of it rubbed off on you.'

He raised his eyebrows.

'You've never realised how totally logical you often are, how boringly-down-to-earth? No wonder you were so traumatised by your first psychic experience.'

'I've never disbelieved in the paranormal.'

'Neither have you embraced such ideas.'

'Why so hostile, Amy?'

The question shook her. 'Oh, Jon, I didn't mean to sound that way. I just want to help, to get you to explore yourself. There must be a link between you and this person, something that's drawing your mind to his.'

'Or vice versa.'

'Whichever. Perhaps it's a two-way thing.'

The notion sent a shudder through him. 'It's not . . . it's not a person, Amy. It's a creature, a malevolent, corrupted being.'

She took his hand. 'After all I've said this evening, now I want you to be logical. This killer is human, Jon, someone who is immensely strong according to your detective friend, but a *person* with a particularly warped mind.'

'No, I've seen into that mind, I've witnessed the horror there.'

'Then why can't you see who he is?'

'He . . . it's . . . too strong, its pressure too overwhelming. I feel as though my own mind has been scoured, ravaged, as if this *thing* is eating away at my psyche, stealing my thoughts. And I see these gross acts because it allows me to, it wants me to see. This creature is mocking me, Amy.'

She took the glass and placed it on the floor, clasping her hands over his. 'I want to stay with you tonight,' she said.

It was his turn to be surprised. 'Your father . . .'

Despite the seriousness of their mood, Amy could not help but laugh. 'Good God, Jon, I'm twenty-three years old! I'll ring Mother and let her know I won't be home.' She made as if to rise and he grabbed her arm.

'I'm not sure it's such a good idea.'

'You don't have to be. I'm staying.'

His tension eased slightly. 'I don't want your father on my doorstep with a loaded shotgun. I don't think I could handle that tonight.'

'I'll tell Mother to hide the cartridges.' She got to

her feet and touched his face for a lingering moment before going into the hallway. Childes listened to her muffled voice, finishing the Scotch in one last gulp. He closed his eyes, resting his neck over the back of the sofa, and wondered if Amy knew how relieved he was that he would not be alone that night.

His murmuring woke her. She lay there beside him in the darkness and listened. He was asleep and the sounds he made were dreamwords.

'. . . you're not there . . . he says no . . . he says . . . you can't be . . . he . . .'

Amy did not wake him. She tried to understand the meaning of his words repeated over and over again.

'. . . you can't *be* . . .'

It had searched the man's mind, puzzled at first but excited by the contact made between them. Who was he? What was his power? And could he be dangerous?

It smiled. It enjoyed the game.

So many images had flowed between them, at times their force and swiftness perturbing, but soon accepted and pleasured in. It had probed, searched, unleashed its own consciousness to find this frightened person, not always successfully; yet the intangible sensory link was becoming stronger. It had sensed and absorbed, and had felt his panic. And even memories had been unable to hide.

The past killings, the murders of the infants, locked away in the deeper recesses of the man's mind, had been uncovered and viewed with surprise and soon with sadistic pleasure. More than observed, for visual manifestation did not apply in the literal sense, they were perceived—experienced. Revelled in. And it understood this man's association with these murders.

There were many other sensory evocations in this person to contemplate, for there was enjoyment for it here, a new torment to be exploited. He could be discovered, for his past was still present in his thoughts, much of it acutely so, and though his physical image could not be perceived, those he knew could be tenuously glimpsed. The moonstone, mysterious though it was that the gem should be in his possession, had been the catalyst to their minds' congress, the breakthrough sudden and almost overwhelming where before it had been tentative and probing. When the infant-killings had been unveiled, the connection with the stone and the police had been established and the man's gift of psychometry comprehended. Those previous murders held the key.

Records of them were easy to find, for the newspapers at the time had gloried in the atrocities and their bizarre conclusion; library microfilm provided the answers it needed.

A week had passed and now it dialled the next number on the list, all the others bearing the same area code, those above already crossed through with a felt-tip pen.

It grinned when the receiver at the other end was lifted and a small voice said, 'Hello?'

THE SUN reclaimed them like returning prodigals as they stepped from the air-conditioned coolness of the Rothschild building, the warmth wrapping itself around their bodies in welcoming embrace. The girls, twelve of them in all, dressed in La Roche's summer blue, chattered incessantly, enjoying every free moment from the college. They gathered on the pavement outside the modern office block while Childes counted heads, making sure no pupil in his charge had gone astray. He felt the visit to the financial company's large computer room had been well worthwhile, even if most of his pupils had been baffled by the operator's highly technical explanation of his machines and their facilities (Childes had smiled to himself as the inevitable glazed looks had come into the girls' eyes). Nevertheless, they now had a glimmering of how computers helped such international corporates to function.

All present and correct, no heads lost, no bodies missing. It had been a good morning. Childes consulted his wristwatch: 11.47.

From where they stood, the wide thoroughfare swept down and around to the harbour, the congregated yacht masts stirring lazily as if gently beckoning.

'We've a while before we have to get back for lunch,' he told the girls, 'so why don't we take a break down by the harbour?'

They squealed delight and quickly fell into an orderly double-line. Childes led them away after suggesting they keep the gabble down to a minimum. For the first time that week he felt some kind of mental equilibrium returning, the bright sunshine, the girls' chatter, the normality of their surroundings having their effect. Not only had the experience with the moonstone left him with a peculiar sense of futility, but his conversation with Amy afterwards had dredged up memories that were better left dormant. During the days that followed, the darker strictures of his upbringing had returned to haunt him, although he realised he no longer hated his father; he had long since learned to repress such emotions along with certain others. And oddly, it was his father who had forced such self-subjugation upon him. That was how he was coping now, with resilience born of his own intrinsic suppression; both the recent macabre events and his own disquieting retrospection could be resisted when sunshine and normality lent their support. Only the dark night hours were allies to dread.

Childes spotted an empty bench overlooking one of the marinas and six of the girls quickly laid claim when he pointed it out to them, squeezing themselves into the limited space with much giggling and groaning. The others leaned against the rail opposite.

The harbour was bustling with tourists and residents alike, cars and white buses making slow progress around its perimeter, the wharves themselves tight with parked vehicles. The two marinas, enclosed by granite arms, were filled with yachts and motorboats of all sizes and descriptions, the island's fishing boats having separate berthing in a quieter section further along the port. A lighthouse rose up at the end of one curved pier while a fort stood watch on its twin, ancient guide and guard. Shops and bistros faced the sea, bright façades, old and new, edging the concrete haven with postcard colours. Here and there steps cut through the terraces in steeply-rising alleyways, the gloomy passages invitingly cool and mysterious, their destination the narrow upper reaches of the town itself.

'Two of you are about to do your day's good deed for the elderly,' Childes told the seated girls as he belatedly approached. They looked up curiously and he jerked a thumb. 'Let teacher have a seat.'

'Does Isobel count as two, sir?' Kelly asked with a cheeky grin, pointing at her plump schoolmate on the other end of the bench, instigating more laughter and one loud protest.

'I think I'll take your place, Kelly,' he said, 'while you perform yet another good deed.'

She rose, no malice in her smirk, but her eyes, as ever, challenging. 'Whatever you say, sir.'

He reached for his wallet. 'You girls have a choice: vanilla or strawberry. No Tutti-Fruities, no Super-Dupe Chocolate with Almonds, no Three-layer Mango, Tangerine and Passion Fruit Delights—nothing to complicate life, okay? And two more volunteers to go get 'em with Kelly.'

Eyes gleaming and with indecent haste, Isobel rose while the others were still exclaiming their pleasure. 'I'll help, sir,' she offered brightly.

'Oh no,' someone moaned. 'There'll be none left by the time she gets back.' More laughter from the others and a miffed glare from the plump girl.

'All right,' said Childes, sitting in the place vacated by Kelly and removing two notes from his wallet. 'How about you going with them, Jeanette?' He smiled at the small girl leaning against the railings, who immediately stiffened to attention. 'I think I can trust you with the loot.' She reached for the money almost timidly, avoiding his eyes. 'You take the orders, Einstein,' he said to Kelly, 'and make mine vanilla. And the three of you watch that road—Miss Piprelly would never forgive me if I returned without the full company.'

They set off, Kelly and Isobel sharing some secret joke, Jeanette lagging behind. Childes kept an eye on them until they were safely across the busy road, then turned his attention back to the harbour to watch the mainland ferry ponderously approaching the docking quay near the end of the north pier. Further out, white sails specked the sea's calm surface like tiny upturned paper cones, while overhead a yellow Trislander, a twelve-seater aircraft used almost as a regular bus service between islands, began its descent, the muted engine sound as much a part of the island's ambience as the summer bee's droning. He reassured himself that the hubbub around him, the constant hum of traffic and passing conversations, was merely a seasonal interruption to the rest of the year's peacefulness, and even so, just gazing out at the sea, with its soft-rippling textures and gracefully swooping gulls, induced a calming effect.

Relaxed himself, he was also pleased that the girls appeared at ease in his presence, obviously enjoying their outing as much as he had enjoyed escorting them. He began asking questions concerning the Rothschild's computer room to discover just how much they had absorbed, but their conversation soon developed beyond mere educational studies; he found the girls' remarks interesting and sometimes amusing, and was reminded that such excursions often led to a more knowing tutor/pupil relationship. Childes planned a similar field-trip with a class from Kingsley but did not anticipate such a pleasurable morning, for it would require a more disciplinarian approach to keep the boys' natural raucousness in order.

Kelly, Isobel and Jeanette returned laden with ice-cream cones to the cheered approval of their classmates who quickly relieved them of their burdens. Childes smiled at Jeanette when she dug a hand into her dress pocket and drew out his change.

'Thank you,' he said.

'Thank you, Mr Childes,' she responded, smiling back, some of her timidity having evaporated.

'Did much of what you saw this morning make sense?' he asked her.

'Oh yes, I think so.' She paused. 'Well . . . a lot of it did.'

'It's not half so scary once you begin to understand, you know. You'll find it'll all begin to click when you've got the basics under control. You'll see,' he added reassuringly, then looked around at the others. 'Hey, who's got mine?'

'Whoops, sorry,' said Kelly, giggling. 'I wasn't going to eat it, I promise.'

The ice-cream cone was already beginning to melt, white streams oozing down the cone and over her fingers. Kelly's own, which was clutched in her other hand and already half-consumed, was dwarfed by the one she held out to Childes.

He took the ice-cream from her and her hand immediately rose to her lips to lick the white stickiness from them.

As she did so, the smell of burning came to him. A peculiar smell. Like meat being cooked. Only worse, far worse. Like flesh being incinerated.

He stared at Kelly, and the hand she held to her mouth was blackened, merely gristled tattered skin clinging to white bone. Her hand was a malformed, charred claw.

He heard laughter around him and the sound came from a long way off, even though it was the laughter of his pupils. He felt the cold stickiness on his thigh, glanced down in reaction, saw the white blob of melted ice-cream sluggishly sliding over his leg.

When he looked back, Kelly was laughing with the others while she licked clean the hand that was now unblemished.

The road was wide and quiet, traffic sparse.

All the houses were detached, with their own garages and small well-kept front gardens. The rear gardens were no doubt ample, for it was that type of neighbourhood, affluent without being wealthy. The car moved along slowly, the driver searching for a particular number, a particular house.

The vehicle drew to a smooth halt and its occupant watched that particular house.

It knew he would not be there: the little girl with the funny squeaky voice of the very young had said on the telephone that Daddy didn't live there any more, that he had moved away to an island. Of course she could remember the island's name, the squeaky voice had insisted, she was seven-and-a-half years old, wasn't she?

It waited in the car, observing and unobserved, for it was early Saturday morning, a time for the dwellings' occupants to relax from the usual weekly haste. Now that the house had been located, the driver would come back when night fell and darkness could assist.

The observer became more alert, though, when a small girl ran from behind the house chasing a black cat. A tingling thrill ran through its gross body.

The cat leapt onto the low wall bordering the garden and froze on seeing the shadowy form huddled inside the parked car. The animal's fur bristled, its tail stiffened, its yellow eyes glared. Then the cat was gone, intimidated into flight.

A little girl's face appeared in its place, peering curiously over the wall.

The figure inside the car watched for a moment longer. Then opened the car door.

FRAN STRETCHED her limbs, her mouth agape in a huge yawn. She settled back into the bed, enjoying the languor of sleep's after-moments, her appreciation voiced in a blissful moan. She turned onto her side, auburn hair spilling over her face to flood the pillow.

A weekend to herself for a change, no commitments, no client pandering-to, no meetings, no phone calls. No cajoling journalists or radio and TV producers for interviews with clients who were just as likely to veto such hard-earned concessions on a personal whim. No fending off grubby-minded business associates (or even clients—no, *especially* clients) who considered any healthy-looking divorcée fair game. A chance to spend time with little neglected Gabby, the greatest kid in the world. Oh God, give me the energy to go down and cook her a decent breakfast for a change. Allow me ten more minutes in bed first, though.

Gabby had already crept in earlier to kiss her good morning and to sneak a warm, snuggly cuddle beneath the bedsheets. After promising a nice cup of tea to revive her weary Mummy, Gabby had left the bedroom, her high-pitched trilling broken only by calls for Miss Puddles.

Fran was relieved that Douglas hadn't stayed the night—not that there had been much chance anyway, with the way he protected his own marriage. Douglas

Ashby was a sound business partner and a splendid, inventive lover; unfortunately for Fran, he was also a considerate husband (apart from one infidelity—herself) and never stayed away from home longer than was necessary. Well, maybe that was okay: one serious man in her life had already proved too much. She knew Gabby desperately missed Jonathan, and there had been times over the past couple of years when Fran had regretted her own uncompromising attitude towards him, but enough had been enough. They had both been forced to face up to the truth of the situation: they were not good for one another.

But oh, it would be nice to have a male body next to her right now. Funny how a glorious love-making session the night before always left her wanting more the following morning. Her muffled moan this time contained a hint of frustration. Tea, Gabby, tea. Save your mother from self-abuse.

Fran pushed herself upright, fluffing up the pillows behind her and leaning back against them. She appraised her image in the dressing-table mirror on the opposite side of the room. Still good, she told herself. Breasts firm and not too many spare inches on her body to pinch. Hair long and lush, its sheen not yet from a bottle. Mercifully her reflection was too far away to discern perfidious lines around eyes and neck. She lifted the sheet to examine her stomach. H'mn, could do with some tummy exercises before 'loose' became 'flab'. No problem with thighs, though: slim and as nicely-shaped as ever. Pity such a well-toned body was so under-used. Fran allowed the sheet to drop.

Her neck arched back and she studied the stippled ceiling. Must do something with Gabby today, she thought. A trip to the shops to stock up, then lunch out somewhere. She'd like that. Perhaps a movie tonight, invite Annabel along—Gabby would like that, too. Got to spend more time with Gabby, to hell with the job. Her daughter was quickly growing mature beyond her age, becoming a little too responsible for one so young. The innocent years were too precious to be brushed aside so speedily. And it was surprising, considering how rare and brief were the times she spent with her father, how like Jonathan she was becoming. Not only were they both short-sighted, but their resemblance went beyond mere physical characteristics.

Fran heard a car outside pull away, the noise of its engine fading in the distance.

She closed her eyes, but it was useless: tired though she was, sleep had absconded, her head, as usual, buzzing with thoughts, most of them trivial. Why, oh why, when she had time to relax, would her brain never let her do so? And where was Gabby with that blessed tea?

Throwing back the sheet, Fran rose from the bed and snatched her flimsy nightgown from the back of a chair; slipping it on, she made for the door. Leaning over the rail at the top of the stairs she called down,

'Gabby, I'm dying of thirst up here. How's the tea coming along?'

There was no reply.

SHE STIRRED and Childes remained still, not wishing to wake her.

One breast lay exposed, delicate curves a temptation to touch. He resisted.

But her lips, slightly parted in sleep, were too compelling not to taste.

He kissed them and Amy's eyelids fluttered open.

She smiled.

He kissed her again and this time she responded, one arm sliding around his shoulders to hold him tight. Although their lips eventually parted, their bodies clung together, each enjoying the other's warmth, the comfort of filling closeness. Her legs parted as his thigh gently pushed between them and the soft pressure caused her to sigh. She ran her fingertips slowly down the ridges of his spine.

They shifted position so that they lay side by side, each wanting to see the other's face, he fondling her nipples which stood so proud from their small, fleshy mounds, she reaching down to caress him with firm but tender motion. Their lovemaking was slow and easy, neither wishing to rush, all frenzy spent the night before: now was a time for leisure, a relaxed joining, a steady exhilaration.

He moistened her with his own tongue and she fought to control her rising excitement, the exquisitely sensuous stabbing movement dangerously irresistible; sensing the ebbing of her resolve he quickly entered her, the penetration so glidingly smooth that she was full with him before realising he had changed position. Her thighs rose around him and she pulled at his lower back.

It did not take long for the tension to break, an intoxicating warmth shuddering through them in waves, only gradually depleting in strength to leave them panting breathlessly. They stayed locked together until their senses became placid once more.

Eventually they parted, both taking pleasure even in that movement, to lie side by side, waiting for their breathing to steady.

'Did you sleep last night?' Amy asked him.

'I didn't expect to, but, yes, soundly,' he replied.

'No dreams?'

'None that I can remember.'

She touched his face and he could smell their bodies on her fingertips. 'You looked so terrible yesterday,' she said.

'I was scared, Amy. I'm scared now. Why did I see Kelly's hand mutilated like that? Thank God the girls were laughing so much they didn't notice how frightened I was.' He gripped her arm. 'What if it was some kind of premonition?'

'You've told me before you're not precognitive.'

'Something's changing inside me, I can feel it happening.'

'No, Jon, you're confused and upset by this business with the moonstone. Someone's playing tricks with your mind, deliberately tormenting you—you've said as much yourself.'

'Putting these thoughts into my head?'

'Perhaps.'

'No, no, that's nonsense. Things like that don't really happen.'

'Christ!' she exploded. 'How can you say that? Why do you keep avoiding the reality of the situation?'

'You call this real?'

'It's happening, isn't it? You've got to come to terms with yourself, Jon, stop resisting something that's unnatural to others but natural to you. Accept whatever extra sense you have so that you can learn to control it! You've already admitted that some outside influence is encroaching on your thoughts, so try to understand your own power in order to defend yourself.'

'It's not that simple . . .'

'I never said it would be. But surely nobody else can determine what you choose to think or see?'

'I know you're right and I wish I could get a grip on myself, but it seems whenever I'm over one shock nowadays, another comes along to knock me rigid again. It's getting tedious. I need to think, Amy. Something you said recently has bothered me since and I need to brood on it a little while longer. There's a door waiting to be unlocked—all I need is the key.'

'Can't we work on this together?'

'Not just yet. I'm sure there's something which only I can resolve, so be patient for a bit longer.'

'If you promise not to hide any answers from either me or yourself.'

'That's an easy promise to keep.'

'We'll see.'

'You hungry?'

'You change the subject so well.'

'Is there any more to say?'

'Lots.'

'Later. What can I get you for breakfast?'

'If you don't have a horse, coffee and toast will be fine.'

'If you're that hungry I can do better than coffee and toast.'

'I'll leave it to you, but wouldn't you rather I cooked?'

'You're my guest.'

'Then I hope I haven't outstayed my welcome these last couple of days.'

'No fear of that. How's Daddy taking it?'

'Stone-faced. I need a bath, Jon.'

'Okay. You bath while I cook.'

'Prude.'

'After the last few nights?'

'Maybe not. Your tub's too small anyway.'

He left the bed and grabbed his bathrobe. 'Give me a couple of minutes,' he called over his shoulder as he descended the stairs.

Amy closed her eyes and soon a frown lined the softness of her features.

Downstairs, Childes quickly electric-shaved and washed, first turning on the bathtaps for Amy. He opened the bathroom cabinet and removed his contact lens case, inserting the soft lenses into his eyes before the mirror steamed up. He ran back up the stairs two at a time and donned faded jeans, tan sneakers and a grey sweater while Amy watched from the bed.

'You need fattening up,' she remarked.

'For which slaughter?' he answered and neither found any humour in the response.

'Your bath's about ready,' he said, running fingers through his dark tousled hair.

'I feel like a kept woman.'

'So do I once in a while, but they're hard to come by.'

'You're cheerful again.'

'It's a habit.' He realised there was a certain truth in his reply: suppression of the unfaceable, he reminded himself.

'A kiss will get me out of bed,' Amy said.

'Yeah? What will get you downstairs?'

'Come and find out.'

'The water will run over.'

'You're no fun at all sometimes.'

'And you're no schoolmarm.' He threw her the robe. 'Food in ten minutes.' Childes couldn't help moving to the bed, though, and kissing her lips, neck and breasts, before going down to the kitchen.

Later, when Amy sat opposite him at the tiny kitchen

table, her wringing wet hair and his blue bathrobe transforming her from schoolteacher to schoolgirl once again, they discussed their plans for the day.

'I'll have to go home and collect some things,' she told him, tucking into bacon, eggs and grilled tomatoes with undisguised enthusiasm.

'Want me to come with you?' He grinned at her appetite, no longer surprised that her trim figure was never affected by the amount of food she consumed. He bit into his toast, all that was on the plate before him.

Amy shook her head. 'Might be better if I went alone.'

'We'll have to have some kind of showdown sooner or later,' he said, referring to Paul Sebire.

'Later's better than sooner. You've got enough to contend with for now.'

'I'm getting used to having you around.'

She stopped eating for a moment. 'Feels sort of . . . okay, doesn't it?'

'Sort of.'

She screwed up her face and continued eating. 'I mean, it feels right, doesn't it? Comfortable. But exciting, too.'

'I think so.'

'You only think so,' she said flatly while chewing.

'Sure so. I could even grow to like it eventually.'

'Should I move in permanently?'

He was taken aback, but she did not appear to notice.

'We could give it a try,' she went on, not even looking at him, 'see how it goes.'

'If you won't think of your father, consider how Miss Piprelly would take to the idea of two of her teachers living in sin together.'

'At least we're male and female—that must be in our favour. Anyhow, Pip need never know.'

'When if someone sneezes at one end of an island this size people at the other end catch a cold? You've got to be kidding. She probably knows what's going on between us right now.'

'No problem then.'

He sighed good-humouredly. 'There is a difference, you know.'

Amy laid down her knife and fork. 'Are you trying to talk your way out of this?'

He laughed. 'Sounds like a great proposition to me. But—'

He stopped. He looked at her, but did not see. His eyes were wide.

'Jon . . . ?' She reached across the cluttered table and touched his hand.

The coffee percolator bubbled in the corner of the kitchen. A fly buzzed against a window frame. Dust motes floated in the rays from the sun. Yet everything seemed still.

'What is it?' Amy asked nervously.

Childes blinked. He began to rise. Stopped halfway. 'Oh no . . .' he moaned, '. . . not that . . .'

His knuckles were white against the table-top and his shoulders suddenly hunched, his head bowing.

Amy shivered when he raised his head once more and she saw the shocked anguish.

'Jon!' she shouted as he lurched for the door, knocking his empty coffee mug from the table, the handle breaking off as it hit the floor.

Amy pushed back her chair and followed him into the hallway. He was standing by the phone, one trembling finger attempting to dial a number. It was no use, he was shaking too much. He looked at her beseechingly.

She reached him and grasped him by the shoulder. 'Tell me what you've seen,' she implored.

'Help me, Amy. Please help me.'

She was stunned to see his eyes glistening with tears. 'Who, Jon, who do you want to ring?'

'Fran. Quickly! Something's happened to Gabby!'

Her heart juddered as if from a blow, but she took

the receiver from him, forcing herself to keep her own nerves under control. She asked him to tell her the number and at first, ridiculously, perversely, he could not remember. Then the figures came in a rush and he had to repeat them slowly for her.

'It's ringing,' she said, handing back the receiver and moving closer to him. She could feel the quivering of his body.

The phone at the other end was lifted and she heard the distant voice.

'Fran . . . ?'

'Is that you, Jonathan? Oh God, I'm glad you rang!' There was a terrible distressed brittleness to her voice and Childes sagged, the dread almost overpowering.

'Is Gabby . . . ?' he began to say.

'Something terrible's happened, Jon, something awful.'

'Fran . . .' His tears were blinding him now.

'It's Gabby's friend Annabel. She's missing, Jon. She came over earlier to play with Gabby, but she never came in. The police are next door with Melanie and Tony right now, and Melanie's almost hysterical with worry. Nobody's seen Annabel since, she's just vanished into thin air. Gabby's distraught and won't stop crying. Jonathan, can you hear me . . . ?'

Only Amy's support kept Childes from collapsing to the floor.

AMY DROVE Childes to the airport, casting frequent anxious looks at his pallid face. He said nothing at all during the short journey.

His relief was mixed with sorrow for the missing girl, for he knew Annabel's fate. *It* had made a mistake, he was sure of that; his daughter was meant to have been the victim. *It* would know by now.

Amy parked the MG while Childes checked in at the flight desk. She joined him in the lounge bar where they waited, neither one saying much, until his flight was called. She walked with him to the departure gate, an arm around his waist, his around her shoulders.

Amy kissed Childes tenderly before he went through, holding him tight for a few seconds. 'Ring me if you get a chance, Jon,' she told him.

He nodded, his face gaunt. Then he was gone, disappearing through the departure gate with the other passengers for Gatwick, his overnight bag slung over one shoulder.

Amy left the terminal and sat in her car until she saw the aircraft rise into the clear sky. She was weeping.

CHILDES RANG the doorbell and saw movement behind the panes of reeded glass almost immediately. The door opened and Fran stood there, a mixture of gladness and misery on her face.

'Jonathan,' she said, stepping forward as if to embrace him; she hesitated on seeing the figure standing behind Childes and the moment was gone.

'Hello, Fran,' Childes said, and half-turned towards his companion. 'You probably remember Detective Inspector Overoy.'

Confusion, then hostility, altered her features as she looked over his shoulder. 'Yes, how could I forget?' She frowned at her ex-husband, questioning him with her eyes.

'I'll explain inside,' Childes told her.

She stood aside to let them through and Overoy bade her good evening as he passed, eliciting little response.

'Let's go into the sitting room,' Fran said, but they heard the scampering of footsteps on the landing above before they could do as she suggested.

'Daddy, Daddy!' came Gabby's excited cry and then she was hurtling down the stairs, leaping the last three into Childes' outstretched arms as he went to meet her. She hugged him close, dampening his cheeks with her kisses and tears, her glasses pushed sideways on her face. He closed his eyes and held her tight.

She was sobbing as she blurted out' 'Daddy, they've taken Annabel away.'

'I know, Gabby, I know.'

'But why, Daddy? Did a nasty man take her?'

'We don't know. The policemen will find out.'

'Why won't he let her go? Her mummy misses her, and so do I—she's my best friend.' Her face was blotchy from crying, her eyes puffed up behind the lenses of her spectacles.

He eased his daughter down and sat next to her on the stairs, taking a handkerchief from his pocket to mop away the wetness on her cheeks. He removed her glasses and polished them, talking softly to her as he did so. Her fingers clutched his wrist all the while.

Overoy interrupted. 'I think I'll call in next door and have a word with Mr and Mrs, er . . .'

'Berridge,' Fran finished for him.

'You go ahead,' said Childes, putting an arm around Gabby's hunched shoulders. 'We'll talk when you're through.'

With a brief nod towards Fran, Overoy left, closing the front door behind him. She immediately locked it.

'What the hell is he doing here?' she demanded to know.

'I rang him before I left,' Childes explained. 'He picked me up at Gatwick and drove me over.'

'Yes, but what's he got to do with this?'

Childes stroked his daughter's hair and Gabby looked from him to her mother, revealing a new anxiety. He didn't want an argument in front of her.

'Gabby, look, you run upstairs and I'll be up to see you soon. Mummy and I have to talk.'

'You won't shout at each other, will you?'

She still remembered.

'No, of course not. We just have to discuss something privately.'

' 'Bout Annabel?'

'Yes.'

'But she's my friend. I want to talk about her too.'

'When I come up you can talk all you want.'

She rose, standing on the first step. Her arms went around his neck. 'Promise me you won't be long.'

'I promise.'

'I miss you, Daddy.'

'You too, Pickle.'

She climbed the stairs, turning and waving from the top before running along the landing to her room.

'Gabriel,' Fran called after her. 'I think it's time you got yourself ready for bed. Pink nightie's in your top drawer.'

They heard a sound that could have been a protest, but nothing more.

'It's been a bad day for her,' Fran remarked as Childes stood once more.

'Looks as though it's been tough on you as well,' he said.

'Imagine the hell Tony and Melanie have been through.' She kept her distance for just one moment longer, watching him uncertainly; and then she was in his arms, her head resting on his shoulder, hair soft against his cheek. 'Oh, Jon, it's so bloody awful.'

He soothed her as with his daughter, by stroking her hair.

'It could so easily have been Gabby,' she said.

He did not reply.

'It's funny,' she said, 'but I felt something was wrong this morning. Gabby was downstairs making tea and I got up to see why she was taking so long.' Fran gave a small, tired laugh. 'Would you believe she'd spilt the sugar and was patiently sweeping up every last grain so I wouldn't find out? Annabel must have come through the garden to play with her around that time. Perhaps she went out onto the main road—nobody knows, nobody saw her. Except the person who took her. Oh God, Gabby and Annabel have been warned so many times about going outside the gate!'

'We could both do with a drink,' he suggested.

'I was afraid to start—didn't know if I'd be able to

stop. I'd be no help to Melanie if I'd got plastered. I suppose it's okay now that you're here, though. You were always good at controlling my drinking.'

They went through to the sitting room, holding each other as though still lovers. Everything was so comfortably familiar to Childes despite the odd pieces of furniture collected after he had gone, five years of living in the house were difficult to forget; yet it was all so remote, no longer a part of him, of his life. It was an odd sensation, and not pleasant.

'You sit down,' he said, 'I'll fix the drinks. Gin and tonic still?'

Fran nodded. 'Still. Make mine a large one.' She slumped on to a sofa, kicking off her shoes and curling her legs beneath her, watching him all the time. 'Jonathan, when you phoned this morning I didn't give you the chance to say much, but I realised afterwards you were already distraught before I spoke. I don't know, there was something anxious just in the way you said my name.'

'D'you want ice?'

'Doesn't matter, just give me the drink. *Were* you upset when you rang?'

He poured a good measure of gin and reached for a tonic inside the glass cabinet. 'I thought something had happened to Gabby,' he replied.

'To Gabby? Why, what . . . ?' Her voice trailed off, and then she closed her eyes. 'Oh no, not again,' she murmured softly.

He brought her gin and tonic over and her gaze never left his as he handed her the glass. 'Tell me,' she said, almost as a plea.

Childes poured himself a Scotch, then returned to the sofa, sitting close to her. 'The sightings are happening again.'

'Jon . . .'

'This morning I had an overpowering feeling that Gabby was in danger.' Could he tell her yet that he had *known* their daughter was in danger, that Annabel

had been taken by mistake? Throughout the day he
had been taunted by this other, perverted, mind, received glimpses of the prolonged atrocity, the creature, whoever and whatever it was, tormenting him,
searching out his mind to inflict painful visions. And
oddly, after a while Childes had learned to inure himself to the sightings, for he had become aware that the
worst had already happened, that Annabel could no
longer feel the torture. She hadn't from almost the
beginning. He had to tell Fran that much at least.

'But it wasn't Gabby, it was her friend, Annabel,'
his ex-wife had already said.

'Yes, somehow I got things wrong in my mind.' It
was the coward's way, but she would have to face
another shock before the whole truth could be told.
Take it slowly, he said to himself, one bit at a time.
'Fran, there's something you've got to know.'

She took a large swallow of gin as if steeling herself,
aware that his 'intuitions' were always bad, never good.
She said it for him, unable to stop herself. 'Annabel's
dead, isn't she?'

He bowed his head, avoiding her eyes.

Fran's face crumpled, the drink spilling over onto
her trembling hand. Childes took the glass from her,
leaning over to place it on the occasional table beside
the sofa. He slid an arm around her shoulders and
pulled her against his chest.

'It's so vile, so wicked,' she moaned. 'Oh dear God,
what will we tell Tony and Melanie? *How* can we tell
them?'

'No, Fran, we can't say anything yet. That'll be up
to the police when . . . when they find her body.'

'But how can I face Melanie, how can I help her
when I know? Are you sure, Jon, are you absolutely
certain?'

'It's like before.'

'You were never wrong.'

'No.'

He felt her body stiffen. 'Why did you think Gabby

had been taken?' She pulled away so that she could look into his face. Fran had never been a fool.

'I'm not sure. I suppose I was confused because it happened so close to home.'

She frowned disbelievingly and was about to say more when they heard the doorbell.

'That'll be Overoy,' Childes said, relieved. 'I'll let him in.'

The detective's expression was sombre when he followed Childes into the sitting room. 'They're taking it badly,' he said.

'What would you expect?' Fran countered with a sharpness that surprised both men.

'Sorry, that was pretty trite,' Overoy apologised. He nodded as Childes showed him the whisky bottle from across the room. 'Can I ask you the same question I asked Annabel's parents, Mrs Childes? Er, it is still *Childes*, isn't it?'

'Childes sounds better on a letter-heading than my maiden name so I never bothered to revert. It's less confusing for Gabriel, too. As for your first question, it's one I've been asked several times today by your colleagues and the answer remains the same: I've noticed no one who could be described as suspicious within the last week or so, or even the last few months. Now let me ask you two a question.'

Overoy took the whisky glass from Childes and their eyes met for a brief moment.

'Take a seat, Inspector, you look uncomfortable standing there.' Fran reached for her gin and tonic, noting her hand was still shaky as she picked up the glass. But she was curious too, a new suspicion forming in her mind. Childes came over and sat next to her.

'It seems peculiar to me that Jonathan should immediately contact you just because he's had another of his infamous sightings, and that you should take the trouble of picking him up at the airport and bringing him here. I mean, why you when he hasn't seen you for—what, nearly three years?'

'I'm familiar with his background, Mrs Childes, his special ability.'

'Yes, I know you've come to believe in it. But to drop everything just to meet him? I wonder if you were even on duty today? It is a Saturday, after all.'

Childes answered this time. 'As a matter of fact I contacted Inspector Overoy at home.'

'Ah, you had his private number.'

'We didn't intend to keep anything from you, Fran. It's just that we thought—*I* thought—that you might be upset enough over Annabel's disappearance without giving you more to worry about.'

A fresh fear was in her eyes. She used both hands to raise the gin to her lips, sipped, then slowly lowered the glass so that it rested in her lap. Her back was rigid and her voice unsteady when she said: 'I think it's time you told me everything.'

The hour was late.

Childes and his ex-wife sat alone at a table in the kitchen, the remains of an unenthusiastically cooked meal before them, the food itself eaten with even less enthusiasm. All was quiet in Gabby's bedroom.

'I should see how Melanie is.' Fran bit into her lower lip, an anxiety habit that he had often chided her over during their marriage.

'It's well after ten, Fran—I shouldn't disturb her now. Besides, Melanie's doctor may have sedated her, so she could be sleeping.'

Fran's shoulders slumped. 'What would I say to her anyway, knowing what you've told me? Can you really be so positive?'

He knew what she referred to. 'I wish I could have some doubt.'

'No, as I said before, you were never wrong about . . . about those things.' There was no jibe in her remarks, only an immense sadness. 'But there is something different going on this time, isn't there? This isn't like those other incidents years ago.'

He sipped lukewarm coffee before answering. 'I've got no explanation. Somehow this monster knows me, can penetrate my mind: how and why is a mystery.'

'Perhaps he's accidentally stumbled upon your access code.'

He regarded her with surprise. 'I don't follow.'

Fran pushed her plate to one side and leaned her elbows on the table. 'Look at it this way, using your beloved computers as an analogy. When you want to gain access to another system, you need that system's special code to open the door, don't you? Once you have that code, you can get inside the other machine's memory bank. In fact, you have dialogue between both computers, right? Well, maybe this other mind got hold of your access code by accident or other means. Or perhaps subconsciously, you have his.'

'I didn't realise you were interested in such things.'

'I'm not as a rule, but what happened to us last time left me a little curious. I did some research—not much, just enough to try and understand. A lot still doesn't make much sense to me, but at least I know something of the various theories on psychic phenomena. Admittedly most appear to be ridiculous, though there is a certain pleasing logic to some. I'm only surprised you never investigated further yourself.'

He became uncomfortable. 'I wanted to forget everything that happened, not pursue it.'

'Strange.'

'What is?'

'Oh, it doesn't matter.' She smiled distantly. 'I remember you never even liked ghost stories. I always put it down to your microchip disposition; you've no room in that technological brain of yours for such romanticisms. How ironic that someone like you should have received psychic messages; it might even have been funny if they hadn't been so horrendous.'

'I've changed at least in some ways.'

'I'd be interested to hear.'

'Computers have taken a back seat. They're just a job, and only part-time at that.'

'Then you really have changed. Any other miracles?'

'Different lifestyle, more easy-going I guess you could say, more time spent relaxing, enjoying the things around me.'

'You weren't some kind of work-ogre when you were here, Jon, although you did put in too many hours. You made time for me and Gabby when you could.'

'I realise now it was never enough.'

'I was at fault too, I had my own unfair demands. But it's old territory now, there's no point in re-exploring.'

'No, as you say: old territory.' He placed the coffee mug back on the table. 'Fran, I'm worried about you both staying here on your own.'

'Then you really do think this monster meant to snatch Gabby?'

'It wanted to get at me through her.'

'How do you know it's the same person?' Her voice rose in anger. 'And why do you refer to him as *it?* My God, he's a ghoul, but of the human kind.'

'I just can't think of it as a man. The feeling of total malevolence is too overpowering, too *in*human. When its thoughts force their way into mine I can almost smell the corruption, I can almost *see* its depravity.'

'God, you have changed.'

He shook his head wearily. 'I'm trying to describe the impression I'm left with, the sense of festering malignancy it imposes upon me. The feeling is ugly, Fran, and terrifying.'

'I can see. Jonathan, I don't doubt these visions, that you actually *suffer* these awful things, but are you sure you're not losing control of your own mind?'

He tried to smile. 'You never were one for holding back. You mean am I going mad?'

'No, I don't mean that. But could these terrible experiences cause you to hallucinate as well? Let's face it, there's precious little that anybody knows about the million functions of the mind, so who can tell what it takes to throw it slightly out of sync?'

'You have to take my word for it: the person, if that's what you want to call this creature, who murdered the prostitute and the old man, and who mutilated the dead boy, is the same one who mistakenly took away Annabel. It knows me and wants to hurt me. That's why you and Gabby have to be protected.'

'But how could he know where we lived? Did he read the address from your mind, too? The whole thing's crazy, Jonathan!'

'I can't hide my past from it, Fran, don't you see?'

'No, I bloody don't.'

'Like the computer, it's all in my memory bank and, as you said, access is easy once you have the code. Maybe it discovered what happened to me before, how I saw those other murders.' A thought occurred to him. 'Fran, did you have this number put back in the phone directory?'

'Not the old one, not after all those crank calls we used to receive. I couldn't stay ex-directory, not in my line of work, so I had a new number listed.'

Childes slumped back in his chair. 'Then that's probably the answer.'

'Oh, it's not human, but it can look up telephone numbers.' She tapped her foot impatiently.

'I've tried to explain. It's a person, but something inside isn't human. This thing's intelligent, otherwise the police would have caught it by now, and it's perceptive.'

'Not perceptive enough to kidnap the right little girl,' she snapped.

'No, thank . . .' He stopped himself from finishing the sentence and that moment of guilt between them somehow eased the tension. 'The point is,' Childes went on more gently, 'it will soon realise the mistake—if it doesn't know through Annabel.'

'The newspapers.'

'All the media.'

Her eyes widened. 'Jon, if they make the connection . . .'

He studied the table top. 'We'll have to go through the whole business all over again. It's too much of a coincidence for another child to be kidnapped right next door to the man who assisted police investigations last time through psychic detection.'

'I couldn't face that again.'

'Another reason for you to move out for a while. Overoy's arranged for someone to watch the house for your protection, but they can't keep reporters away. As it is, the pretext is that the police are keeping an eye on Tony and Melanie, but that won't fool any journalist for long. They're going to have a field-day when they learn the truth.' He was cautious with his next suggestion. 'I think it would be a good idea if you both came back with me for a while.'

'There's no way I could do that, Jon,' she responded immediately. 'I've got my job, remember? And Gabby has school.'

'A couple of weeks off for her wouldn't hurt, and you must be due for some leave.'

She shook her head. 'Uh huh, the agency's too busy right at this moment and we can't afford to turn away clients. Besides, Gabby and I would have to come back eventually, so what would happen then?'

'Hopefully this killer will have been caught.'

'I'd like to know how. Your idea's impractical, Jon, but there is a compromise: I could stay with my mother. She'd love to have Gabby in her clutches and she's not too far out of town, so travelling in to work would be easy for me.'

'Why not let Gabby return with me on her own?'

His ex-wife's reply was sharp and unequivocal. 'The court gave me custody.'

'I didn't contest.'

'You were wise not to. Anyway, hasn't it occurred to you that you're the danger point in this situation? Haven't you wondered if your so-called tormentor didn't come to this house looking for you?'

That possibility had been discussed between Overoy

and himself during the drive from the airport. 'You may be right, Fran, there's no way of being sure; but that would prove it doesn't know where I live now.'

'The more delving into your mind he does, the more he'll discover about you.' She persisted in not referring to Annabel's kidnapper as 'it'.

'The power doesn't work that way, the thoughts aren't that definitive. It will have some idea of surroundings, but not location. Don't you recall how I could describe only the area where the murdered children were to be found?'

'You were pretty accurate but, all right, I take your point. You're still a danger, though.'

He had to concede. 'You'll have to be guarded even if you do go to your mother's.'

'She'll adore the excitement, you know what she's like.'

'Yeah, I do. You'll keep Gabby away from school?'

'If you think that's best. Maybe we'll find another close to Mother's.'

'Better still.'

'Okay, I agree.' Fran ran a hand through her auburn hair and seemed to relax a little. 'Would you like more coffee?'

'No, I'm sinking fast. Is it okay if I stay the night?'

'I was assuming you would. Despite everything that's happened between us in the past, you know you're always welcome here.' She touched his hand across the table, the gesture only slightly awkward, and he responded by squeezing her fingers, then letting go. 'We may not have made each other very happy in the long run, but we did have a certain something going for us, didn't we?'

Tired though he was, Childes managed to smile back. 'They were good years, Fran.'

'To begin with.'

'We changed in ourselves, became unfamiliar to each other.'

'When—' she began to say, but he interrupted.

'Old territory, Fran.'

She lowered her gaze. 'I'll fix up the bed in the spare room for you. If that's where you want to sleep. . .' The words were deliberately left hanging in the air.

He was tempted. Fran was no less desirable than she had ever been and the emotions wrung out by a fraught day had left them both in need of physical comforting. Moments went by before he answered.

'I've got kind of close to someone,' he said.

There was a trace of resentment in Fran's question. 'A certain fellow-teacher?'

'How did you know?' Childes was surprised.

'Gabby was full of the nice lady teacher she met last time she came back from visiting you. It's been going on for quite a while, hasn't it? Don't worry, you can speak freely; I'm long past jealousy, not that I have that particular right any more so far as you're concerned.'

'Her name is Aimée Sebire.'

'French?'

'Just the name. I've known her for more than two years now.'

'Sounds serious.'

He did not reply.

'I just get involved with married men,' Fran sighed. 'I suppose I never did choose very well.'

'You're still beautiful, Fran.'

'But resistible.'

'Under different circumstances, I—'

'It's okay, I'm deliberately making you squirm. Independence for a woman isn't all it's cracked up to be, even in this day and age; a warm body to cuddle up with, a strong male shoulder to fall asleep on, can still be a necessity for us liberated ladies.' She rose slowly from the table and for the first time he noticed the shadows beneath her eyes. 'I'll get the bedclothes. You haven't told me yet what you and Inspector Overoy plan to do about our friend the ogre.' She waited by the kitchen door for his reply.

He twisted in his chair to face Fran and the tone of his words and their implications chilled her. 'So far it's been searching for me, probing my mind. Overoy thinks it's time I tried to reverse the situation.'

He awoke and sensed someone else was in the room with him. For a few brief seconds he was disorientated, the dim light unfamiliar, subdued shapes unidentifiable. The events of the day crowded back in on him. He was home. No, not home. Temporarily back in his old house with Fran and Gabby. The light was from the streetlamp outside.

A shadow was moving closer.

Childes sat up, the movement sharp and rigid, stiffness caused by sudden fear.

A weight on the bed, and then Fran's quietened voice.

'I'm sorry, Jon. I can't sleep alone, not tonight. Please don't be angry.'

He raised the covers and she slid in beside him, pushing close. Her nightdress was soft against his skin.

'We don't have to make love,' she whispered. 'I'm not here for that. Just put your arms around me and hold me for a while.'

He did so. And they did make love.

HE AWOKE again in the night, much later, when sleep had a firmer hold.

A hand gripped his shoulder: Fran had been roused too. 'What is it?' she hissed.

'I don't—'

The sound came again.

'Gabby!' they both said together.

Childes scrambled from the bed, Fran following, and made for the door, the coldness of terror abruptly roughening the skin of his naked body with tiny bumps. He fumbled for the light-switch in the hallway, giddy for a moment, the light hurting his eyes.

They saw the black cat standing outside Gabby's open bedroom door, back arched, a million needles bristling. Miss Puddles glared ahead, eyes venomous, jaw wide in an angry, pointed-tooth grin.

Gabby's cry again, calling piercingly.

The cat's stiffened hairs ruffled as if disturbed by a draught. She disappeared down the stairway.

They rushed along the landing and when they entered their daughter's room, Gabby was sitting bolt upright in the bed. She was staring into a far corner by the doorway, the weak glow from the nightlight casting deep shadows across her features.

She did not look at them when they ran to the bed, but kept watching the darkened corner, seeing something there. Something that was not visible to her mother and father.

When Fran hugged her close, she blinked rapidly as if emerging from a dream. Childes looked on with concern as Gabby pulled away and scrabbled around her bedside cabinet for something; she found her glasses and quickly put them on. Once more she peered into the shadowy corner.

'Where is she?' Gabby's words were tearful.

'Who, darling, who?' asked Fran, holding her comfortingly.

'Has she gone away again, Mummy? She looked so sad.'

Childes felt the hair on the back of his neck prickle. His forehead and the palms of his hands were clammy with cold sweat.

'Tell me who, Gabriel,' said her mother, 'tell me who you saw.'

'She touched me and she was so cold, Mummy, so *freezing*. Annabel looked so sad.'

Deep within Childes, a long-forgotten memory stirred.

THE PACKAGE arrived by first post Monday morning and it was addressed to JONATHAN CHILDES. Both the name and his ex-wife's address were hand-written in small, neat, capital letters. The brown envelope was a standard ten-by-seven size.

Inside was a narrow, four-inch-square cardboard box.
Inside the box was crumpled tissue paper.
Wrapped in the tissue were six objects.
Five were tiny fingers and thumb.
The last was a smooth, white moonstone.

LIFE WENT on; it always does.

Childes returned to the island after two days of intensive questioning by the police and having seen his ex-wife and daughter safely away to Fran's mother, who lived in a quiet village not many miles from London. He had not accompanied them, wanting no impressions of the journey imprinted on his mind.

Although there had been no more help he could give the investigating officers, he suspected that only Detective Inspector Overoy's assurances had persuaded them to allow his departure. Neither the postmark (a suburb of the city) nor the neat handwriting of the address on the macabre package provided any useful clues. There had been no saliva traces on the gummed envelope flap, for it was of the self-adhesive kind, and no clear fingerprints could be established on the paper or on the box inside. Mention of the semi-precious stone found among the mutilated human fingers had been kept from the media: copycat crimes were never encouraged by the police. That there was a 'probable' connection between the kidnapping and possibly three other crimes already under investigation could not be withheld, but the authorities declined to say why they believed there was a link.

Childes benefited from their discretion and had managed to leave the mainland before conclusions could be drawn by outsiders. His psychic contact with the killer had remained a closely guarded secret. The pathologist's report stated that the fingers had been severed from a victim already dead. There was mercy in that alone.

Annabel's body was not recovered and no vision of its whereabouts came to Childes. He tried earnestly to probe with his mind but to no avail.

Nothing more was to happen until a few weeks later.

In the dream he watched the dark-haired boy and knew the boy was himself.

He sat upright in the narrow bed, sheets bunched around him, and he was young, very young. He was speaking, the same words repeated over and over again like a senseless litany.

'. . . you . . . can't . . . be . . .'

The figure of a woman stood at the end of the bed, an ivory statue, unmoving in the moonlight, watching as did he, the dreamer. A terrible sorrow ebbed from her and, just as the sleeping observer knew that the boy was his younger self, he knew the woman was his mother. But she was dead.

'. . . he . . . says . . . you can't . . . you can't . . . be . . .' mumbled the boy, and the sadness between woman and child, mother and son, became immense.

And the son then became aware of the observer, his startled eyes looking upwards, into the darkest corner of the room. He looked directly at himself.

But the moment was gone as heavy, lumbering footsteps sounded along the corridor outside. So, too, was gone the spectral vision of his mother.

The dark shadow of a man stood swaying in the doorway and Childes, the onlooker, was almost overwhelmed by the wretched anger exuding from his father in threatening waves, a guilt-ridden fury that charged the atmosphere. Childes cringed, as did his younger self, the boy, when the drunken man lurched forward, fists raised.

'I told you,' the father shouted. 'No more! No more. . .' The boy screamed from beneath the bedclothes as the blows fell.

Childes tried to call out, to warn his father to leave the boy alone, that he could not help seeing his mother's ghost-spirit, that she had returned to reassure him, to let him know that her love had not perished with her cancer-riddled body, that love always continued, the grave was no captor or gaoler or executioner, that she would ever love him and he could know that through his special gift which allowed him to see . . . But his father would not listen, did not hear, his wrath over-riding all other senses and emotions. He had told his son there was no life after death, the dead could never come back to torment, that his mother had died full of hate and had deserved the lingering suffering because God willed such upon those whose hearts were corrupted with hatred, and she could not rise again to talk of love when she was filled with an odious loathing of him, her husband, the boy's father, and there were no such things as spirits or ghosts or hauntings because even the Church denied them, and there was nothing like that, nothing at all, *nothing. . .!*

The boy's screams had sunk to sobs and the beating this time was worse than any of the others. Soon his consciousness began to fade as he closed away his mind, deliberately rejecting what was happening, what *had* happened. And Childes, the man, the dreaming witness, was aware that the boy's mind had closed against what *would* happen.

He awoke whimpering, as he had all those years ago when only a boy.

'Jon, are you all right?'

Amy was leaning over him, her hair brushing his cheek. 'You were having a nightmare, like before, saying the same words, and then yelling at someone, screaming for them to stop.'

His breathing was shallow, fast, his chest rising in sharp movements. She had turned on the bedside lamp and her sweet face, anxious though it was, was a relief from the nightmare.

'He . . . he made me . . .' he whispered.

'Who, Jon? And what?'

Alertness was swiftly returning. Childes lay there for a few more seconds, gathering his thoughts, then pushed himself up so that his back was against the wall. Amy half-knelt beside him, shadows accentuating the soft curves of her body as the bedsheet fell around her waist. She smoothed away dark hair that hung over his forehead.

'What did I say in my sleep?' he asked her.

'You mumbled, but it sounded like: "It can't—" no, "—*you* can't be". You kept saying the same thing over and over again and then you started shouting.'

Although the hour was late, there was no chill in the air; not even a breeze came through the open window.

'Oh, Amy, Amy, I think I'm beginning to understand,' he said, and the words were almost a moan.

Her arm went around his body and she rested her head against his shoulder. 'You frighten me so much,' she said. 'Talk to me now, Jon, tell me what you think it is you understand. Please don't hide anything away from me.'

He caressed her back, absorbing the warmth that was more than physical through sensitive fingertips. He began to talk, speaking in a soft, low voice, hesitant at first, the words as much for himself as for her.

'When Gabby . . . when she saw . . . when she thought she saw Annabel that night . . . after Annabel had been . . . taken . . . something was revived in me, a thought, a feeling, a memory. Something kept hidden away for a long, long time. It's complex, and I know I won't be able to explain it all, but I'll try, if only for my own sake.'

Amy eased away so that her weight was not on him.

'I suppose no one really wants to hate their father,' he went on, 'and remember, for so many years he was my only parent, so that guilt may have played some small part in my refusal to admit certain facts about myself. I can't be sure, I'm just searching, Amy, trying to come up with some answers, a *rationale,* if you like.'

He fell silent, as though searching his own thoughts, attempting to bring some order to them, and Amy tried helping. 'Your dream, Jon. Perhaps you should start there.'

Childes' fingers pressed against his closed eyelids. 'Yes,' he said after a while, 'the dream, that's the key. Only I'm not sure it was just a dream, Amy.' Reaching for her hand, he held it in his lap and looked towards the window on the far side of the room. 'I saw myself as a boy—about Gabby's age, I think—and I seemed to be looking down at him—at *myself*—as if hovering over his bedroom. The boy was sitting up in bed, afraid, yet somehow I felt there was a kind of happiness about him. Someone else was in the room, standing in the moonlight, watching the boy as I was. A woman. I know it was my mother.'

Childes breathed in deeply while Amy quietly waited. His face was drawn and the glistening in his eyes indicated both sadness and the subdued excitement of discovery. She tensed when he said, 'But my mother had been dead for over a week.'

'Jon—'

'No, just listen, Amy. Gabby wasn't dreaming when she saw Annabel that night. Don't you see? She has my gift, she's psychic, mediumistic—I don't know what term you'd use because it's a subject I've evaded most of my life. Gabby and I are the same, she's inherited the power from me. But my father, God help him, beat such notions out of my head; he refused to ac-knowledge such a power and wouldn't let me *accept* it! In my dream I watched him come into the room and beat the boy—beat me!—until I lost consciousness. And that hadn't been the first time, and I don't think it was the last. He made me reject this ability, this extra-sensing, forced me to black the power from my mind.'

'But why should he—?'

'I don't know! I had a feeling from him, though, in the dream. He was confused and angry—and God, yes, he was frightened—but there was guilt also! He may have blamed himself in some way for her death, or . . .' he squeezed his eyes shut to concentrate, to remember '. . . or maybe for the way he couldn't cope with her last weeks of dying. He was a drunkard, a selfish man who could never face up to his own responsibilities. I don't think he could take her suffering, he wasn't able to help her through the pain. He may even have treated her badly and later was ashamed. My father wanted to shut out her memory totally, but my visions, my "sightings", wouldn't allow that. I was destroying the barrier he'd erected around his own emotions.'

He paused, to regain his breath, for the words had been an unleashed torrent. 'I don't think I'll ever know the whole truth, Amy; I can only tell you what I've sensed. Consciously I've spurned anything to do with the supernatural, as any kid who has been constantly taught that something is wrong or unnatural might eventually, yet the power has always stayed locked away inside me. Can you imagine the conflict that must have gone on inside my young mind? I loved and missed my mother, wanted her comfort, yet my father forced me to reject her, and with her, my own special perception. I suppose the conscious side of my mind finally won the battle, but it wasn't a victory that could be maintained for ever.'

Amy took her hand from his so that she could touch his face. 'It could explain so much about you,' she said, and smiled. 'Perhaps even why you chose such an ultimately logical career. The only wonder is that you're not full of neuroses.'

'Who says I'm not?' He shifted in the bed, aware of his own tenseness. 'But why now, Amy? Why has all this bubbled to the surface, now?'

'It hasn't just happened, don't you see? The process began three years ago.'

'The murders of those children?'

'Isn't that when the extra sense began to surface again? But who knows what else you perceived in this special way that you put down to mere intuition?'

He was thoughtful, then said slowly, 'Maybe it took another mind to trigger it off.' He added more quietly, 'Somebody may have found my code.'

'What?'

'Something Fran said to me, equating minds with computers and access codes. The comparison isn't important, but the principle could be.' He suddenly raised his knees and leaned forward. 'Another point I've remembered about my dream tonight, if that's what it can be called. The boy saw me. He was aware of me.'

She shook her head. 'I don't understand.'

'He looked up at me from his bed. I looked up at *myself*, Amy! No, I didn't dream tonight; it was a memory, a recall. I remember my mother's spirit coming to me, showing me her love, telling me that death wasn't final; and I remember a different pair of eyes watching me on that particular night—*I swear to you I remember that night from the boy's point of view*—and those eyes belonged to someone who cared, like my mother, someone who was concerned for me. Amy, do you understand now? I had the power then to see my future-self! Am I insane, Amy, or is that the truth of it? I had the power to see my future-self and tonight I had the power to go back and see my *past*-self!'

He shuddered and she clung to him. 'It's strong in me,' he told her. 'God, I can feel the power so strong in me. And . . . and . . .'

The glow was before him, a vaporous shimmering,

yet he knew the image was inside his head, not there in the room. Small to begin with, gradually growing solid, becoming rounded, taking form.

A moonstone.

But no. Still growing, altering in shape, in texture. Not a moonstone any longer.

Fissures and craters scarred its surface. Mountain ranges shadowed its whiteness.

He saw the moon itself.

And with the image came a dreadful, a stomach-wrenching foreboding.

JEANETTE SPRINTED across the circular lawn, heading for the science department and praying that no staff member would catch her trespassing on hallowed ground. She skirted around the statue of the school's founder, dark hair flailing loosely behind, books for the next lesson tucked tightly beneath one arm. Fortunately, the lesson was Computer Studies and Mr Childes seldom got really cross, although occasionally he could get quite stern if the girls misbehaved *too* much.

She was relieved to be off the lawn and on the gravel turning circle for visitors' cars. Taking the stone steps two at a time, Jeanette pushed through the glass entrance doors and pounded up more stairs to the computer room which was on the first floor with the science laboratory, spilling her books near the top so that she had to pound down again to gather them up. Once more she made the ascent.

Outside the computer room she paused in order to compose herself. Three deep breaths, a swift combing of hair with clawed fingers, and she entered.

'Hello, Jeanette,' Childes greeted her with a trace of a frown. 'You're a little late.'

'I know, sir, I'm sorry,' she said, still breathless despite her efforts to steady herself. 'I left my program sheet in the dormitory this morning and didn't have the chance to fetch it between lessons.' She regarded him apprehensively and he smiled.

'That's okay ' he told her. 'Let's see, you'll have to share with Nicola and Isobel, then take your turn with the screen when they're finished. Hope you worked out a decent program to try.'

'A spelling test, sir.'

Somebody giggled.

'Well, that's a little basic, Jeanette, but it'll be fine,' said Childes, then added for the benefit of the rest of the class: 'Everybody has to find their own way with computers, there are no short cuts to begin with. Takes a while for the sheer logic of it all to sink in, but once it has, you'll be up and running.'

Jeanette pulled up a chair behind Nicola and Isobel and looked over their shoulders at the monitor screen they were using. She saw they were playing an anagram game.

Childes went from machine to machine, offering advice and suggestions as to how his pupils could increase the information in their programs and make them more interesting.

He lingered behind Kelly and nodded with pleasure. She was devising sailing times from and into the local marina, assuming she had a yacht or motorboat moored there, having taken the trouble to visit the harbour master for detailed information on traffic flow and regulations. Kelly became aware of his interest and glanced round at him, a smile on her upturned face.

As usual, he thought, you're just a trifle too smug, Kelly, but there's no denying you're my brightest. He said, 'That's a good exercise, Kelly. Looking towards the future?'

'Yes, Mr Childes, the very-near future. But my yacht's more likely to be in the Bahamas.'

He held back the grin. 'I don't doubt it.'

She turned back to the machine and he watched her deft fingers tap decisively at the keyboard. The only blemish on her hand was an ink stain and he won-

dered, not for the first time, what had caused him to
see the limb so horribly burned those few weeks ago.
Premonitions were not part of the strange ability he
possessed. Yet, as a boy, hadn't he seen his future-
self? He was confused and afraid, but no longer willing to be a compliant victim of this terrible curse, nor
of the monster who had taunted him through his own
mind. Childes had finally began to probe himself, a
tactic he had agreed with Overoy to try, searching for
the perverted psyche of his tormentor. The burning
down of the psychiatric hospital had still not officially
been attributed to any particular person, but neither
he himself, nor Overoy, had any doubt it was the same
one who had mutilated and murdered before. He supposed he ought to have been grateful for the detective's belief in him, and Overoy had certainly worked
hard behind the scenes to prevent Childes' name being
linked with Annabel's disappearance. Overoy was making amends for mishandling the publicity surrounding
their past association, yet Childes could not find the
willingness to fully trust the man. The last time they
had spoken, just three days before, Overoy had told
him that he was now the chief liaison officer in charge
of investigations into all four crimes, his involvement
with Childes being the prime factor in the appoint-
ment; unfortunately, there had been no solid leads as
yet to follow up. Was there any more information
Childes could give him to save him from looking a
total jackass? None at all, Childes had replied, then,
almost apologetically, he had mentioned the curious
vision of the moonstone which had gradually changed
into the moon itself. What did it mean? Who the hell
knew? And no, there still had not been any contact
with the other mind. In fact, after finally accepting he
possessed an extra-sensory ability, Childes now wondered if the power had left him, like some spectre that
vanished when focused upon.

He wondered: Is it all over? Had the creature, like
the child-murderer before, ceased to exist, become its

own executioner? Had the terrible visions and the nightmares ended?

'Sir. Sir!'

Kelly's voice had broken into his thoughts. He quickly glanced up to find she had twisted towards him once more, this time with a look of consternation on her face.

'What is it, Kelly?' he asked, rising from the desk.

'Something's gone wrong with my computer.' She turned back to the screen and stabbed at the keyboard below.

'Whoa!' he said, going over. 'Don't take it out on the machine. Let's just go through the thing logically.'

He leaned over her and froze, further words locked in his throat. His hand gripped the back of her chair as a soft pressure nudged at his mind.

'What made you write this on the display, Kelly?' he forced himself to say calmly.

'*I* didn't do it,' she retorted indignantly. 'It just appeared and everything else went off.'

'You know that's impossible.'

'Honest, sir, I didn't do anything.'

'Okay, clear the screen and start again.'

The girl touched the RETURN key. Nothing happened.

Childes, not sure if she were playing stupid games with him, impatiently leaned forward and pressed the same key. It had no effect.

'Kelly, have you—?'

'How could I? There's no way I could make the computer do that.'

'All right, let me take your seat.'

She stood and Childes eased himself into the chair, watching the monitor warily as if disbelieving his own eyes. His hands hovered nervously over the keyboard. Other girls in the classroom were looking round curiously at them.

'We'll try RESET.' Childes murmured, keeping his voice steady, disguising the panic bubbling inside. He could not hide the beads of perspiration that had rapidly formed on his forehead, though.

He fingered the key.

The screen went blank and he sighed with relief.

The single word appeared again.

'Why's the computer doing that, sir?' Kelly asked close to his shoulder, both astonished and fascinated by the phenomenon.

'I've no idea,' he replied. 'It shouldn't happen, it should be impossible for it to happen. Could be an outsider's somehow tapped into your circuit.' Extremely unlikely, he thought and then remembered Fran's computer/mind analogy. Nonsense, that had nothing to do with this! He pressed RESET again.

The word disappeared. Then reappeared.

'I don't want to lose your program,' Childes told Kelly, his voice more even than the turmoil inside his head should have allowed, 'but I'm afraid I'll have to.'

This time he tapped HOME.

The screen went blank, became a dark void. He rested back in the chair.

And sat rigid when the word shone from the blackness yet again.

He stared transfixed at the screen, his eyes wide, the green glowing word reflected in his contact lenses. The small, computer-typed word said:

MOON

Some of the other girls had gathered round, but sudden cries came from those who had remained at their machines. Childes pushed his chair back and went to each one. The same single word was impossibly displayed on every monitor.

In a desperation that alarmed the girls, he reached underneath the benches and yanked out all the plugs, cutting off the power supply to each computer so that the screens blinked to a lifeless grey. He waited in the centre of the classroom, his chest heaving, the girls beginning to huddle together as if he were mad.

Cautiously he approached the computer which Kelly had been operating. He knelt, picking up the power plug once again, and slid it into the socket.

The computer screen came to life, but now the word that had frightened him so much was missing.

He found Amy after the lesson had finished, having barely managed to show his pupils a calm face throughout the rest of the period, explaining that what had occurred was due to some peculiar malfunction or the intrusion of another computer. The explanation was hardly feasible, but the girls appeared to accept his word.

Childes drove Amy away from the school, grateful that the lesson had preceded the lunch break, giving them the opportunity to be alone. He did not stop until they had found a remote point on the clifftops.

He switched off the engine and looked out at the sea. Only after a few more moments when his breathing had steadied did he turn to her and say: 'It's here, Amy. It's here on the island.'

THE DAY was perfect. Only a few small clouds clung to the sky like glued cotton-wool buds, seemingly stuck fast to a vividly blue board, unable to drift, with no breeze even in the upper reaches. The sun, a brilliant fireball, gloried in its dominance. A faint low mist spread over the sea, and other islands were merely hazy smudges in the distance.

Scores of small motor-powered boats left short white plumes in their wakes, while yachts searched in vain for the slightest wind that would allow use of canvas. Further in, closer to the shore, wind-surfers drifted astride their boards, colourful sails resting flatly beside them in the water. Sandy beaches were full, only the less accessible coves and inlets still quiet and uncrowded, refuges for those who valued their peace enough to undertake arduous climbs.

On the clifftop overlooking one such secluded bay, stood La Roche Ladies College, its white main structure a beacon lit by the sun.

A perfect Saturday for Open Day, when staff and girls and classrooms preened themselves under inspection. An important day for the school: prize-giving, awards and certificates for excellence (or even plain usefulness), and general school or house achievements throughout the year; speeches by the principal, Miss Estelle Piprelly, and a member of the governing board,

Conseiller Victor Platnauer; a recitation by La Roche's head girl of the year's events within the school related in obligatory (by tradition) rhyming verse, a test of nerve and ingenuity (and often of perseverance by the assembled guests); the luring of more fee-paying parents. A fun day for the school: various raffles, a lottery, games, a second-hand uniform sale; a strawberry-and-cream stall, a jam, sweets and cake stall, a hot-dog stall and barbecue, a wine and orange-squash stall, a gymnastic display, light choral singing, country dancing; and all to be enjoyed on the lawns.

A day for things *not* to go wrong.

Milling parents, arriving vehicles jostling for space in the overcrowded carpark and driveway, schoolgirls excited and pretending not to be, giggling though under threat to be on best behaviour. Childes had left the computer classroom when the mandatory parent/teacher discussion period was over. Now he watched the activity with restless attention. He tried not to let his close scrutiny of each passing face appear too obvious, but more than one parent was made to feel uncomfortable under his gaze.

And after a while he, too, had the feeling of being studied. He turned quickly and found Miss Piprelly, only yards away and supposedly in conversation with a group of parents and staff, staring intently at him. Their eyes met and a curious recognition passed between them, a *knowing* that had never been present before. An anxiety shadowed the principal's features and Childes watched as she said something to those around her, then broke away from them, striding in her stiff-backed manner towards him.

She acknowledged greetings from other visitors she passed with a brief smile that was polite yet rebuffed conversation, and then she was before him, looking up into his face. He blinked, for he had seen the energy glowing from her, an aura of vitality that was of many subtle colours. The phenomenon was extraordinary

and something he had witnessed more than once just
recently, the radiance like a gentle many-hued flame
that flared briefly to fade when concentrated upon,
leaving him perplexed and slightly spellbound. The
unusual effect vanished when Miss Piprelly spoke and
his attention was diverted.

'I'd rather you didn't stand there inspecting everybody with quite such intensity, Mr Childes. Perhaps
you could tell me if there is something wrong?'

That uncanny *awareness* in her eyes. He was slowly
beginning to view the school's principal in a different
light, catching glimpses of deeper sensitivities beneath
the somewhat brittle exterior. Yet their relationship
had not changed. He wondered if these fresh insights
into the woman were due to the confusing developments within himself.

'Mr Childes?' She was waiting for an answer.

'The urge to tell her everything was almost overwhelming, but how could she believe him? Estelle
Piprelly was a rational, no-nonsense headmistress, en-
ergetic and diligent in her pursuit of educational excellence. Yet what was it in her that puzzled him so, what
elusive—or camouflaged—quality did she possess that
belied her image?

She sighed impatiently. 'Mr Childes?'

'I'm sorry, I was miles away.'

'Yes, I could see that. If you'll forgive me for saying
so, you seem unwell. You've looked haggard for a
while now, since your few days absence, in fact.'

A minor illness, a summer cold, had been how he
had accounted for his time spent on the mainland after
Annabel's disappearance. 'Oh.' He shrugged. 'Well,
summer term's nearly over, so I'll have plenty of time
to rest up.'

'I wouldn't have thought your curriculum is exactly
full, Mr Childes.'

'Perhaps not.'

'*Is* there something on your mind?'

He faltered, but it was neither the time nor the

place to be frank with her. She would have probably ordered him off the premises if he had, anyway.

'No, I was, uh, interested in the parents, trying to associate them with their offspring. Just a little game I like to play. Have you ever noticed how like their mothers or fathers some of the girls are, while others are total opposites? Incredible, really.'

She was not satisfied, but she was far too busy to indulge him. 'No, I don't find it incredible at all. Now I suggest you forget your "game" and mingle a little more with our guests.' Miss Piprelly began to turn away, but paused. 'You know, Mr Childes, if there is some kind of problem, my door is always open to you.'

He avoided her stare, feeling uncomfortable, for there was more in her remark than a casual invitation. Just how much did she really know about him?

'I'll remember,' he told her, then watched her walk away.

Amy spotted Overoy endeavouring to resemble a visiting parent but succeeding only in looking like a plain-clothes policeman on the lookout for pickpockets, his intent look and alert stance the giveaway. She could not help smiling: maybe he only looked like that to her because she knew who he was and why he was there. She resisted the mischievous urge to wave and call out, 'Inspector!' Instead, she said to the two thirteen-year-old girls helping her on the strawberries-and-cream stall, 'Take over for a while and make sure you give the correct change. And only *four* strawberries to a basket otherwise we'll run out too fast and without even showing a profit.'

'Yes, Miss Sebire,' they replied in unison, delighted to be in charge.

Amy made her way from behind the stall, exchanging hellos with any parent she recognised. Overoy was standing beneath a tree, sipping wine from a plastic cup, shirtsleeves rolled to the elbows and jacket hanging over an arm.

'You look hot, Inspector,' Amy said when she drew near.

He turned in her direction, surprised for a moment. 'Hello, Miss Sebire. You seemed busy on your stall.'

'Strawberries and cream are in great demand on a day like today. Would you like me to bring you some?'

'That's very kind, but no, thank you.'

'They would add to your disguise.'

He grinned at the mild leg-pulling. 'I stick out that much, do I?'

'Probably only because I know who you are and what you're doing here. At least your numbers are discreet.'

He gave a wry shake of his head. 'Yes, I know. I'm sorry about that, but as it is, I'm on my own time. Difficult to convince my governors that an undercover team was needed for this little exercise—not that we have any jurisdiction on the island anyway. Fortunately Inspector Robillard is an old friend, so I'm here on a weekend social as his guest.'

'I thought I'd seen him wandering around with his wife.'

'Like me, he's on unofficial duty, keeping an eye on things.''

'Looking for our monster?'

'Yeah, bit difficult when you don't know what he looks like, though.'

' "It", you mean: Jon refuses to accept the killer as human.'

'I'd noticed.' Uncomfortable, Overoy scratched his cheek with a nicotine-stained finger, careful not to spill the wine. 'Mr Childes is, er, a strange man in some ways, Miss Sebire,' he said.

Amy smiled sweetly. 'Wouldn't you be if you'd been through what he has, Inspector?'

'No, I'd be worse: I'd be out of my brain by now.'

A quick frown replaced the smile. 'You can be sure he's not.'

He held up the plastic cup between them as if a shield. 'I'm not suggesting anything, Miss Sebire. In fact, I find him a remarkably down-to-earth character, considering. I just mean this ESP business is a bit odd, that's all.'

'I thought you'd be used to it by now.'

'He isn't, nor am I.'

'Jon is beginning to accept the ability.'

'I accepted that in him a long time ago, but that doesn't mean I'm used to it.'

A passing group of parents waved to Amy and she called out a hello in return. She faced the policeman again. 'Do you really think this person could have come here to the island?'

Overoy sipped the wine before answering. 'He knows Childes is here, so it's possible. I'm afraid this business may have turned into a personal vendetta against Childes.'

'But you really think he could read Jon's mind in that way?'

'To find his location, you mean? Oh, no, he didn't need to. Childes' daughter, Gabriel, took a funny phone call a day or two before her friend was abducted— she couldn't remember exactly when—and we're assuming it was from the kidnapper.'

'Jon mentioned that to me.'

'We didn't find out for some time after, when we questioned Gabriel again and specifically asked if she or Annabel had spoken to any strangers in the days or weeks before Annabel was taken. She remembered the call then.' His eyes ranged over the crowds, but he was recalling something unpleasant. 'Gabriel couldn't describe the voice, so she did an impression for us. It made my flesh creep just to listen.' He finished off the wine and looked around for somewhere to dispose of the plastic cup. Amy took it from him.

'Please go on,' she said.

'The voice was weird, a kind of low growling. Rough, but with no particular accent, nothing for us to latch on to. Of course, she's just a kid and anyway the caller could have been deliberately assuming a different voice to normal, so even that doesn't help us much. Unfortunately, when he asked to speak to her father, Gabriel said he didn't live there any more, that he was here, on the island.'

'Then when he went to the house . . .'

'He specifically went there for Gabriel, or at least to do some mischief. We haven't mentioned our notion to Annabel's parents—it would be heartless and at this stage, there'd be no point—but we believe he mistook Annabel for Childes' daughter. She'd told her mother that she was off to play with Gabriel, so we reckon she was in the Childes' garden when she was abducted.'

'You still haven't found her body?'

Overoy shook his head. 'Not a trace,' he said dismally. 'But then the killer doesn't need her body to be found: he's already presented us with the moonstone, along with the little girl's fingers.'

Despite the heat of the day, Amy shuddered. 'Why should he do such a thing?'

'The moonstone? Or do you mean why the mutilations? Well, the desecration of the bodies has all the hallmarks of ritual, and the moonstone could play some part in that.'

'Did Jon tell you about his dream?'

'The moonstone changing into the moon? Yeah, he told me, but what does it mean? And why did the word "moon" appear on the computer screens in his classroom? And was it *really* there?'

Amy was startled. 'I don't know what you mean.'

'The mind is a funny thing, and Childes', apparently, is a little different from most. What if he *imagined* he saw the word on the monitor screens?'

'But the girls in his class saw it too.'

'Pubescent girls at their most sensitive age, minds open to suggestion. I'm talking about a form of mass hypnosis or collective hallucination. Such things aren't rare, Miss Sebire.'

'The circumstances weren't like—'

He held up a hand. 'It's merely a consideration we have to keep our *own* minds open to. I wouldn't be here if I thought Childes was making the whole thing up, and I'm working on one particular theory that might throw some light, but I need to do more research.'

'Couldn't Moon be somebody's name?'

'First thing that occurred to me, so I checked whether the prostitute who was murdered had any associate or regular clients by that name. So far, nothing. I also did a run-through of the list of staff and inmates at the hospital, but drew a blank there, too. Something's bound to turn up sooner or later, though—it's the natural order of events in most criminal investigations.'

'Is there any way in which I can help?' Amy offered.

'I wish there were—we need all the help we can get. Just keep an eye out for anyone acting suspiciously around Childes. And for that matter, around yourself. Remember, the killer tried to get at him through his daughter; next time it could be you.'

'Do you . . . do you think this person is here today?'

He sighed, still looking around. 'Hard to say. After all, what do we have? A word on a computer screen? Doesn't tell us much, does it? But if he is here, he'll know where Childes lives—all he has to do is look in the phone book and find there's only one Childes listed.'

'But surely you're keeping a watch on the cottage,' said Amy, alarmed.

'I've got no authority here, Miss Sebire.'

'Inspector Robillard . . .'

'What can he do? I've had a hard enough job getting my own people to listen, so what can Inspector Robillard, who thinks I'm slightly out of my head anyway, tell his superiors?'

'But that leaves Jon so vulnerable.'

'We may come up with something today. Childes

has one of his feelings about the safety of the girls, that's why I'm here and why I've persuaded Geoff Robillard to give me a hand. Not much of a task force, I admit, but under the circumstances, all you're going to get. It had crossed our minds to let the principal in on our little secret, but what sane reason could we give for our presence? You know, I'm not at all sure of this myself, but I'd hate anything to happen here without at least taking a few precautions.'

Amy had been quietly appraising Overoy while he spoke. 'I think Jon has been fortunate to find an ally in you,' she said. 'It's hard to imagine any other policeman taking him too seriously.'

Overoy glanced away, embarrassed. 'I owe him,' he said. 'Besides, he's a definite link—why else would this lunatic send him a moonstone? Frankly, Miss Sebire, Jonathan Childes is all we've got to go on.' He continued to search among the strolling people, looking for a certain indefinable something, a guarded look in someone's eyes, an awkwardness of movement betraying an unnatural self-consciousness—any small nuance that would make an individual subtly conspicuous to the trained eye. So far, all appeared normal; but the day was still young.

Amy was about to walk away when Overoy said, 'Did he tell you about his daughter's dream?'

She stopped. 'When Gabby saw Annabel after she'd been taken?'

He nodded.

'Yes, he did.'

'It wasn't just a dream, was it?'

'Jon's already told you.'

'He was vague. He said that he and Mrs Childes heard Gabby call out in the middle of the night from another room along the hallway and when they got to her she was sitting up in bed, very upset and claiming to have dreamt about Annabel. Those were his words. I'd like to know if she really had been dreaming. It's not important, Miss Sebire; I'm just curious. Does

Gabby have the same gift as her father?' He failed to notice that something he had said had shaken Amy.

'Jon doesn't believe it was a dream,' she replied, distractedly. 'He may have told you that to protect her—'

'From me?'

'You let matters get out of control last time; he wouldn't want Gabby to go through what he had to. I'm surprised he even mentioned it to you.'

'He didn't. Mrs Childes told me and later he explained it as a sort of nightmare.'

'Perhaps I shouldn't have said otherwise.'

This time he was aware that her initial cheerfulness had been dampened and, mistakenly, he assumed she regretted her disclosure. 'Like I said, it's not important, so let's leave the matter there. I'm sorry he still doesn't have confidence in me, though. I'd hate to think Childes would keep anything important from me.'

'I'm sure he wouldn't, Inspector. Jon is a very frightened man at the moment.'

'To be honest, he's not the only one: I've seen the forensic photographs of what this maniac can do.'

'I don't think I want to know any more than I do already.' Amy looked over at the strawberries-and-cream stall. 'I'll have to get back and help the girls; they're being swamped with customers.'

'You'll see me and Inspector Robillard wandering around throughout the afternoon, so let either one of us know if anything suspicious catches your eye. I don't think anything's going to happen with all these people around, but you never know. Oh, and Miss Sebire,' he added as she turned away, 'if you do casually bump into me again, try not to call me Inspector.' He smiled, but her mind was obviously now on other things, for she did not respond in kind.

'I'll remember,' was all she said, and then she disappeared into the throng milling around the stall.

*   *   *

He checked his wristwatch: soon it would be time for the gymnastics and dancing to begin.

Childes kept careful watch as visitors and staff began drifting towards the main lawn at the rear of the school. He continued to feel uneasy, even though nothing had occurred as yet to give him cause for concern. He had come across nobody who appeared in the least bit out of place, no one who made his spine stiffen or the skin on the back of his neck crawl, a reaction he instinctively knew he would have once he set eyes on the person—creature—he sought. *The creature who sought him.* Could he have been wrong? Was the idea that it was on the island a misguided assumption? He did not think so, for the feeling was too strong, too intense.

Childes followed the visitors, spotting the island policeman, Robillard, among them; Overoy would not be too far away.

Lively chattering around him, smiling faces, movement of bright colours and the buzz of activity—all conspirators to the air of normality. Why did he doubt so? There had been no warnings, no sensing of overt danger; only a trembling within, a creeping unease, a certain tenseness. No recognition, but a heavy, shadowy awareness without definition, without clarity. He felt eyes upon him and was suddenly afraid to turn. He forced himself to.

Paul Sebire stood three yards away, supposedly in conversation with Victor Platnauer, but his gaze boring into Childes. The financier abruptly excused himself and strode towards him.

'I don't intend to create a scene here, Childes, but I think it's about time you and I had a serious talk,' Sebire said gruffly when he reached the teacher.

For a moment, Childes forgot his main concern. 'I'm ready to discuss Amy at any time,' he replied with a calmness he scarcely felt.

'It's *you* I want to discuss, not my daughter.'

They stood facing one another, the crowd flowing around them like a river around boulders.

'I discovered certain things about you,' Sebire went on, 'that were rather alarming.'

'Yes, I guessed it was you who initiated the investigation into my background. It must have come as a surprise to learn that Amy knew all about my past.'

'Whether or not you'd already informed her doesn't concern me. What does is the fact that you've been under police investigation.'

Childes sighed wearily. 'You know what that was all about; I don't have to explain myself.'

'Yes, I grant that you were cleared of any suspicion, but I have to say one thing, Childes: I don't believe you to be a very stable man. You revealed that when you were my dinner guest.'

'Look, I'm not going to argue with you. You can think what you like about me, but the truth is, I love your daughter and it should be fairly obvious even to you that she returns that love.'

'She's blinded by you for the moment, though God knows why. Do you realise I haven't seen Aimée since she moved in with you?'

'That's between you and her, Mr Sebire; I certainly haven't kept her away from you.'

'She's not for someone like you.' His voice had risen a tone and passers-by looked in their direction.

'That's for Amy to decide.'

'No, no it isn't—'

'Don't be ridiculous.'

'How dare—'

Another figure smoothly interposed itself between the two men. 'Paul, I think we should make our way to the main lawn,' Victor Platnauer said soothingly. 'The performances are about to begin and I'm afraid I have my usual speech to make.' He gave a short laugh. 'I'll try not to bore you too much this year, you gave me enough stick after last time. Please excuse us, Mr Childes. Now there's a point I want to raise about. . .' He gently led the financier away, continuing to speak placatingly, obviously anxious to avoid any upset to the day's proceedings.

Childes watched them go, regretting the brief but vitriolic exchange with Sebire, yet dissatisfied that nothing had been resolved. He hadn't meant to fall so deeply in love with Amy—what man or woman consciously rendered themselves so vulnerable?—but since he had, he would do his utmost to keep her. Though arguing with her father in public was hardly going to help matters. Come to that, nor was sleeping with Fran. He pushed the thought away, but guilt was a lingering reprover.

There were not too many people left around him by now, most having made their way to the rear of the college. Instead of following, Childes took the long way round, checking the quieter areas of the school grounds, keeping a wary eye on the bordering shrubbery and woodland, peering into the recessed doorways and shadowed corners of the building itself and the annexes.

Gulls wheeled lazily above, suddenly swooping out of sight as they dived below the nearby clifftops; the sound of surf breaking on the rocks came to him when he stopped for a few seconds and listened intently. A huge, furry bumble bee staggered sluggishly across the path before him, unable to fly, victim of premature summer mating. The sun beat down relentlessly, causing a shimmer above the ground in the near-distance.

Childes walked on, carefully stepping over the stumbling insect. A slight rustling somewhere to his left brought him to a halt once again until he saw, with relief, that the bushes from where the noise had come were low, incapable of concealing anything other than a smallish animal or bird. He resumed walking.

The hubbub of voices hit him as soon as he rounded the corner, the bustling panorama in sharp contrast to the quiet emptiness behind. Benches and chairs were laid out in long lines facing the building, leaving a wide expanse of green between them and the terrace to accommodate the display which was to be followed by speeches and prize-giving. Visitors and schoolgirls filled the benches, presenting a vibrant mixture of restless colours across the clear sweep of lawn. A yellow island-hopper plane flew low overhead, while a backdrop of trees behind the assemblage stood lush against the strikingly blue sky.

Childes made his way along the gravel path fringing the lawn and, seeing that all the seats allocated to staff and guest dignitaries had been taken, moved on towards the back rows. Finding an empty place, he sat and waited for the activities to begin.

On the terrace, Miss Piprelly was seated alongside members of the governing board, representatives of the parents' association and chosen teachers, before a long table containing trophies, rolled certificates, raffle prizes and a somewhat ancient-looking microphone. A short, wide flight of stone steps led up to the terrace, and the old grey stone building which housed classrooms and dormitories loomed up darkly behind, while the white tower of the more recent building, which housed the assembly hall and gymnasium, reigned over all.

The crowd settled as La Roche's principal rose to speak and Childes, with the warmth of the sun on his back, seriously began to doubt his earlier misgivings.

JEANETTE lay on her bed, head propped up by pillows and cushions, knees raised high with the hem of her light blue dress stretched over them, white-stockinged feet digging into the quilt beneath her. A less than immaculate black-and-white Pierrot doll sat on her stomach, back resting against her thighs, wide stiffened ruff framing its smooth face with its tearfully sad expression. She despondently picked at the cotton buttons of the doll's tunic.

Jeanette should have been outside with the other girls in her class, but had sneaked away, wanting only to be alone. *They* all had their parents and brothers and sisters with them, while she had no one, and to be among them only made her miss her own parents more. Besides, she hadn't been chosen for the dancing display and certainly had no gymnastics prowess, and knew there would be no awards or certificates waiting on the prize table for *her*. There never were! Oh yes, once she'd won a merit badge for embroidery, but the earth had hardly moved for that. Perhaps it was just as well that her parents hadn't flown all the way from South Africa just to sit with her on the sidelines and watch her friends collecting their prizes. Her father was an engineer of some kind—she never quite understood *exactly* what he did—and used the island as a base for his various journeys to other parts and different jobs, her mother often accompanying him. They'd be away for eighteen months this time—*eighteen months!*—but at least she would stay with them for two months as soon as the summer term was over. She missed them terribly, but didn't know if they missed her. They said they did, but then they would, wouldn't they? Of course we love you and miss you, darling, but it just isn't practical for you to be dragged halfway around the world and have your education broken up in such a way. Of course we want you with us, but learning must come first. Jeanette allowed Pierrot to tumble off her body and slide from the bed onto the floor. His woebegone expression had been making her miserable.

She closed her eyes for a few minutes, face pointed towards the ceiling, her single plait of hair (she told herself it was in the style of Miss Sebire) spread on the pillow. If anyone caught her in the dormitory she'd be in trouble; fortunately all the teachers would be too busy toadying up to fee-paying parents to patrol the school's upper floors, otherwise she would never have risked being there. She liked occasional solitude, but found the only trouble with being alone was that it got lonely.

Jeanette sighed, pictured Kelly confidently marching forward to receive her trophies—best debater, highest grade in maths and physics, special award for progress in computer studies, etc., etc., etc.—and wished she could be like her. Kelly was *so* pretty, too. It was wrong to be jealous, Jeanette knew that, but sometimes, *oh, sometimes,* she wished she were like her classmate. She never would be, though, Jeanette had to accept that, but everybody had to have at least *one* quality, something that made them as good as the rest; it was just a little bit difficult to discover what hers was. Someday it would shine through, though. Perhaps soon. And perhaps when her periods started her spots would disappear and her breasts start to grow. And her head would be less dreamy all the time and she might even grow taller and—

—And the mobiles were beginning to move.

Of course, windows were open on the upper floors on such a brill day, so a draught was moving them. Jeanette was annoyed at herself. The other girls often accused her of being frightened of her own shadow and sometimes she was forced to agree with them. She didn't like dark corners, didn't like scary movies—*hated* crawly things—didn't like the creaking of the old building or the rattling of windows when she lay awake in the middle of the night while others around her slept. And shadows did frighten her, especially those under beds.

Jeanette sat up, but did not immediately swing her legs to the floor. She crouched forward and peered under the bed first.

Satisfied no beast was lying in wait to reach out and pull her into its dark lair, Jeanette allowed her stockinged feet to touch the floor. She remained on the edge of the bed for a little while, listening intently and not quite sure what she was listening for. Perhaps the crack of floorboards in another room, a mysterious scratching that might or might not be a tiny mouse, the slithering of some loathsome slime-covered creature that wandered empty corridors, or a huge cloaked figure lurking just beyond the doorway, waiting for her to come out, clawed, scabby fingers with long curling nails waiting to—

Stoppit! She was frightening herself again. Sometimes Jeanette hated her own stupid imagination for conjuring up such self-inflicted spectres. It was broad daylight, the school grounds were full of people, and she was deliberately teasing herself with scary thoughts. Jeanette reached for her shoes, deciding it was time to join the rest of the world.

Her toes had wriggled into one shoe, two fingers hooked into the heel, when she heard the footsteps approaching. She watched curiously as the fine hairs on the back of her bare arm stiffened and began to rise. The crawling sensation on her flesh reached the sharp ridge of her spine.

Jeanette straightened. Listened. Looked towards the dormitory's open doorway.

The footsteps were heavy, almost lumbering. Drawing closer. Their sound mesmerising.

Her heart seemed to be beating unusually loudly.

The footsteps stopped and, for a moment, she thought that so, too, had her heart.

Could she really hear the sound of breathing beyond the doorway?

Jeanette slowly rose, the shoe slipping off her foot. She stood by the edge of the bed, barely able to breathe, Pierrot staring blankly up at her, still frozenly weeping.

She did not want to walk towards the doorway; something—perhaps confrontation with her own silly fears—compelled her to. Her stockinged feet were silent on the polished floorboards as she stealthily crept forward, and her hands were clenched into tight fists.

She hesitated just before she reached the open door, suddenly more afraid than she had ever been in her life.

Beyond the opening, something waited.

The dancing and gymnastics display was over. Miss Piprelly had given her usual incisive and succinct oration before introducing *Conseiller* Victor Platnauer, whose discourse was more leisurely and contained at least a modicum of humour. Nevertheless, Childes found it difficult to concentrate on either speech, for he constantly searched the crowd in front of him for some telltale sign, the slightest indication that one person among the guests was not quite what he seemed.

He not only observed nothing out of the ordinary, but *felt* nothing that gave cause for concern. All was as it should have been: attentive spectators, splendid weather, although perhaps a trifle too warm, fine exhibitions by the pupils themselves, and adequate speeches.

Prize-giving had just begun when a movement caught

his attention. He blinked, not sure if it had only been a trick of the light, a reflection in one of the windows across the lawn. Yet something in his vision was not quite as before and that change was sensed rather than seen. His eyes were drawn towards one particular spot high in the building opposite.

A face was at an upstairs window.

Blurred, too far away to be identified, but he instinctively knew whose face it was.

His very blood was suddenly chilled.

Stunned, Childes could only sit there, a burdensome dread pinning his body to the seat. His mouth opened to speak, to cry out, but it was as if a fist, a cold, steel, clenched fist, had blocked his throat.

The face was still, and it seemed that its eyes were on him alone.

Then the whitish blur was gone.

Childes staggered to his feet, his limbs feeling almost too heavy to move; somehow he managed to step over the back of the bench. He looked around for Overoy, the semi-paralysis of shock beginning to fade, but failed to locate him in the crowd. He couldn't wait. Something was wrong inside the school, something awful that sent a sharp terror knifing through him.

He skirted the rows of seating and hurried back along the gravel path towards the school building. Applause broke out behind as a pupil went up to receive her prize. Only a few people noticed his rushing figure, one being Overoy, who had been loitering beneath a tree at the edge of the gardens, a position that had provided a good view of the proceedings. Unfortunately, he was on the far side of the lawns and some distance away from the path Childes had taken; the detective decided it would be easier if he went in his own direction and met Childes on the other side of the building. Overoy slipped on his jacket and briskly strode towards the front of the school.

Childes entered the first door he came to, shivering

involuntarily as he stepped into the cooler atmosphere.
He took a short flight of stairs and found himself in
the main hallway running centrally along the length of
the building. The face had been at a window on the
third floor where the older girls' dormitories were; he
ran down the hallway in the direction of the main
stairway, footsteps echoing off the half-panelled walls
around him.

He passed the library, the staffroom and parents'
waiting room, before reaching the wide stairway where
he paused, craning his neck to look into the upper
reaches as if expecting to find someone peering down.
The stairs were deserted.

Not giving in to his trepidation, Childes began the
ascent.

Overoy cursed himself. He had forgotten that the
college's layout was not conventional, for various wings
and annexes had been added over the years. The
detective had found himself cut off from Childes by
the white structure with its high tower, attached to the
older section at right angles. He could either go around
and join up with Childes on the other side, or go
through. He found the nearest door and went through.

First floor. Childes scanned the corridor leading off
in both directions. Empty. But a sound from above.

He leaned over the balustrade. Sharp sounds, scuf-
fling. He looked up.

'*No!*' he shouted. '*No, don't!*'

He ran, mounting the stairs three at a time, using
the handrail to pull himself up with each step, not
even the exertion overcoming the sudden pallor of his
features.

Second floor. The noise from above had ceased. He
kept climbing. A kicking sound.

As he went higher, he heard a strangulated wheezing.

Nearly on the third floor and a shadow—an ungainly, lumbering shadow—seemed to dissolve away at
the top of the stairs. He thought he heard footsteps,
but his attention was on the small thrashing figure
dangling over the empty space of the stairwell.

As she swung in his direction, he saw her face was already turning a mottled bluey-purple. Her eyes bulged wildly as she tried to tear at the coloured noose around her neck. The girl's stockinged feet kicked out at the air.

'*Jeanette!*' Childes cried.

He was almost at the top when he tripped, skidding onto the landing and instantly rolling over, ignoring the wrenching pain as his knee grazed against wood. He did not even try to rise, but scrabbled on all fours to the balustrade, reaching through, grabbing at the twisting body below, finding her arms, gripping them tightly and supporting her weight.

He thought he sensed movement behind but concentrated on holding the hanging girl. He pulled, but his position was awkward. He could only lie there, sprawled and gasping, straining to maintain his grip.

He could feel her beginning to slip.

'Don't struggle, Jeanette. Just try to keep still . . . please . . . don't fight against me!'

But she could not help herself. Her choking became a wheezing sibilance. Her fingers clawed at her own neck, drawing speckles of blood.

Childes felt the girl slipping from him.

Running footsteps on the stairway. Overoy staring up at them, not breaking his stride, tearing up the stairs with all the speed and strength he possessed.

Childes clung to Jeanette, his legs spreadeagled behind, body flat against the floor and face pressed against the metal struts of the balustrade. As he willed himself not to let go, the struggle slowly becoming too much, an object lying close to the edge of the landing caught his eye.

It was tiny. It was round. It was a moonstone.

TRAFFIC WAS heavy going through the island's main port-
town, and Childes forced himself to drive with extra
care, his nerves still ragged and hands less than steady.
Beside him, Amy was pensive, obviously shaken by
what had happened, yet strangely reserved.

He stopped the Mini at traffic lights on a junction
overlooking the harbour. Tourists strolled in the comfortable warmth of early evening, while in the marina
yacht crews relaxed on deck, sipping wine and discuss-
ing the day's unfortunate lack of sailing breeze. Day-
trippers returning from one of the other islands
disembarked from a hydrofoil docked at the far end of
the long, curving pier. Light green cranes used for
loading and unloading cargoes stood along the quay-
sides near the harbour entrance, jibs leaning at odd
angles as if in conversation with each other.

He glanced at Amy. 'You okay?'

'I'm frightened, Jon.' She turned to him briefly,
then looked away again.

'You and me both. At least there'll be closer police
surveillance here from now on.'

'Poor little Jeanette.'

'She'll recover. Her throat was bruised and her lar-
ynx and windpipe badly compressed by the school tie
this maniac found to use as a noose, but she'll mend.'

'I'm thinking of the damage to her mind. Will she
ever get over such an ordeal?'

The lights changed and Childes took his foot from the brake pedal to ease down on the accelerator, swinging the wheel right to drive along the harbour front.

'She's young, Amy, and time dulls even mental trauma.'

'I hope so, for her sake.'

'Just thank God Overoy got to us—I couldn't have held on much longer.'

'He didn't see . . . anyone else?'

'No. But then he had Jeanette and me to think about. The police think the fire stairs were used as an escape route, and from their exit it would have been easy enough to slip through the school grounds into the woods. La Roche isn't exactly a secure property.'

Past the harbour, the road began to slope upwards into a steep winding hill; soon they were beyond the outskirts of the town.

'I wish your detective had seen him,' Amy said abruptly.

Childes cast a quick surprised look at her.

'Did you notice how some of the police were watching you when they were asking questions?' she went on.

'Yeah, suspiciously. I've come to expect that. No one else caught even a glimpse of this lunatic, least of all Jeanette herself. From what we can gather—and remember, she's still in a state of shock and her throat injuries make talking difficult for her—she came out of the girls' dormitory and someone grabbed her from behind, throwing the tie around her neck before she could cry out. She fought as hard as she could, but was forced along the corridor and tossed over the stairway and left to hang there while her attacker tied her to the balustrade. Can you imagine the strength it would take to do that? I know Jeanette is small for her age, but it would require considerable power to carry out such a feat. If anyone other than Overoy had discovered us, they couldn't be blamed for assuming I was the one trying to hang Jeanette, but even they'd have to admit I don't have the kind of physique to manage anything like that.'

He turned off into the narrower country lanes which would eventually lead them to his cottage. Tall hedges and old walls screened off the countryside around them.

'Why should he come here?' Amy had shifted in her seat now, and her expression was earnest. 'And why pick on the children?'

'To torment me,' he replied grimly. 'It's playing a game, knowing it'll be caught sooner or later, especially now it's trapped on the island, and I don't think it cares one way or the other. But until that happens, there's fun to be had with me.'

'But what *is* the connection? Why you?' She sounded desperate.

'God help me, Amy, I don't know. Our minds have met and that seems to be enough. Maybe I represent a challenge, someone to show off to as well as taunt.'

'You need protection. They've got to keep a watch on you.'

'Overoy might be able to persuade them, but I doubt I'll get anything more than an occasional patrol car passing by the cottage. I think the Island Police will be more concerned with guarding La Roche until the end of term.'

Trees formed a canopy over the roadway, darkening the car's interior. Childes rubbed his temple with one hand, as if to soothe a headache.

'Surely Inspector Overoy will insist you have proper protection.' Shifting light speckles, the evening sun's rays diffused by overhead leaves, patterned Amy's face as they sped along the lane.

'I'm sure he'll do his best, but Robillard told me at the hospital that his force is stretched to the limit because of the tourist season. You know how sharply the crime rate rises during the summer months.'

She became quiet again.

Childes pulled into the side of the road as another

car approached from the opposite direction. The driver waved an acknowledgement as he eased past; the Mini picked up speed again.

Amy broke her silence. 'I spoke to Overoy earlier this afternoon, before the speeches: he wondered if Gabby might be like you, Jon—psychic.'

'I've wondered myself. Of course Gabby may have been so overwrought she only *thought* she saw Annabel, although she was adamant when we got to her.'

'When you and Fran got to her?'

'Yes.'

'Where were you both when you heard Gabby call out, Jon?' Her voice was steady, her eyes on the road ahead, but Childes sensed the intent behind the question. 'We've not discussed that particular point before, have we? But you and Fran arrived in Gabby's bedroom together, from what I can gather.'

'Amy . . .'

'I need to know.'

He pulled at the wheel to avoid a branch extending dangerously from a hedge. 'I was sleeping on my own that night in the spare room.' Easier, so much easier, to lie. But he couldn't, not to Amy. 'Fran was upset, she came to me.'

'And you slept with her?'

'It just happened, Amy. I didn't mean it to, I didn't want it to. Believe me, it just happened.'

'Because she was upset?'

'Fran needed comforting. She'd been through an awful lot that day.'

He stole a glance at Amy. She was weeping. Childes reached for her hand. 'There was no meaning to any of it, Amy, just a comforting, nothing more.'

'So you imagine that makes things okay?'

'No, I was wrong and I'm sorry. I don't want you to think I was involved—'

'I don't know what to think any more. In a way I suppose I understand—you were married to her for a long time. But that doesn't lessen the hurt.' She moved her hand from his. 'I thought you loved me, Jon.'

'You know I do.' There was a gradually expanding pressure inside his head that had nothing to do with the conversation with Amy. 'I . . . I just couldn't turn her away that night.'

'Like doing an old friend a favour?'

'That isn't far from the truth.'

'I hope Fran didn't realise.'

The road dipped, became more gloomy.

'Don't let what happened ruin what there is between us.'

'Can we be the same?'

A crawling sensation at the back of his neck, similar to the feeling earlier in the afternoon when he had looked up to see the face at the window.

'It . . . it wasn't im-important . . .' he stammered, his fingers beginning to tingle on the steering wheel. He felt his shoulder-blades contracting inwards.

'I don't know, Jon. Perhaps if you'd told me before. . .'

'How . . . how could I? How could I have explained?' A heavy, cold hand had reached from the gloom of the back seats and was resting on his shoulder. But when he looked, there was nothing there.

'Amy . . .'

He saw the eyes peering at him from the rear-view mirror. Wicked, malevolent eyes. Darkly gloating.

Amy looked at him, feeling his tension, seeing the horror on his face. 'Jon, what's—?'

She turned to the empty back seats.

Childes saw the eyes glow larger in the mirror, as the thing—the grinning thing—in the back was leaning forward, was reaching out for him, strong, numbing fingers touching his neck, nails pressing into his skin . . .

The car veered to one side, scraping the hedge.

'*Jon!*' Amy screamed.

The gloating eyes. Steely fingers clamped around his throat. Fetid breath on his cheek. He pulled at the hand and touched only his neck.

The car swerved to the right, hit a low stone wall on that side. Sparks flew off metal as the Mini sheered along the wall's rough face. Bushes and branches lashed at the windows.

Amy grabbed the steering wheel, tried to wrench it to the left, but Childes' grip was solid, frozen. The rending of metal screeched in her ears.

He could hardly breathe, so constricted was his throat. His right foot was hard against the accelerator as he tried to flee from the snickering thing behind. But how could he escape when it was in the car with him?

The road curved. He pulled at the wheel, turned it slightly, just enough to swerve the car, not enough to carry it through the bend. He jammed his foot on the brake pedal, but too late. The car skidded, the wall seemed to rise up and throw itself at them.

They crashed at an angle, the vehicle brought to a shattering halt, Childes thrust against the steering wheel, his arms reflexively bearing his weight, softening the blow.

But Amy had nothing to cling to.

She hurtled forward, the windscreen exploding around her, screaming as she pitched over the car's short bonnet to land writhing and bloody beyond the wall.

CHILDES LEANED forward and rested his head in his hands, the dull throbbing inside making him nauseous. There was an aching in his chest, too, and he knew it had been bruised by the steering wheel. But he had been lucky. Amy hadn't.

A double-door swung open at the end of the long corridor and a figure in a white coat came through. The doctor spotted Childes waiting on the cushioned bench and strode briskly towards him, stopping to speak to a passing nurse on the way. The nurse hurried on, disappearing through the same doors from which the doctor had emerged. Childes began to rise.

'Stay there, Mr Childes,' Dr Poulain called out and, on reaching him, said, 'I could do with a sit-down myself—it's been that kind of day.' He sat, giving a grateful sigh. 'And, it would seem, an eventful day for you.' He scrutinised Childes with a professional eye. 'Time to have a look at you,' he said.

'Tell me how she is, Doctor.'

Poulain ran his fingers through tousled prematurely-grey hair and blinked at the other man through gold-rimmed spectacles. 'Miss Sebire has extensive lacerations to her face, neck and arms, one or two of which I'm afraid will leave small but permanent scars. I had to remove some glass fragments from one of her eyes—

now don't be alarmed: they had hardly penetrated the sclerotic coating and were nowhere near the iris or pupil, so her vision shouldn't be affected; the damage there was purely superficial.'

'Thank God.'

'Yes, He is to be thanked. I wish the States government would follow the mainland's example and declare it unlawful not to wear seat-belts in cars, but I'm sure they'll continue to dither for years to come.' He clucked his tongue once and gave a shake of his head. 'Miss Sebire also sustained a fractured wrist as well as severe bruising and lesions to her ribs and her legs. Nevertheless I'd say she's a very lucky girl, Mr Childes.'

Childes released a long-held breath and rested his head in his hands once more. 'Can I see her?' he asked, looking back at the doctor.

'I'm afraid not. I want her to rest so I've given her a sedative; she'll be sleeping by now, I should think. She did ask for you, by the way, and I told her all was well. Miss Sebire seemed very happy about that.'

At once Childes felt totally and utterly exhausted. He watched his hands shaking uncontrollably before him.

'I'd like to take you down to an examination cubicle,' Dr Poulain urged. 'You may have been injured more than you know. There's a rather nasty bruise developing on your cheekbone and one side of your lower lip is swelling considerably.'

Childes touched his face and winced when his fingers found the bruising there. 'I must have turned my head when I hit the steering wheel,' he said, gingerly probing the puffed lip.

'Take a deep breath and tell me if it hurts,' Poulain told him.

Childes complied. 'Feels stiff, nothing more,' he said after releasing the air.

'H'mn. No sharp pain?'

'No.'

'Still needs checking.'

'I'm all right. A little shaky, maybe.'

The doctor gave a short laugh. 'More than just a little; your nerves have been shot to pieces. This afternoon, when you came in with the schoolgirl—what was her name? Jeanette, yes, Jeanette—I recommended a mild sedative for you, but you refused. Well now I want to suggest something stronger, something you can take when you get home and which will make you sleep soundly.'

'I think I'll sleep okay without any help.'

'Don't be too sure.'

'How long will Amy have to stay here?'

'Much depends on how her eye looks tomorrow. She'll need a couple of days under observation even if all's well in that department.'

'You said—'

'And I meant it. I'm almost positive her eye hasn't been seriously damaged, but naturally we have to take precautions. Incidentally you haven't explained how this accident occurred.' He frowned at the fear that abruptly changed the other man's countenance.

'I can't tell you,' Childes said slowly, avoiding the doctor's gaze. 'Everything happened so fast. I must have been distracted for a moment just as we hit the curve.' What could he say that Poulain would believe? That he had seen eyes reflected in the rear-view mirror, staring eyes that were somehow obscenely evil and which were watching him? That he'd seen someone in the back of the car who wasn't there at all?

'By what?'

Childes looked at the doctor questioningly.

'You were distracted by what?' Dr Poulain persisted.

'I . . . I don't remember. Maybe you were right—my nerves were shot to pieces.'

'That's now. Earlier today you were most definitely shaken up, but not quite that badly. Forgive my curiosity, Mr Childes, but I've known the Sebire family for a number of years and Amy since she was a child, so it goes beyond mere professional interest for me. Had you been quarrelling with her?'

Childes could not answer immediately.

Dr Poulain went on. 'You see, I think you might have to explain to the police the other marks that are beginning to show around your throat. A discoloration that looks to have been caused by a hand—the pressure points are quite clear.'

A wild, momentary panic seized Childes. Could there be such power? Was it possible? He had *felt* the hand, the tightening fingers; yet no one other than Amy had been with him in the car. He forced the panic away: no one—*nothing*—could physically mark another by thought alone. Unless the victim was a helpless accomplice and the injury self-induced.

There was no time for further speculation on his part, or more questions from the doctor, for the lift doors along the corridor opened and Paul Sebire and his wife stepped out. Childes had rung the Sebire home soon after arrival at the hospital and had spoken to Vivienne Sebire, telling her of the accident. Paul Sebire's concern instantly turned to anger when he saw Childes who, with the doctor, had risen from the bench.

'Where is my daughter?' the financier asked Poulain, ignoring Childes.

'Resting,' the doctor replied, then quickly informed them of Amy's condition.

Sebire's expression was grim when Poulain had finished. 'We want to see her.'

'I don't think that's wise at the moment, Paul,' the doctor said. 'She'll be asleep and you might be more upset than necessary. In this kind of accident injuries often look much worse than they are. I've just advised Mr Childes here that she shouldn't be disturbed.'

Pure hatred shone from Sebire as he turned to the

younger man. Vivienne quickly reached for Childes' arm. 'Are you all right, Jonathan? You didn't say too much on the telephone.'

'I'm fine. It's Amy I'm worried about.'

'This would never have happened if she hadn't been such a fool over you,' snapped Sebire. 'I warned her you were nothing but trouble.'

His wife interposed once more. 'Not now, Paul, I think Jonathan has been through enough for one day. Now Dr Poulain has assured us that Amy will recover without permanent injury—'

'She may have been scarred for life, Vivienne! Isn't that permanent enough?'

Poulain spoke. 'The scarring will be minimal, nothing that minor plastic surgery won't easily repair.'

Childes rubbed at the back of his neck, the movement awkward because of the painful stiffness in his chest. 'Mr Sebire, I want to say how sorry I am.'

'You're sorry? You really think that's good enough?'

'It was an accident that could have . . .' *Happened to anyone?* It was a sentence Childes could not complete.

'Just stay away from my daughter! Leave her now before you cause her more harm.'

'Paul,' Vivienne warned, catching her husband's sleeve as he moved towards Childes.

'Please, Paul' said Dr Poulain 'there are patients on this floor to consider.'

'This man isn't what he seems.' Sebire stabbed a finger at Childes. 'I sensed it from the very start. You only have to look at what happened this afternoon at the school to realise that.'

'How can you say that?' his wife protested. 'He saved the little girl's life.'

'Did he? Did anyone else see exactly what happened? Perhaps it was the other way round and *he* was attempting to murder her.'

The last remark was finally too much for Childes.

'Sebire, you're being your usual kind of fool,' he said in a low voice.

'Am I? You're under suspicion, Childes, not just from me but from the police as well. I don't think you'll be returning to La Roche or any other school on the island where you can hurt helpless children!'

Childes wanted to lash out at the financier, to vent his frustration on someone, anyone—Sebire would be ideal—to strike back in any way he could. But he didn't have the energy. Instead he turned to walk away.

Sebire clutched his arm, swung him round. 'Did you hear me, Childes? You're finished here on this island, so my advice to you is to get out, leave while you're still able to.'

Childes wearily pulled his arm away. 'You can go to hell,' he said.

Sebire's fist struck his already bruised cheek and he staggered back, caught by surprise, going down on one knee. He heard a jumble of sounds before his head fully cleared—footsteps, raised voices—and regaining his feet seemed an unusually slow and difficult procedure. Someone else's hand under his shoulder helped. Once up, he felt unsteady, but the person by his side supported his weight. He realised it was Overoy who held him and that Inspector Robillard was restraining Sebire from attacking him further.

'I'd have hated to have read your horoscope this morning,' Overoy said close to his ear.

Childes managed to stand alone, although he had to resist the urge to slump onto the nearby bench. His limbs felt sluggish, as if their blood flow had thickened, become viscid. Vivienne Sebire was pale beside her husband, her eyes full of apology. Sebire himself still struggled against restraint, but his efforts were slack, without vigour, the thrust of his anger dissipated in that one blow. Perhaps there was even an element of shame behind the rage.

'Come on, Jon,' Overoy said, using Childes' Christian name for the first time. 'Let's get you out of here. You look as if you could use a good stiff drink and I'm buying.'

'Mr Childes hasn't been examined yet,' the doctor quickly said.

'He looks okay to me,' Overoy replied, gently tugging at Childes' elbow. 'A little battered maybe, but he'll survive. I can always bring him back later if need be.'

'As you wish.' Poulain then spoke to Sebire in an attempt to diffuse the situation. 'Perhaps it would be all right for you to look in on Amy, as long as you're quiet and she isn't disturbed.'

The financier blinked once, twice, his face still a patchy red from fading anger, then finally tore his gaze from Childes. He nodded and Robillard released him.

'Let's go,' Overoy said to Childes, who hesitated, opened his mouth to say something to Amy's mother, but then could not find the words. He walked away, the detective at his side.

Inside the lift, Overoy pressed the G button and said, 'The officer keeping watch on the schoolgirl got word to us that you were back at the hospital. You must like the place.'

Childes leaned back against the panelled wall, his eyes closed.

'We heard you ran off the road.'

'That's right,' was all that Childes would say.

The lift glided to a stop, its door sliding open to admit a porter pushing a wheelchaired patient, a grey-haired woman who gloomily surveyed the arthritically-deformed knuckles of her hands folded in her lap and who barely noticed the men, so quietly immersed in her own infirmity was she. Nobody spoke until the doors opened again at ground level. The porter backed out the wheelchair and whisked away his sombre patient, whistling cheerfully as he went.

'I've hired a car for the weekend so I'll drive us somewhere quiet where we can talk,' said Overoy, holding the doors before they could close on them. 'Even if your car were still driveable, I don't think you're capable. Hey, we're here, ground floor.'

Childes was startled. 'What?'

'This is as far as we go.'

'Sorry.'

'You sure you're okay?'

'Just tired.'

'What condition did you leave your car in?'

'Sick.'

'Terminal?'

'They'll mend it eventually.'

'So like I said, we'll take mine.'

'Can you get me home?'

'Sure. We need to talk, though.'

'We'll talk.'

They left the hospital building and found Overoy's hire-car parked in a doctor-reserved bay. They climbed in, Childes relieved to sink back into the cushioned passenger seat. Before switching on the engine, the detective said, 'You know I have to leave tomorrow evening?'

Childes nodded, his eyes closed once more.

'So if you've anything more to tell me . . . ?'

'It made me crash my car.'

'How d'you mean?'

'I saw it looking at me, Overoy. I saw it in the back seat. Only it wasn't really there!'

'Easy now. You thought you saw someone in the back of your car and that's what caused you to crash?'

'It was there. It tried to choke me.'

'And Miss Sebire can verify this? She saw this person?'

'I don't know. No, she couldn't have, it was in my own mind. *But I felt its hands choking me!*'

'That isn't possible.'

'I can show you the marks. Dr Poulain noticed

them.' He pulled at his shirt collar and Overoy flicked on the interior light.

'Can you see them?' asked Childes, almost eagerly.

'No, Jon. No scratches, no bruising.'

Childes swivelled the rear-view mirror in his direction, stretching his neck towards the glass. The detective was right: his skin was unmarked.

'Get me home,' he said wearily. 'Let's do that talking.'

It stood inside the blackness of the ancient and solitary tower, perfectly still, perfectly silent, relishing the void. The dark oblivion.

The sound of waves crashing against the lower cliffs drifted through openings, echoing around the Martello's circular walls like many whispers. The thing in the dark imagined they were the hushed voices of those lost to the sea, forever mourning in their starless limbo. The thought was amusing.

Strong stenches hung in the air inside the crumbling tower—urine, faeces, decay—the abuse of those who cared little for monuments and even less for their history; but these odours did not offend the figure lurking in the comforting blackness. The corruption was enjoyed.

Somewhere in the night a tiny creature screamed, prey to another more swift and more deadly.

It smiled.

The forces were building. The man was part of that building. Yet he did not know.

He would. Before very long.

And for him, it would be too late.

ESTELLE PIPRELLY searched the darkness, the incomplete moon consumed by thick clouds so that little was visible below her window. The lawns were still there, the trees were still there—and the sea still battered the lower cliff faces—but for all she knew there might be no existence beyond the confines of her room. So acute was her aloneness that life itself could well have been an illusion, a fantasy invented by her own mind.

Yet that could easily be borne, for loneliness was nothing new to her, despite crowded days, duty-filled hours; it was this new, threatening emptiness arousing a deeper, soul-touched, apprehension that was hard to bear. For the night's mood presaged menace.

She turned away, leaving the soft ghost of her reflection, a slight bending of her famously ramrod-straight spine appearing to change her character, render her frail. There was an aimlessness to her step as she paced the room which was part of her living quarters in the college, a listlessness in her movement. Lines frowned her face and her hands curled into tight balls inside the long, knitted cardigan she wore. Her lips were less firm, less severe than usual.

It was not just the sable bleakness of the night that haunted La Roche's principal, nor the unsettling quietness of late hours: Death had bid her a mocking hello that day. And its unholy visage had been present in the faces of a certain number of her girls. Just as many years before, when the mere child who could not understand but who could be *aware* had observed the imminent mortality of certain of the island's occupying forces, she had now discerned the death masks of her own pupils.

The disquiet weakened her, forcing her to sit. On the mantelshelf over an unlit fire, a dome-shaped clock, its face set in lacquered wood, counted away the moments as if they were the beats of an expiring heart. She pulled the cardigan tight around her, clutching the wool to her throat, the chill from inside her rather than the air around.

Miss Piprelly, swiftly aged and almost tremulous, pushed her thoughts outwards, wanting to—desperate to—perceive, but knowing ultimately that the strength was not within her, the faculty not that great. By no means comparable to Jonathan Childes'. How strange that he himself did not know his own potential.

The enigma of the man frightened her.

She turned as a breeze brushed against the window. Had she expected Death himself to be peering in?

Miss Piprelly wondered how secure the school was. True enough, a policeman guarded the main gate, frequently leaving his vehicle to prowl the grounds, checking doors, windows, shining his torch into surrounding shrubbery. But could a solitary policeman prevent somebody from entering one of the buildings, with their numerous access points, the irregularity of the complex itself making surveillance difficult and providing easy concealment for skulking figures. She had spoken with Inspector Robillard that very afternoon, voicing her concern (and, of course, unable to explain the reason) and he had assured her that the area in and around the college was regularly patrolled, had been since the attempt on Jeanette's life. He understood her anxiety perfectly well, yet felt it was misplaced: he doubted the attacker would return to La Roche now that the police had been alerted. The principal wished with all her heart that she could accept the policeman's calm assurances.

Her thoughts dwelt on Jonathan Childes once more—as they often had over the past few days. Reluctantly, Miss Piprelly had asked him to stay away from the college—no, she had insisted, he was not on suspension, neither was he under suspicion; but his presence at La Roche appeared to have put her girls at risk, and their welfare must always be her prime concern. She, Victor Platnauer, and several other members of the governing board had discussed the matter with Inspector Robillard and it was deemed wise, for the time being, that Childes should be kept away from the school (she had not mentioned that Victor Platnauer had insisted Childes be instantly dismissed). As there were less than two weeks left of summer term, it did not seem unreasonable that Childes should accede to their request. He had. And without hesitation.

When she had called him to her study on that Monday morning just three days ago, his intensity had been disconcerting. He had hardly seemed to hear her words, yet had not been inattentive. His mind was grappling with inner confusions, while still acutely aware of everything around him. Of course he was distressed not only by Jeanette's terrible ordeal, but also by the injuries to Miss Sebire in the car crash on the same day; however, she felt his inward preoccupation had little to do with shock. The man was seeking—she had *felt* his probing inside her own head—but his searches were random, speculative. He had recognised the gift in her, although he had not spoken of it. At times she sensed a vibration all around his form, a psychic field constantly expanding and contracting. Its fluctuating levels disconcerted her, yet he appeared unaware of these invisible emanations.

Her body juddered as the terrible violence to come, a jagged, cutting thought only, pierced her brain like a heated knife. Her mind no longer lingered on the days past. Now was the real nightmare.

Some alien presence was inside the school.

With the notion, the shadows of the room pressed in closer, the ticking of the clock grew louder, both seeking to intimidate, to influence reason.

Miss Piprelly's initial reaction was to call the island's police headquarters and she actually pushed herself from the chair—*pushed herself because the pressure from the enclosing shadows and the thunderous ticking of the clock sought to smother all movement*—and walked—*staggered?*—over to the telephone. But her hand stayed on the receiver, did not lift it.

What could she tell them? *Please come, I'm alone and frightened and somebody is with me here in the school, someone who wishes us harm, and my girls are sleeping and I've seen death in their faces and they're so young, so unknowing, their lives unlived, and they have no idea of the danger . . .!* Could she tell the police that?

Had she heard a break-in? they would ask. Their man had reported nothing unusual, but they would radio through, ask him to check the grounds more closely, report back to them. No need to worry, Miss Piprelly (an old spinster grown frightened of her own shadow), all was well, their man was on duty, call again later if you're still anxious.

She could lie, *pretend* to have heard noises. And if they arrived in force to find no sign of an intruder, what then? Raised eyebrows, condescending smiles? Mocking chuckles on the return journey?

That consideration straightened her back, set her face into firmer lines once more. She would not be belittled by the apprehensions of one night. Miss Piprelly headed for the door. She would look for herself and on finding the *slightest* evidence that all really was not well, she would contact police headquarters. The barest indication . . .

But her resolve faltered for an instant when she opened the door and fear touched her like a skeletal hand from the darkness.

CHILDES AWOKE.

There had been no nightmare, no chasing demons, no horror to jolt him from sleep. His eyes had merely opened and he was awake.

He lay in the darkness and listened to the night. Nothing there to disturb him. Only the wind, a breeze, a guileless whispering of air.

But still he rose from the bed, naked and quickly chilled, to sit there on the edge, unsure, uncertain of the tingling expectation that gnawed at him. The outline of the nearest window was a grey patch among the black. Mellowed patterns of ragged cloud edges shifted in the frame.

After fumbling at the bedside table for his glasses, Childes slid them on and went to the window.

His hands clutched at the sill as something cold and vicious inside his chest clamped hard.

In the distance, near the clifftops, La Roche glowed red.

Unlike before, there was no setting sun to flush the school's buildings. This time, flames coloured the walls as they fluttered upwards from windows to lick at the clouded sky.

As Estelle Piprelly descended, her footsteps unusually loud in the emptiness of the corridors and stairway, an unexpected smell wafted upwards to meet her. A smell unfamiliar only because it was not in context with the school's normal odours of age-mellowed wood, polish, and the constant but subtle taint of transient human bodies. Life itself.

This was not part of that common texture.

She paused, one hand on the thick stair-rail. Listened to a silence that was more ominous than peaceful. The aroma, still mild because its origin was not close, was faintly cloying and reminded her of an outhouse in the school grounds where garden machinery was stored. A small, ramshackle brick building full of tools, lawn-mowers, hedge cutters and the like, which always reeked of earth, oil and . . . petrol.

Now that she knew the source her disquiet increased tenfold, for the malodorous scent was a precursor, an indication that perhaps her own intuitive dread was not unjustified. The prevailing urge was to retrace her steps, climb the stairway to the top floor where her charges slept, rouse the girls and lead them from this unsafe place. But another impulse weighed against that course of action. An irresistible force lured her downwards.

Curiosity, argued her own rationalising thoughts. A

need to substantiate her suspicions so that she would not be accused of crying 'wolf'. But a tiny voice, a whisper almost, tucked somewhere deep in her consciousness, hinted otherwise. This voice alluded to a morbid compulsion to confront the ghost that had constantly haunted her in the unknowing faces of those soon to die.

She descended further.

On the last step, the hallway widening, corridors stretching from right to left, Miss Piprelly lingered once more, sniffing the air and wrinkling her nose at the now powerful fumes. The floorboards were damp with sleek liquid. Light came from the stairway behind, so that the farther reaches of the corridors were but gloomy tunnels. The large double-door entrance to the school building was directly opposite the stairway, a distance of perhaps thirty feet. A bank of light-switches was on the wall next to those doors.

Thirty feet was not too far. So why did the expanse appear so formidable? And why the graduating blackness so menacing?

Because she had become a silly old maid who would soon begin looking beneath the bed each night, she scolded herself, but knowing that was not the reason. The darkness *was* menacing, the distance from there to the doors *was* immense.

And she had no alternative but to cross. Returning upstairs would mean the spilled petrol would be lit. Turning on the lights might possibly flush out the intruder, hopefully frighten him off. At least the lights would attract the policeman on watch.

One brown, chunky-heeled shoe touched the floor. The other followed. Miss Piprelly began the long journey across the hallway.

Again, only halfway there, she halted. Had she heard something, or had she *felt* it? Was there someone in the corridor to her left? Was there a shadow moving among the other shadows? Miss Piprelly journeyed on, the thin layer of inflammable liquid spread over the floorboards sucking at her feet. Her pace quickened as she neared the doors.

There was someone lurking in the covering gloom, someone who wished ill on her and her school. The sense of it was overwhelming, tightening her chest so that her breaths came in short gasps. Her heart raced with her legs, her hands stretched outwards long before she was in the proximity of the switches. The *presence* was closer, drawing near, still unseen but undoubtedly reaching for her, soon to touch, soon to feel.

She had to get out!

She would find the policeman, call him to her, inform him of the intruder inside. He would know what to do, he would prevent the petrol from being lit! He would save her!

She was at the doors, almost crashing into them, scrabbling hurriedly for the handles, the lock, sobbing now with relief that she was there, soon to be free from the impending threat behind.

She knew it was close, but would not turn to look, sure that the prickling of her neck was due to this intruder's cold breath.

A vague wondering at why the doors were already unlocked, and then she was twisting the handles, a small cry of triumph mixed with fright escaping her. She pulled the doors inwards. Chilled air ruffled in.

And the shape, a dark blankness against the night, was standing before her on the porch steps *outside*, unmoving and impassable.

Miss Piprelly's legs buckled and her voice was merely a sighing moan as the shape reached for her.

CHILDES BROUGHT the hire-car to a lurching halt outside the tall open gates of La Roche, hands locked tight on the wheel and foot hard on the brake pedal. Despite the steadying grip, his body shot forward with a jolt, then rocked backwards with the moton of the vehicle.

His eyes widened as he stared down the long driveway, lit by the Renault's headlamps, at the college buildings.

They were darkened and impassive, the whiteness of the main building reduced to a heavy grey by the cloud-dense sky. No flames leapt from the windows, no redness scorched the interiors. There was no fire.

He hadn't heard sirens during the brief, frantic journey from his home to the school, hadn't met any other vehicles similarly racing to La Roche. The roads were deserted. And why should they be otherwise at that late hour when there really wasn't any blaze?

He shook his head, bewildered. Then saw the patrol car waiting just inside the gateway, lights and engine switched off. Childes shifted into first and gentled the Renault through the gates as if the police vehicle were some slumbering animal he had no wish to disturb. He pulled up alongside. The car was empty.

Wasn't it?

Then why the compulsion to leave his own car and

look through the window of the other? And why the counter-compulsion to turn the hire-car around and flee from these forbidding, ill-defined grounds, their moonlight mastered by massed, scarcely-moving clouds?

Why indeed? spoke a low, mocking voice somewhere outside his own dimension.

The silvery patterns of cloud edges streaked the black sky like stilled lightning; a lively breeze swept in from the sea to unsettle leaves and branches; the headlights beamed a vignetted tunnel towards the tall, weighty buildings. Beyond any doubt, Childes knew he would look inside the patrol car, then drive up to the school itself, as though the rules had already been laid down for him, the pattern already set. His will was still his own, and he could deviate from the course at any time he chose, but a certain destiny had been predetermined. He would follow it through, but would not succumb. He prayed he would not succumb.

Childes left the Renault and walked around its bonnet to the other vehicle. He peered through the open window.

The policeman had slid down in his seat, his knees high behind the steering wheel. For one hysterically funny moment, Childes thought the man had fallen asleep, but the black stain spreading from his throat like an infant's bib onto his light-coloured shirt told otherwise. Even so, he reached in and nudged the policeman, careful not to touch the slick mess that was still seeping outwards. There was no response to the touch, as he knew there wouldn't be. He pulled at the handle and opened the door a fraction, just enough for the interior light to come on.

The uniformed man's chin rested on his chest so that the neck wound could not be seen. He was plump for a policeman, the overhead light throwing a shiny highlight on his balding head. His eyes were partially closed as though he were looking down, contemplating the inky crimson spoiling his shirt. Hands resting placidly at his sides, fingers unclawed, relaxed, they looked as if death had arrived too quickly for combat. He appeared in repose, unmindful of his fate.

Childes closed the door, its soft *clunk* the sound of a coffin lid falling into place. He leaned against the roof of the car, head bowed onto forearms. The victim, unaware, extreme violence rare in his career on the island, had been watching the school, the car's side-window open so that any inconsistent sounds could be heard. Probably his attention had been focused upon the complex of buildings ahead, or/as well as the shrubbery surrounding them, not—for a few moments, at least—on the roadway behind. A knife, a razor—a sharp steel blade of some kind—had quietly thrust through the opening to slice his throat, deep and neat, the movement taking no more than two, perhaps three, seconds. Had the policeman cried out, the noise would have been no more than a throttled gurgling, all that the wound would have allowed.

It was here, in the school. The thing he knew only as Moon.

The notion curdled inside his lower stomach and the walls of his lungs became hardened, stiff, barely able to pump air. He raised his forehead from his arms and looked down the long drive, gravelly surface traced by the light beams, towards the buildings that now stood gaunt and sullen. Overcast.

The agonised moan was inside his head but did not come from him. It belonged to someone behind the doors of the tallest, grey building. Someone beyond those stout walls was in mortal terror.

And something *in there was enjoying that terror.*

Now, in the lower-floor windows of La Roche's main building, Childes saw a rapidly spreading orange glow, the fire no longer a precognitive vision of his mind, but there in reality before him.

MISS PIPRELLY lay on the floor, unable to move, her head twisted at a grotesquely odd angle.

She was conscious and she was terribly afraid. And she was aware in a strangely detached fashion—for there was no pain, only paralysis—that her neck was broken, the bones snapped easily by rough, powerful hands that had reached for her from the darkness outside as her legs had given way. In that one terrifying instant of confrontation, the principal had realised that the intruder had hidden outside the doors at the sound of her approach.

Miss Piprelly had not seen her assailant, had perceived only an image of bulk, *black unremitting bulk*, that shuffled forward to ensnare. Stale, noxious breath. A raspy, grunting satisfaction. The twisting—*the snapping*—of her own neck column when her head, viced between palms as hard and grazing as rock, was sharply turned sideways. The ungainly moving away of the raven form, *clump, clump,* on bare floorboards. Its return. The splashing of liquid over her clothes, her body, smooth coldness running through her hair; shutting her eyes against the wetness.

Lying there, limbs useless, her voice only a weakened garbling. The stinging of her eyes as fluid drained from her forehead into them. Blinking—at least she could blink her eyelids—clearing her sight, but the burning sensation still there, impeding her vision.

Then just able to see the lumbering shape at the end of the corridor, and crying out in dread, the sound inside her own head, unable to be released.

The sudden and distant flare that was a match being struck. Its slow, plunging fall to the floor, the bright effulgence as the petrol exploded into flame.

The creature lit by the fire, smiling . . . grinning . . . grinning at her!

The flame snaking fast—so very, very fast—along the corridor towards her own soaked, unmoving body . . .

THE FIRE was all but consuming the ground floor, the conflagration widening before Childes' eyes as he raced towards the buildings, flames eager to gorge themselves on the old, dry timber inside. Window after window became a fierce reddish orange. At the blaze's core glass had already began to burst outwards with the heat. As he drew near he saw the shimmering glow was quickly moving upwards to the first floor. Ringing of alarm bells, set off by smoke sensors, came faintly to him.

His footing almost skidded away as the surface beneath changed from gravel to night-damp grass; he recovered, scarcely breaking stride, and pounded across the circular lawn of the school's turn-around drive. La Roche's sculptured founder impassively watched the burning, his countenance taking on a ruddy glow.

Childes leapt the few steps to the main entrance, expecting the double-doors to be locked, yet, because they were the easiest access to the stairway, having to try that way first. He pushed at a metal handle and to his surprise one half of the doors swung inwards. A scorching blast of heat sent him spinning sideways, his back coming to rest against the closed section.

Shielding his eyes against the searing glare, his brown-rimmed glasses also acting as a thin barrier, Childes took a fast look back inside, skin on his hands and face immediately scalded by the exposure, breath torn, it seemed, from his throat by molten fingers. He staggered away again, varnish on the wood he had rested against beginning to bubble and crack, the door ready to ignite.

The stairway was ablaze. And closer, near to the entrance and within the flames, something black sizzled. Only briefly did he wonder whose body it was.

Childes wanted to run, to leave the grounds, to get away from there; afraid for himself, yet aware of the danger for those on the upper floors, the boarders and few members of staff who lodged at La Roche. The alarm bells would have aroused them by now and they would be confused, panic-stricken, their first thought to escape by the easily accessible main stairway, not knowing its lower reaches were already destroyed, perhaps fright and haste overcoming the carefully indoctrinated fire-drill they had rehearsed so often.

Before running to the rear of the building where the fire-exit was located, Childes reached into the inferno with one hand and grasped the door's handle, shouting out in pain at the touch of scorched metal. Forcing himself to maintain a grip, he banged the door shut, knowing it was a small gesture to prevent a draught being sucked in to aid the flames in their journey up the staircase, but hoping the action might make some difference. The door bounced against its partner, the wood already warped from its original shape. Childes left it and jumped down the steps, running alongside the school, passing dazzling windows, ducking as glass shattered.

Turning the corner, coolness hit him like air from an opened freezer door, changing perspiration on his face into cold liquid drops. He was in darkness, no fire-glow on that side—*yet*. Areas of reflected light began appearing on the lawn as lights were switched on in dormitories and corridors. Feeling the wall to his left for guidance, Childes hurried forwards, turning a corner again, soon reaching the fire-door itself. Finding it already open, a glass pane smashed at waist level where a hand could be put through to pressure the lock bar inside.

Childes wasted no time pondering the who or the wherefore: he pushed his way in, reaching for the light-switch he knew to be nearby.

Acrid smoke had searched out that part of the building although, as yet, the swirling clouds were thin and nebulous. The alarms, so much louder inside, served to stoke his fear with their incessant shrill, but he forced himself onto the stone steps, taking them three at a time, jangled nerves reminding him of a similar upward flight only a few days before. This time, though, there was more than one life at stake.

Smoke grew thicker as he went and the crackling rumble of the fire itself could be heard. Then voices, footsteps descending, growing louder. More light from above, glimpses of movement on the stairs. Thank God, they were on their way down!

He paused on the first floor, both hands resting on the iron stair-rail, and scanned the corridor running off from that landing. The far end was an inferno, rolling flames filling the space from floor to ceiling. Sweltering heat roared from the passageway to wash over him.

Onwards. Foolish to stop, even for a second. Foolish to take time to consider the danger.

The voices were near, now perhaps only one flight above, and Childes continued to climb, smoke beginning to sting his eyes, the air itself becoming parched, somehow burnt dry, even though the heart of the blaze was some distance away. It made him wonder how much ground the fire had gained below. The first stumbling figures appeared above and he quickly covered the distance between them.

A girl of no more than ten or eleven tumbled into

his arms, her face streaked with tears, the hem of
her nightdress flapping loosely over bare ankles and
feet.

'You're safe,' he told her, looking over her head
towards the other girls crowding behind. 'You'll soon
be outside.'

'Mr Childes, Mr Childes, is that you?' came a breathless voice from somewhere in their midst.

A figure, taller than most of the girls, worked her
way through. Like the pupils, she was in night attire
and she clutched her dressing gown around her as if
for protection against the mounting heat. Incongru-
ously, she wore normal flat-heeled walking shoes. For
a moment, he thought it might have been La Roche's
principal, but he quickly recognised Harriet Vallois,
history tutor and one of the house-mistresses.

'Are all the girls out of their dormitories?' he asked,
shouting over the noise of the alarms and frightened
girls; some of the girls were coughing into cupped
hands because of the worsening atmosphere.

'Matron and Miss Todd are checking,' the teacher
replied, a quivering of her lips suggesting that she,
too, was close to tears. 'They sent me on with this
group.'

He clasped her shoulder, more to steady her than to
comfort. 'Is Miss Piprelly with them?'

'N-no. I passed her rooms and knocked at her door,
but there was no reply. I assumed she would have
gone straight up to the dormitories, but . . . but there
was no sign of her!'

The burning thing in the hallway!

Childes shuddered. The body might well have been
that of the arsonist, destroyed by its own intent, caught
in its own trap. He couldn't *really* be sure that it had
been Estelle Piprelly lying there, a frizzling lump of
blackened meat; he couldn't really be sure, yet somehow he was, somehow he had no doubts.

Harriet Vallois was looking back up the stairway,
her eyes wild, desperate.

'Get the girls out!' he snapped, sharply increasing his grip on her arm. The sudden pain made her spin round towards him once more.

'Get them out!' he repeated, pulling her forward and handing over the girl still clinging to him. 'Keep them all together and don't stop for anything.' Then, closer to her ear, 'You haven't got much time.'

Her alarm increased. 'Won't you help me?' she pleaded.

Oh yes, he would love to help by leading her and the girls away from that place of impending death in which a body lay crisped and inhuman in the main hallway, where God-only-knows-what might still be roaming the corridors and where ravenous flames ate away the very innards of the building.

'You'll be okay,' he reasoned with her, 'there isn't much further to go. I've got to try and help those still left upstairs.'

He gave her a firm but gentle shove downwards and reached for the nearest girls, encouraging them to follow. The rest quickly fell into step and he urged them to take care not to lose their footing, reassuring each one as they went by. He estimated that at least thirty had passed him and more were continuing to trickle down. Childes had no idea of how many of La Roche's three hundred pupils were boarders, but a calculated guess put the figure at sixty or so. Apart from Estelle Piprelly, only two staff members and the matron were in charge of the girls at night. His pace quickened even though the effort of climbing was becoming harder, the air more difficult to breathe. The higher he went, the more dense the rolling smoke became. The soot-filled fumes were like some insidious scout, exploring and seeking out, giving gleeful warning of its master's seething approach. Louder, also, was the grumbling resonance of the fire itself, with timbers cracking somewhere deep within the furnace like rifle shots. And over all were the stridulous alarms inciting their own special panic.

Beginning to choke, he drew out a handkerchief and held it to his mouth. More girls appeared, their spluttering cries preceding them.

'Keep going!' he shouted to them, though they did not need his bidding. Two older girls were supporting another whose hysteria had virtually rendered her helpless. Childes was tempted to lift the screeching girl and carry her down himself, but realised that despite their difficulties the trio would make it to the exit.

Someone staggered into him and he held out his arms to prevent the figure from falling.

'Eloise!' he said, recognising the other teacher who lodged at the school.

Miss Todd gaped at him, bewildered, unsure, her plump chest rasping noisily as she sucked in spoilt air.

'How many are left up there?' he yelled close to her face.

She shook her head, impatient to be away.

'For God's sake, try to think!'

'Let me go,' she begged. 'There's nothing we can do!'

'How many?' he insisted, gripping her flailing arms tightly.

'We looked, we searched! Some were so frightened they were hiding in the bathrooms. Others were screaming from windows.'

'Did you get them all out?'

'Oh let me go let me go!'

He held her rigid. 'Did you get them all out?'

Girls pushed past, all of them clinging to the stair-rail for guidance, shoulders jerking and eyes streaming tears. Their screams had merged into a kind of wailing. The teacher broke away from Childes and joined them in their flight, her arms going around the shivering shoulders of one, giving comfort in spite of her own desperate fear.

She turned to call back to him. 'Some of the girls went in the other direction, towards the main staircase! Matron went after them!' Then she hurried away, pushed on by those behind.

Childes wasted no more time. Covering his mouth with the handkerchief, he mounted the remaining flights, passing no one else on the way. He had lost count, but he suspected that most of the boarders were on their way down.

He arrived at the top floor where the smoke was almost overpowering. His eyes were blurred, his throat painfully dry. With dismay he saw that the flames had reached that level, for there was a glow from further down the corridor he now faced. It was considerably softened by the whirling haze, but he was sure its source was the other stairway.

Bending low to avoid the worst of the smoke, Childes ran along the passageway, looking into dormitories as he passed.

A bout of coughing made him clutch his chest and sink to his knees. Realising he was near one of the washrooms, he crawled inside to find the air much clearer. He staggered to a basin and turned on a tap, removing his spectacles and splashing water on his face. He grabbed a towel, throwing it into the basin to soak, then wrapped it around his neck like a scarf, pulling the sodden material up over his nose and chin.

First checking toilet cubicles and bathrooms, he went back out into the corridor, the wet towel serving as a mask against the fumes. The fire's sound had become a low roar and the heat was stifling as he drew near the main stairwell. He was about to enter another dormitory when a different noise caught his attention, faint under the mêlée of alarm bells and burning, splintering wood, but distinct from them. The screaming seemed to come from the heart of the blaze itself.

Pulling the towel over his head and holding one end across most of his face, Childes moved along, touching the wall on that side for support as much as guidance.

Sparks leapt upwards from the stairwell, shooting into the air like volcanic debris, while writhing flames were consuming tongues, licking at walls, woodwork, rolling in white-hot balls towards the ceiling. The landing was not yet ablaze, but the flooring was beginning to smoulder, smoke rising like steam.

Childes went to the rail, quickly pulling back his hand when he touched the peeling wood.

The girls were bunched in a corner just below, opposite where he stood, the stairs ahead of them in flames. As were the stairs behind. They had attempted to leave that way and had been stopped by a rapidly advancing wall of fire. When they had rushed back up, they had found their line of retreat cut off by flames that had leapt ahead of them, currents of displaced, turmoiled air sweeping them upwards.

Several of the girls appeared to be unconscious, while the rest huddled or pushed against each other, hands and arms covering their faces from the approaching heat. There were six or seven girls down there (they were grouped so closely, it was impossible to count) and the matron was with them, her back to the fire, arms stretched out as if to protect her charges.

Childes moved around to the edge of the stairs, descending a little way, but the heat soon drove him back. A blazing impenetrable wall blocked the wide staircase. Maybe he could leap through the flames onto the landing below where the girls crouched, but what good would that do him? *What good would that do the girls?* He hurried back to the balcony.

'Matron!' he called. 'Mrs Bates, up here!'

He saw the matron raise her head and he yelled again.

Her face turned in his direction, looked up. She saw him. Childes thought there was a sudden look of hope

in her expression, but shimmering heat distorted
everything.

The matron left the girls, advancing only a few feet
to the edge of the landing. 'Is—is that you, Mr Childes?
Oh, thank God! Please help us, Mr Childes, please get
us away from here!'

Several of the night-clad girls were staring up at him
now, although they still cowered back in the corner.

Help them, yes; but how? *But how?* He couldn't get
down to them, and they couldn't reach him.

The matron was bent over, retching and choking,
the air itself boiling. She stumbled back, away from
the inferno. A sudden flare-up of yellow-white light
sent Childes reeling back, too. Flames shot towards
the ceiling, biting into rafters there. They just as quickly
diminished, disappearing back into the well to become
part of the broiling mass. The rafters, however, had
not been left unscathed; they had begun to burn fiercely.
There was very little time left.

A ladder might have helped, angled between the
balcony and the landing below. But there was no time
to go back down and find one. A rope, then. They
could loop one end beneath their arms and he could
pull them up, one by one. How many could he save
before his strength gave out, though? And where the
hell would he find a rope in the dormitories?

'*Help us!*' came the cry again. The girls, too, had
begun to call out to him.

'Keep away from the stairs!' he shouted, seeing that
some of them had ventured forward to stand by the
matron. Childes recognised Kelly among the group,
her face darkened with smoke-grime, tear trails descending through the dirt on her cheeks. She stretched
out a beseeching hand towards him, a vulnerable weeping child, and the memory of a charred and gristled
arm hit him, freezing his movement, shocking him
rigid.

He moaned, swaying there, the towel—now almost

dry, its moisture sucked by the heat—falling limply around his shoulders. Thick, choking smoke weaved and dodged around him, tufts of fire sprang up between the floorboards. Shrieks brought him to his senses and a splintering crashing of wood made him peer over the balustrade again.

A section of stairway had fallen inwards, leaving a deep, seething chasm before the landing on which the group sheltered. The girls and the matron had retreated into the corner once more, where they huddled together, those on the outside beating at the air with clawed fingers as if they could push back the terrible engulfing heat. More had slumped against and over their companions.

'I'm going to get something to lower down to you!' he yelled. 'I'll be back soon!' He did not know if they even heard. And would it be a useless gesture anyway? Could he really haul every one of them across that inferno? Childes pushed the begging questions from his mind.

He could feel the scorching heat of the floor through the soles of his shoes as he scrambled away. A thick swirling fug filled the corridor. He sensed the building pressure—like steam trapped inside a boiler because of a faulty valve-release—the atmosphere itself seeming to become combustible, ready to explode into one huge incandescent fireball. He sucked in oxygen-starved air and was instantly seized by a choking fit. His lungs felt scorched dry.

Childes did not stop. On hands and knees, chest and shoulders heaving, he crawled onwards, his palms tender against the hot timber, until he found an open doorway. He scrambled through, kicking the door shut behind, rolling onto his back, allowing himself the briefest, gasping respite. The haze was not as thick inside the dormitory, although the rows of beds were seen through a swift-curling fog. Pushing himself to his knees, he reached for the nearest bed and pulled off sheets.

Still crouched, he tied two sheets together, scrambled to another bed and tore off more, refusing to accept the hopelessness of his efforts.

It was when he was tying one of these to the two already joined, his eyes blurred, a pain in his chest as if a knife was lodged sideways there, that Childes heard the muffled sobbing.

He looked around, unsure of the source. He heard only the crackling rumble of the fire. Bending low to the floor, he searched beneath beds and found no crouched figures. He completed knotting the sheets, then stumbled towards the closed door.

The sobbing again.

He whirled, his back slamming against the door, and scanned the room, eyes skimming over rumpled bedclothes, discarded dolls, past crazily whirling mobiles, over posters that were beginning to curl downwards from their corners. His glasses were grimed with soot and his own perspiration; using a corner of sheeting, he wiped them clean, still listening for the sobbing as he did so. The sound was soft, quiet, but had become more distinct from the other noises. His gaze came to rest on a store cupboard set in the wall at the far end of the room.

No time. There was no time to look. He had to get back to the girls on the landing.

Nevertheless, dropping the sheets, he ran the length of the dormitory.

He pulled open the cupboard doors and the two whimpering, sobbing girls, crouched there in the darkness among hockey sticks and tennis rackets, hanging raincoats draped over their heads and shoulders, screamed and cowered away from him.

Childes reached in and the girl whose shoulder he touched flinched and screamed even louder, forcing herself deeper into the recess. He took her arm and pulled her away from her companion, using his other hand to bring her face round towards him. He just had time to see she was one of the juniors when the lights went out.

He lost her in the darkness and screams pierced all else. Childes dropped to his knees and groped forward, finding their shivering bodies and encompassing them with his arms.

'Don't be frightened,' he said as soothingly as possible, conscious of the tightness in his own voice. 'The fire's burnt into wires downstairs, that's why the lights have gone out.' Still they pulled away from him. 'Come on now, you know me. It's Mr Childes. I'm going to take you out of here, okay?' He tugged at them, but still they resisted. 'All your friends are waiting outside for you. They'll be getting anxious by now, won't they?' *The others on the landing—Oh God, he had to get back to them before it was too late!* 'Come on, we'll just go right on downstairs, then you can tell your friends how exciting it was. Just a quick walk downstairs and we'll be out.'

The scared little voice fought hard to stem the sobs. 'The . . . the . . . stairs are all on . . . f-fire.'

He stroked her hair, pressing close. 'We'll use the other staircase. Don't you remember fire-drill and the stone steps that lead out of the building? They can't burn, so there's nothing to be frightened of there. And you remember me, don't you? Mr Childes? I bet you've come into my computer classroom at some time to have a look, haven't you?'

As if by silent, mutual consent, they threw themselves into his arms and he held their small, trembling bodies close, feeling the dampness of their tears on his neck, against his chest. Without further words, he lifted the two girls and made his way back between the short rows of beds, carrying them on either arm, their combined weight hardly encumbering him for those few moments. He stumbled once, twice, using a red-glowing line he knew to be from beneath the closed door as a guide.

Yet another sound now mingled with the general muffled roar, this one distant, beyond the school itself, and growing louder with each passing second. Approaching sirens.

The two schoolgirls, one in pyjamas, the other in an ankle-length nightie, buried their faces against him, bouts of coughing jerking their bodies.

'Try not to breathe in too deeply,' he told them, swallowing with some difficulty to relieve his own parched throat. The towel had fallen from his shoulders and become lost.

When they were at the door, Childes put down the girls and fumbled around the floor for the discarded bedsheets. His fingers closed around the material and he drew it up, remaining on one knee, the two frightened girls staying close.

He forced himself to speak easily, discarding any hint of panic. 'I know you both, I'm sure, but for the life of me I can't remember your names. So how about telling me, eh?'

'Sandy,' a quivery voice said close to his ear.

'That's nice. And what about you?' he asked, pulling the other to him. 'Aren't you going to tell me yours?'

'R—Rachel,' came the stuttered reply.

'Good girl. Now listen, Sandy and Rachel: I'm going to open this door and go outside, but I want you to wait here for me.'

The fingers dug into him.

'I promise it'll be all right. I'll only be gone for a short while.'

'Please don't leave us here!'

He couldn't tell which one had cried out. 'I've got to help some of the others, some of the older girls. They're not far away, but they're in trouble. I've got to go and fetch them.' He pulled their arms free, hating what he was doing, but having no choice. They struggled to keep hold of him, but he stood, the sheets over one shoulder, and felt for the door knob. Was it warmth from his own hand, or was the metal really hot? He yanked open the door.

To squint against the torrid glare, his skin contracting against the harsh blast of heat that swept in.

Shielding his eyes, he peered into the corridor and was dismayed at how much more the fire had spread.

The awful, splintering roar came just as he stepped out from the dormitory. No shrieks and no cries for help accompanied that sound—at least, none that he heard—but he knew its source, he *knew exactly* what had happened.

Yet he had to make sure. He had to be certain. If there was the slightest chance—

'*Stay there!*' he screamed at the two clutching, terrified ten-year-olds. He ran, crouching low, ignoring the peeling sensation of his skin, knowing it was only drawing tight around his bones, not really breaking, that it only felt that way. He bumped off the wall as he ran, the tied sheets trailing behind.

Childes reached the wider area overlooking the main staircase, only a few areas of unburnt flooring left. Overhead, curious rolling waves of fire swept the ceiling.

He could no longer touch the balustrade that was part of the balcony over the stairs, for the wooden beam was engulfed, a burning log amidst a greater fire. But he could see sections of the stairway through occasional gaps in the flames.

Only there was no stairway any more, just bits of burning timber protruding from the walls. And there was no longer any landing below. Everything had collapsed into the screeching volcanic pit.

Childes returned to the dormitory, too numbed for emotional tears, his blurred vision caused by stinging smoke-whirls. The three tied bedsheets lay further back along the corridor where he had dropped them and were already beginning to flame. He staggered, an arm resting against the wall, but kept moving, knowing it would be fatal to stop. His pace quickened when he saw that the two girls were no longer by the doorway. He prayed that they had obeyed him, had not run off in the opposite direction, away from the oncoming fire. If they got lost in the thickening smoke . . .

The door was still ajar and he pushed it back so that the wood smacked against a bedside cupboard behind. His shadow was black against a yellow-red patch of shifting, soft-edged light and Sandy and Rachel, cuddled together on the nearest bed, watched him with wide fearful eyes.

'Come on,' he said, and they both felt the deadness in his voice. 'I'm taking you out.'

They ran to him and he scooped them up, one in each arm. Now they were heavy, but he would manage. Whatever it took, he would at least save these two. Childes backed out and headed down the long corridor, away from the worst of the flames, everything around them—walls, ceiling, floorboards—sizzling, ready to ignite, to explode into one huge conflagration. He could barely see and there was a steady growing numbness inside his head, a constricting of his throat. Flames shot out from the floor near a wall, forcing him to turn his back and face the opposite wall to squeeze by. There wasn't a murmur from either of the girls. Their arms were around his neck and they kept perfectly still, terribly afraid yet trusting. Perhaps they had sobbed out the worst of their terror inside the cupboard.

They were in semi-darkness for a while, smoke obscuring even the light at their backs, but another soft-hued glimmer soon came into sight ahead. Although this flickering glow acted as a beacon, it was unwelcome; he had hoped that the fire stairs were far enough away to be still untouched by the fire below.

After groping his way along, almost blind, sliding his back along the wall at one side, they finally reached the stone landing over the stairway. Childes all but collapsed onto hands and knees. Sandy and Rachel squatted by his side, waiting for his coughing fit to ease, they themselves choking into open palms.

Recovering enough to pull himself up by the metal railings of the stairs, Childes looked over the top. The stairway acted as a chimney, smoke pouring upwards to swill into the corridor they had just left. Through the sweltering clouds he could see several fires emerging from corridors below.

There was still a chance to get out—if they didn't choke to death on the way down.

He gathered the two girls to him, kneeling so that his face was on a level with theirs. 'We're going to be fine,' he said, his voice dry and strained. 'We're walking down the stairs and we'll be outside within minutes. The stairs are concrete, as I told you, so they can't catch fire, but we'll have to keep away from the corridors.' He reached into his pocket. 'Rachel, you keep this hanky over your mouth and nose.'

Obediently, she took the handkerchief from him and pressed it to her face.

'Sandy, I'm afraid we'll have to spoil your nightie.' He reached for the hem and tore off a long strip of material, then tied it around her neck so that the lower half of her face was masked. He stood, but still crouched low. 'Okay, here we go,' he said.

Childes took their hands and led them down the first flight of stairs, keeping to the wall and away from the rising fumes.

The deeper they went, the fiercer the heat became.

Sandy and Rachel hung back and Childes had to tug at them to keep them moving. Reaching a corner between first and second floors, he closed them in, protecting their bodies with his own. Rachel's knees were sagging as she leaned into the corner and he could see in the red light that she would never make it all the way down. He shrugged off his jacket and draped it over her head, then lifted her. She slumped against him, only half-conscious. Maybe that was just as well; she'd be easier to handle. He took Sandy's hand once more and continued the descent, shielding her as best he could.

'Not far now!' he said loudly to encourage her.

In response, her other hand curled around his upper arm, holding tight. For an instant, Gabby's bespectacled face swam before him and he almost cried out her name. It was he who now faltered, sliding down the wall to sit on the steps, Rachel cradled in his lap, completely covered by his jacket and almost oblivious to what was going on. And it was Sandy who tugged at his shoulder, who worried him into rising again, refusing to let him rest for even a moment.

He looked into her upturned, dirt-streaked face, flickering shadows playing over her features, and she repeated his own words: 'Not far now.'

Not far, he kept telling himself, not far now, soon be on the last flight of stairs. But his strength was fading fast, was really leaving him this time, the last reserves expelled with his now ceaseless dry-retch coughing, each lungful of air taken in filled with asphyxiating fumes; and he could hardly see where to place his next step, so full were his eyes with running, stinging tears which made the rims of his eyelids so sore that it hurt even to squeeze them shut . . .

. . . and Sandy was pulling him down, her exhausted little body unable to cope any more, her bare legs giving way so that she began to sink lower and lower until he was finally dragging her down the stone steps by her arm . . .

. . . and his senses were reeling, full of images of moonstones and Gabby's face and torn mutilated bodies and piercing malevolent eyes that leered mockingly through flames, and Amy, cut and bleeding and writhing, and the glistening white and smooth moon shining through the whirling smoke layers, its lower curvature seeping dark blood . . .

. . . and he was fading, slowly sinking with each blundering step downwards, losing his grip on Sandy, his hand touching warm concrete, taking his own weight so that he could gently lower himself, let his body fold up to rest, succumbing to the choking heat, even though there was only a short way to go, just one more flight, one more—

A tiny part of his flagging senses revived a fraction, became alert to something that was happening below. His length sprawled on the stairs, he raised himself on one elbow.

Voices. He could hear voices. Shouting. Dark silhouettes against flames that billowed from a corridor on the ground floor. Figures on the stairs. Coming towards him . . .

MOONSTONE
(potassium aluminium silicate KA $1Si_3O_8$)
Density: 2.57
Hardness: 6
Indices of refraction: 1.519 - 1.526 (low) A variety of orthoclase feldspar, moonstone exhibits a faint but characteristic fluorescence when subjected to X-ray radiation.
Moonstone, so called because when held to light, presents silvery play of colour not unlike that of the moon. Colour, usually white, known to mineralogists as schillerisation, from German word 'schiller' meaning iridescence. Found in Sri Lanka, Madagascar and Burma.

OVEROY STUBBED out the remains of his cigarette, rubbing his tired eyes with thumb and forefinger of his other hand. He sat at the dining-table, a light hanging so low over the smoked-glass surface that the room around him was cast in shadows. The living area was beyond a squared archway, two small rooms made into one large, an alteration he had tackled himself when he and Josie had moved nine years before, a distant time when he possessed energy for both career and domestic enterprises. Only a single lamp shone in that room, the television in grey suspension, curtains closed against the summer's night.

Nothing. He looked down at his notes and said the word: 'Nothing.'

The tiny gem was no more than some kind of kinky calling-card. But calling-cards were a reference.

So why a moonstone?

A reference to the moon?

With one hand he spread the notes before him, sweeping them in an arc like a winning hand of cards.

Amy Sebire had suggested that Moon was a name. Yet Childes had psychically seen the moon as a symbol.

A symbol representing a name?

Overoy reached for the cigarette pack, found it empty, tossed the carton towards the end of the table. He stood, stretching his arms out behind his back, taking a short walk around the table. He sat once more and ran his hands over his face and around to the back of his neck, entwining his fingers there.

How was Childes coping? he wondered. Against all the rules, Overoy had left scene-of-crime evidence with him. A tiny piece of evidence, the moonstone itself. Childes had wanted the gem. So why not? It was useless to the police. But the stone had some significance for the killer. Checking jewellers in and around the London area had yielded nothing so far, even though the gem on its own wasn't a usual item for sale. The person they were looking for was obviously shopping around, never using the same place twice.

His weary eyes ranged over the pile of books heaped on the dark glass, most of them unhelpful, the information he needed sifted only from a few. That information was all to do with the moon; or more precisely, the mystical aspect of the moon.

Moon-madness, Josie had scolded him before leaving him in the gloom for their bed.

Not my moon-madness, Josie; someone else's.

Ask any policeman how the crime rate, usually with violence, inexplicably increased during a full moon. Even headshrinks believed a full moon tended to bring out the loonies. Overoy had underlined a note he had made: *If the moon has an effect on the earth's water masses, then why not also on the brain, which is semi-liquid pulp?* It was a thought.

And two *new* moons in one single month was said to be calamitous by those who believed in such things. There had been two new moons in May when the Moonstone atrocities had begun. That point had been underscored in his notes as well.

Another common belief among many people was that the moon's maleficent character (despite his weariness he smiled at himself, thinking of the old Man in the Moon and his cranky ways) could be manifested here on earth as a baleful emanation by those who had occult powers. Interesting but not a point to put before the commissioner.

He picked up a red felt-tip and circled the capital-letter word MUTILATIONS, then drew a line from it to another: RITUAL. Close to that he now wrote: SACRIFICE?? Perhaps a better word was OFFERING.

Offering to what? The moon? No, there had to be some kind of reasoning, even if only a crazy man's reasoning. To a moon god then? Goddesses seemed to dominate that area of worship, so let's make it moon goddess. Oh boy, if the boys in blue could see him now.

All right. There were a few moon goddesses to ponder on. Let's run through the list again:

DIANA
ARTEMIS
SELENE

Then three who were the same:

AGRIOPE - Greek
SHEOL - Hebrew   } HECATE
NEPHYS - Egyptian

Hecate. Why did that one ring a bell, albeit a very distant bell? Coming across that name in his researches had prompted further investigation into moon worship and the relevant gods and goddesses. (She seemed to be the most popular, but why should that mean anything? Let's have a look at her.) *Hecate.* Goddess of the dead. Necromantic rituals devoted to her. Daughter of the Titan Perses and of Asteria. Protector and teacher of sorceresses. (Was he really taking all this seriously?)

Hecate. Keyholder of Hell, dispatcher of phantoms from the underworld. At night she would leave Hades and roam on earth accompanied by hounds and the souls of the dead, her hair like bristling snakes and her voice like a howling dog. Her favourite nocturnal retreat was near a lake called Armarantiam Phasis, 'the lake of murders'. (Nice lady.)

Hecate. Possessor of all the great dark knowledges, mother of witches. (What was it about the name?)

Hecate. Like the moon she was fickle and inconsistent of character. At times benign and motherly, acting as midwife, nurse and foster-mother, watching over crops and flocks. But the other side of her nature, the dark side, gradually superseded her kinder side. She had become an infernal deity, a snake goddess with three heads—a dog's, a horse's, a lion's. (Real Edgar Allen. Hell, he couldn't believe he'd written it all down. At least he'd been wise enough to carry out his research at home.)

Overoy reached for the half-drunk mug of coffee lurking behind the pile of books, his lips curling back in disgust on tasting the tepid dregs. He put down the mug again and relaxed back in the chair. Where was he getting with all this? Was the research mere time-wasting or did it really have some relevance? They were dealing with someone who had a sick, deranged mind, someone who desecrated the dead, mutilated murdered victims. Someone who left a moonstone as a calling-card, and someone who got a kick out of psychological torment. Not a pleasant person. But a moon-worshipper? Or, more accurately, a moon-goddess worshipper?

Nah, no sense to it.

But their quarry was demented anyway.

Why had Hecate stuck in his mind? What was familiar about that name? Something he'd seen somewhere . . .

He groaned. No good, he was too tired to think any more. Everything was buzzing around inside his head and none of it settling. Bed. Sleep on it. Talk with Josie—whoops, was that the time? Talk to her in the morning; she always helped clear his thoughts. Maybe he'd got it all wrong anyway. Moon-goddesses, moon-worshippers, moonstones. Psychics. Life was simpler on the beat.

Overoy rose from the dining-table and, hands tucked into trouser pockets, took one last look at his spread notes.

Finally shrugging, he turned off the light and went up to bed . . .

. . . And awoke at dawn, the answer there before him like a faint neon sign seen through fog. Not much, no big deal, but a glimmer.

All grogginess instantly gone, he scrambled out of bed.

Full moon . . .

'To whom am I speaking to?'

'Hello, Daddy!'

'Hi, Pickle.'

'Daddy, I've started a new school.'

'Yes, I know, Mummy just told me. Have you made any new friends yet?'

'We-ll, one. Two really, but I'm not sure of Lucy yet. Do I have to stay at this school, Daddy? I miss my proper one.'

'Only for a little while, Gabby, just until summer holidays begin.'

'Then will we go home to our own house?'

'Don't you like it there at Nanny's?'

'Ooh yes, but home is nicer. Nanny spoils me, she thinks I'm still a baby.'

'She doesn't realise you're a big girl now?'

'No. But it's not her fault, she has good pretensions.'

He chuckled. 'Make the most of it, kiddo, you're a long time old.'

'All grups say that.' 'Grups' was their special word for grown-ups. 'Are you coming to see me soon, Daddy? I've done some pictures for you, I did them with finger-paints. Nanny's cross about the walls, but she didn't smack me, she never does. *Are* you coming to see me, Daddy?'

Childes hesitated. 'I'm not sure, Gabby. You know I want to, don't you?'

'Are you too busy at your schools? I told my new friends you were a teacher, but Lucy didn't believe me. She said teachers didn't teach video games. I tried to explain, Daddy, but you know how thicko some children can be. When it's holiday time, can I come and see you?'

So many uncertainties in his mind, but he told her yes, anyway.

'But I don't want to go on a boat this time, Daddy,' she said after her initial pleasure, her voice becoming low.

'No, you'll come by plane.'

'I mean there—I don't want to go on a boat like last time.'

'When we cruised round the island on that little motorboat, when we went to all those sandy beaches? I thought you enjoyed that.'

'I don't like water any more.'

That was all she would say.

'Why not, Gabby? You used to.'

Silence for a while. Then: 'Can Mummy come too?'

'Yes, of course, if she'd like to. Maybe Mummy'll let you stay on for a month or so.' Forget those black uncertainties, he told himself. Let these promises bring you out on the other side. Think of them as weapons against . . . whatever was about to happen.

'Really? D'you really mean it? I can stay with you for more than two weeks?'

'It's up to your mother.'

'Will you ask her now—*please?*'

'Uh, no, Gabby, not just yet. I've got something that needs . . . well, it needs clearing up first. Then I'll know everything for certain.'

'But you won't forget you promised?'

'I won't forget.'

'Okay, Daddy, Miss Puddles is here and she wants to say hello.'

'Tell her *meow* from me.'

'She says *meow* back. Not really, but I can tell she's thinking it. Nanny's bought a basket for her, but she likes sleeping on top of the fridge.'

'Nanny does?'

'Silly. D'you want to speak to Mummy again? She's going to read me a story in bed.'

No, he wanted to ask her about the water. Small children often developed sudden and irrational fears that bothered them for a while, then disappeared just as quickly, but Childes had been disconcerted by what Gabby had said. Perhaps she'd seen a bad TV movie, or one of the other kids had told her a drowning story. No matter; he hadn't been keen on water himself for some time. 'Yes,' he said, 'find Mummy for me. Listen, I'll speak to you soon, all right?'

'Yes. Lubboo, Daddy!'

For a fleeting, terrifying moment, Childes felt he might never hear his daughter say that to him again. The feeling passed, a cold breeze rustling through a tree.

'I love you, too, Gabby.'

She mouthed six rapid kisses down the phone and he returned one big one.

Just before Gabby rested the receiver, she said, 'Oh and Daddy, tell Annabel I miss her and tell her about my new school.'

He heard the *clunk* as the phone was laid down and Gabby's voice growing fainter as she went looking for her mother.

'Gabby—'

She was gone.

Had he misheard? More probably, Gabby had meant to say Amy. Tell Amy I miss her . . . Her little friend Annabel was dead, Gabby knew that by now. Fran had explained that Annabel wouldn't be coming back.

'Me again, Jon.' Fran's voice sounded rushed as usual.

Childes gave his head a little shake—or was it a

shudder?—to clear his thoughts. 'Fran, has Gabby been acting okay lately?'

'Hardly. The move's upset her more than she lets on and starting a new school is always a mite traumatic anyway.' Her tone changed. 'I get a weird feeling when you start asking about Gabby nowadays.'

'No premonitions, Fran. Honest. Has she mentioned Annabel to you?'

'Several times. But she's not as distressed as you'd have thought. What makes you ask?'

'I just get the impression she believes her friend is still alive.'

Fran did not answer immediately. Eventually she said, 'Gabby's been dreaming a lot recently. Not particularly bad dreams, nightmares, anything like that; she's taken to talking in her sleep a lot.'

'Does she mention Annabel's name?'

'She did once or twice at first; not any more, though. I think she's accepted she'll never see her again.'

'Why is she suddenly afraid of water?'

'What?'

'She seems to have gone off boats and water.'

'That's a new one on me. Fire I could understand, after what you've been through. But water? That I can't figure.'

'You told her about La Roche?'

'Sure. Her daddy's a hero; she's entitled to know.'

'Hardly a hero.'

'Modest, too.'

'A few over here would like to know how I got to the school so fast, even before the Fire Department had been alerted.'

'The police surely don't suspect you?'

'I wouldn't put it that strongly, but let's say nobody's clapped me on the back yet.'

'Oh, Jon, I can't believe this. They can't be that stupid! You barely got out of there alive yourself. And you rescued those two little—'

'I left seven others to die.'

'You *tried* to save them, you did your best. You told me that, Jon.'

'What happened was because of me.'

'Stop being such a bloody martyr and start talking sense. Just because some psychopath has chosen you for a crazy personal vendetta, it doesn't mean you're to blame. None of what's happened has been within your control. Now tell me what these hick policemen are up to.'

'You have to see things from their point of view.'

'Like hell I do.'

'They wanted to know what had made me go to the school *before* the fire started.'

'That must have been difficult to explain. Explain it to me again.'

'I've told you, Fran; let's not do a re-run. Anyway, their questions came thick and fast even while I was still in a hospital bed having oxygen pumped into me.'

'The ungrateful—'

'They had a burnt-out school, lives lost, a murdered policeman—what would you expect? That's twice I was ahead of anyone else at the scene of a crime.'

'So they suspect you of arson and murder. That's terrific. Jon, why the hell don't you get back over here, right now, take a late plane, or the first one tomorrow morning? Why put up with all this?'

'I don't think they'd like that.'

'They can't hold you there.'

'Maybe they can. I'm not leaving, Fran. Not yet.'

Her exasperation bordered on raw anger. '*Why?*'

'Because *it's* here. And while that's so, you and Gabby are safe, don't you understand that?'

She did. She said so. Quietly.

Childes went through into the sitting room, heading for the small array of drinks kept on the bookshelf opposite the door. He lifted the whisky bottle, twisted the top. And stopped. That's not going to help, he told himself. Not tonight.

He returned the bottle.

The room was shaded, only a table lamp providing light. The curtains were drawn back at both ends of the sitting room, open to the night, and he saw the sky was sheened an eerie metallic blue. Childes closed the curtains nearest to him, those at the front of the cottage, then walked the length of the room to the other window. Outside, the moon, white and only faintly smudged, not yet high in its cloudless territory, resembled a communion wafer, flat and delicately tissue thin. He drew the curtains against the night.

Hands tucked deep into the pockets of his cord jeans, Childes went to the coffee table near the room's centre, his movement slow, almost sauntering (except there was nothing casual in his demeanour). A two-day stubble darkened his chin and there was an intensity to his fixed gaze that was oddly both weary and alert as he stood over the low table, looking down. In his eyes, too, was a steady resoluteness.

He lowered himself onto the edge of the sofa facing the coffee table, leaning forward, elbows on knees, observing the tiny round object on the smooth wooden surface.

The lamp's reflection infused a hint of warmth into the moonstone's translucent coldness, while liquid blue, toned to indigo, shimmered a wintry variegation.

He stared into the moonstone's depths, like some old-fashioned clairvoyant gazing into a crystal ball, as though fascinated by the subtle shades; in truth, he looked beyond that interior, seeking perhaps the inmost part of his own self. But searching for something else as well: grasping for a link, a connection, *an access code.*

All he found was names. And unearthly faces. Kelly, Patricia, Adele, Caroline, Isobel, Sarah-Jane. And Kathryn Bates, Matron. All dead. Ashes. Estelle Piprelly. Ashes.

Annabel. Dead.

But: Jeanette, alive. Amy, sweet Amy. Alive. And Gabby. Alive.

Strangely, these last three were not as strong in his vision as the others; thoughts of them were shallow, somehow irrelevant, not part of this new thing.

His thoughts lingered with the dead.

Even those he had not known.

The prostitute. The boy, violated in his grave. The old man with the top of his head sawn off. Others in the asylum. He did not want to envisage them, nor hear their voices, for he sought something—someone—else; but their images and sounds pulsated before him, throbbed inside his mind . . . palpitating . . . growing, fading . . . growing, fading . . . expanding, contracting . . . a swelling, deflating, incorporeal balloon . . . a misty white ball . . . a moon—

—He gasped, his hand jumping to his forehead, the pain sudden and sharp, cutting through the dull ache that had troubled him throughout the day. He slumped back on the sofa.

His mind had almost touched . . .

'Vivienne?'

'Yes?'

'It's Jonathan Childes. I'm sorry to bother you this late.'

The silence at the other end of the phone lasted for a while. 'Just closing the door,' Vivienne said. Childes imagined Paul Sebire was on the other side of that door. 'How are you, Jonathan? Have you recovered from that dreadful experience?'

'I'm okay,' he replied. Physically, at least, he added to himself.

'Amy's very proud of what you did. So am I.'

'I wish—'

'I know. You wish you could have saved those other girls, too. But you did all you could, you must realise that. I just hope they soon catch the madman responsible. Now, I don't suppose you want to waste time chatting to me. Amy's resting in her room, but I can put you through to her. I know she isn't sleeping because `I've only just left her—we were discussing you, as a matter of fact. She'll be glad you called.'

'You're sure it's okay?'

Vivienne laughed quietly. 'Positive. Um . . . I'll have to sneak upstairs and tell her rather than call up.'

'Her father?'

'Her father. He's not as bad as you might think, Jonathan, he just likes to give that impression. He'll come round eventually, you'll see. I'll put the phone down now, and go up to Amy.'

He waited, his head still aching, the dull throb of before. A click, then Amy was on the line.

'Jon? Is anything wrong?'

'No, Amy. I wanted to hear your voice, that's all. I suddenly felt the need.'

'I'm glad you rang.'

'How're you feeling?'

'Same as when you called this afternoon. Sleepy, but that's the pills I'm taking. No problems. The doctor called earlier this evening and he says the cuts aren't half as bad as he at first thought. "Healing nicely", to use his words. I can get up and out tomorrow, so guess where I'm heading.'

'No, Amy, not here. Not just yet.'

'I *know* where I want to be, Jon, and who I want to be with. It's useless arguing. I've had time to think over the past few days and I think I can put any jealousy I have over you and Fran to one side. Not easily, I admit. But I can do it.'

'Amy, you have to stay away.'

'Tell me why.'

'You know the reason.'

'You think you're a danger to me.'

'I'm a danger to anyone at the moment. I even had to consider the risk when I phoned Gabby tonight. I'm frightened to *think* about her in case this monster discovers where she is through me.'

'The police will find him soon. There's no way he can get off the island.'

'I don't think it cares about that any longer.'

A sharp, probing, pain again. Childes drew in a quick breath.

'Jon?'

'I'll let you rest now, Amy.'

'I've had plenty of rest. I'd rather talk.'

'Tomorrow.'

There was an uncomfortable vagueness in the word.

'Is there something going on that you won't tell me about?' she asked almost cautiously.

'No,' he lied. 'I guess I'm just tired of standing on the sidelines while this mayhem goes on.'

'There's nothing you can do. It's for the police to bring it to an end.'

'Maybe.'

Again she didn't enjoy his tone. For all its solemnity, there was an anger there, a contained but inwardly seething rage; she had felt its potency when she had picked up the phone, incredibly even before he had spoken, as if beams of furious energy were coursing through the lines. She was thinking the impossible, and Amy knew that; yet why did she feel so ill at ease, so weakened by this—imagined?—force?

'Sleep now, Amy,' he said. 'Rest.'

And she suddenly felt so tired, almost as if he'd given an order that her body dare not disobey. She was *unbelievably* tired.

'Jon . . .'

'Tomorrow, Amy.'

His voice was hollow, the tail end of an echo. The receiver felt awkwardly heavy in her hand.

'Yes, tomorrow, then,' she said slowly, her eyelids ridiculously weighty. *What is this—hypnosis by phone?* 'Jon . . .' she began to protest, but somehow not having the energy left to complete the sentence.

'I love you more than you know, Amy.'

'I do know . . .'

The phone clicked, the connection was dead. The sudden deep sense of loss almost roused her again. But he had told her to rest, to sleep . . .

The receiver slipped from her fingers.

Childes put down the phone and wondered if the pills Amy was taking were making her so tired. They probably contained a sedative as well as a painkiller. He went into the bathroom to douse his face, also feeling weary—but paradoxically, also acutely aware. Filling the basin with cold water, he bent low and splashed his face, holding his wet fingers against his closed eyelids for several moments each time. Eventually, he straightened, confronting himself in the cabinet mirror; he stared into his own eyes, noticing the bloodshot coronas around the soft contact lenses he wore.

And if mirrors had reflected auras, he might also have observed short dancing white-to-violet rays of ethereal energy dazzling from his own body.

Childes wiped his face and hands dry, then went back into the low-lit sitting room. Once more he sank into the sofa near the coffee table, and once more he resisted the urge to pour himself a large whisky. He wanted his senses clear, would risk nothing that might dull them. The moonstone seemed brighter, the bluish flare inside diminished.

Pain in his head again, tiny repeated knife jabs this time. But he would not desist. Only the sudden urgent need to speak to Amy had interrupted the long, long, process—and before that, the urgent need to hear Gabby's voice—and now there could be no more intrusions, for Amy and Gabby were safe, away from harm. He could concentrate his mind. It hurt, though; God, how it hurt. He closed his eyes and still saw the stone.

He opened them when he heard whispers.

Childes looked around. The whispering stopped. He was the room's only occupant. He shut his eyes again.

And again heard the hushed whispers.

He allowed his mind to go with the sounds, to absorb them and be absorbed by them, and it all came so fast (so fast after hours of probing, sending out his thoughts, seeking) like tumbling into a snowy pit, the sliding plummet soft and smooth, landing with scarcely a jar, sinking into cushioned earth.

Whispers.

Voices.

Some he recognised. Some belonged to girls from La Roche Ladies College, those who had been fused into one melting mass of flesh when they had plunged together into the fiery maelstrom, incinerated into ashes, cremated into no more than a collective powdery heap.

Others.

A small squeaky voice, like Gabby's, but not Gabby's.

Others.

Demented even in death.

He could almost *feel* their presence.

Voices warning him.

Voices welcoming him.

His head reeled with them. And the moonstone that was now the moon throbbed and pulsated, grew large, encompassing . . . threatening . . .

. . . And this time he touched wholly the malignant and diseased other mind . . .

IF POLICE Constable Donnelly had not considered all life sacred—even that of rabbits who squatted, paralysed by headlamps, in the middle of the road late at night—then probably he would never have lost the car he was supposed to be following.

As it was, he had watched Childes leave his cottage from the darkness of his patrol car, the teacher easily visible under the moonlight glare, observed him climb into the hired Renault and drive off into the deeply-shadowed lanes. After first radioing HQ to let them know their target was loose, the policeman had followed, keeping a safe but reasonable distance between himself and his quarry.

The rabbit (or had it been a hare? They said hares had a special affinity with the full moon and would run senseless before it) had appeared near a bend in the road and Donnelly had braked only just in time—in fact swerving to the left a little to avoid the stupid animal, the patrol car brushing the hedge on that side.

The rabbit (or hare—he could never quite remember the difference) had stayed crouching there on the road, directly in his path, stunned and shivery, one black and glistening eye watching with dumb blankness, and the agitated policeman had had to leave his car and actually shoo the silly creature away.

When PC Donnelly had finally resumed his journey

and rounded the bend, the Renault's red tail-lights were nowhere to be seen.

It was as if the car, driver and all, had been swallowed up by the moon-bleached landscape.

First the ringing doorbell disturbed Amy's sleep, then the sound of voices roused her into wakefulness. One of the voices was unmistakably her father's, and it was angry. She pulled back the bedclothes, wincing slightly at the effort, and went to the bedroom door, limping only slightly, opening it just enough to listen.

The voices were still muffled, but her father was evidently complaining about the lateness of the hour. She thought she recognised both the other speakers. Amy joined her mother who was in her dressing gown on the landing, peering over the balustrade at the three men grouped in the downstairs hallway. One was Paul Sebire, fully clothed, obviously having been working late. The two other men were Inspector Robillard and Overoy. Amy wondered what Overoy was doing back on the island. She stood beside her mother and listened.

'This is ridiculous, Robillard,' Paul Sebire was saying. 'Why on earth should we know where he is? Frankly, it would suit me fine if I never laid eyes on the man again.'

It was Overoy who replied. 'We need to know if Miss Sebire has heard from him.'

'I believe he may have telephoned my daughter occasionally over the last few days, but I'm sure Aimée would have no idea of his whereabouts tonight.'

Amy and her mother exchanged glances.

'Find your dressing gown and come down,' Vivienne quietly told her daughter, moving round to the head of the stairs.

'Inspector,' Vivienne said, descending, 'Amy did receive a call from Jonathan earlier tonight.'

Paul Sebire looked up at his wife in surprise and then annoyance.

'Ah,' said Overoy and waited for her to reach the hallway. 'Would it be possible, then, to have a word with Miss Sebire? It *is* a matter of urgency.'

'Look here,' interjected Paul Sebire, 'my daughter is sleeping and shouldn't be disturbed. She still hasn't recovered from her accident.'

'It's all right,' came Amy's voice.

Sebire turned to see that now his daughter was coming down the stairs. Amy hardly gave him a glance—indeed, she had hardly spoken to him since she had learned he had struck Childes at the hospital.

Overoy frowned at Amy's bandaged eye and the plaster-cast from hand to elbow on her left arm. She walked with an awkward stiffness, limping a little. Healing cuts on her face and hands marred the smooth, light-tanned skin that he remembered so well from their previous meetings; he sincerely hoped none would leave permanent marks.

'We're sorry to disturb you at this hour, Miss Sebire,' apologised Robillard, looking distinctly uncomfortable standing there in the hallway, the front door still open behind him, 'but as we've already explained to Mr Sebire, the matter is rather important.'

'That's quite all right, Inspector,' Amy replied. 'If it concerns Jon, I'm only too willing to help. Is there something wrong?'

'You should be resting, Amy,' Paul Sebire remarked rather than rebuked.

'Nonsense. You know the doctor said I could be up and about tomorrow.'

Overoy spoke up: 'I was sorry to hear of your accident. Jon told me about your injuries. Er, your eye. . .?'

Although impatient to learn of the reason for their visit, Amy managed the flicker of a smile. 'Apparently there is no serious damage, my sight won't be impaired. The bandage is really only there to prevent infection and to force me to rest the eye. Now you must tell me what this is all about. Please.'

Vivienne moved close to her daughter and slipped an arm around her waist, drawing her close.

'Mr Childes disappeared from his home earlier tonight,' Inspector Robillard said. Over his shoulder and through the door, Amy could see that more than one police car was parked in the drive. She felt a tightness in the back of her throat. 'One of our patrolmen,' the inspector went on, 'who was, uh, on watch, lost his car in the lanes, I'm afraid.'

She gave a small shake of her head, not understanding.

'We wondered if Jonathan might have phoned to let you know where he was going,' said Overoy, a nicotine-stained finger scratching his temple.

Amy looked from one policeman to the other. 'Yes. Yes, he did call, but he didn't mention anything about going out. If anything, he sounded tired. But why do you want to know? Surely he's not under suspicion?'

'He never has been as far as I'm concerned, Miss Sebire,' replied Overoy, eyeing his colleague with mild but apparent disdain. 'No, I caught the last flight over here tonight because I wanted to talk to him. I also hope to help the Island Police make an arrest.'

He paused to take in a breath, looking at each of them. 'You see, we've discovered the identity of the person responsible for this madness. Someone we've checked on and know is still here on the island. Someone who might get to Jonathan Childes before we do.'

CHILDES SAT in the Renault for a while, suddenly terribly afraid.

It had drawn him here to this place, inducing an image of a large moonlit-smooth lake. Yet no lake of that immensity existed on the island. But there was one such vast area of water, a valley that had been flooded a long time before, covering trees and the deserted houses alike to form a reservoir, a great concrete dam built across that valley to prevent its rivers from reaching the sea.

A voice—no, less than that: a thought—had enticed, had *lured,* him there with a promise.

The thought's instigator had no shape, no substance. When Childes concentrated, his own consciousness drew its periphery inwards to almost a defined line of thought, only a soft-brimmed radiancy formed at a point behind his eyes, a moon-shape that shimmered hugely on the wall of his mind and excluded all other images and all other rationality.

It wanted him here, and Childes had not resisted.

The promise? The incentive?

An end to the killings. An end to the torment. An answer, perhaps, to Childes' own mystery.

The notion made him push open the car door, just as it had impelled him to drive through the empty lanes to reach this point. He had felt sure he was being followed when he had left the cottage—presumably by a police patrol car, for he assumed he was now under observation night and day—but the lights of the vehicle behind had soon disappeared, the other driver having turned off somewhere along the way. Maybe he, Childes, had finally become paranoid; and who could blame him?

The night was chilly despite the season, cool air breezing in off the sea to soothe the land after the heat of the day. Sweater and cord jeans could not prevent that chill from causing a back-juddering shiver; he pulled up the collar of his jacket, closing the lapels around his throat. The full moon was still unsullied by clouds and bathed the countryside in a stark luminescence, rendering it peculiarly flat, while shadows were deep and uncompromisingly black. So brightened was the sky by its round hanging lamp that stars, untold millions of them, were visible only beyond the far-reaching candescence. As Childes walked towards the dam, it seemed that the landscape was frozen beneath the eerie gleam.

His senses were alert and acutely clear, his eyes ceaselessly searching the area around him, well aware that any inert creature would easily blend in with the surroundings, so dark were they in places, so oddly-shaped in others. Here, a lone bush might be a crouching animal; there, a tree stump with thick roots stretched outwards could be a sitting man; a clump of trees to his left might easily hide a lurking figure, while a spread of undergrowth ahead could provide a concealing canopy for some waiting predator.

He wondered now if he wasn't disappointed that he had not been followed by a patrol car. Perhaps he should have rung Robillard before he left the cottage. But then, how would he have explained to the police inspector, who was sceptical to say the least, that earlier that evening his mind had finally fused with another's? The difference this time was that the fusion had been whole, with Childes on the offensive, seeking out and delving, surprising the other with his strength at first, then becoming absorbed by it.

By It!

Explain the silent, torturous mental battle that had followed as the creature taunted him with horrors that had come to pass, revealing the deaths to him again like some edited movie rough-cuts, with each frame containing feelings, smells, the pain and fear of the real event, a new stupendous dimension in cinematography. 4D. All in random order:

The old man feebly protesting against the saw edge cutting into his brow.

Jeanette's abject terror as she dangled over the stairway, hung there and choked by a knotted tie, to be saved but not spared the ordeal of near-death.

The prostitute, whose torn innards Childes had sighted at the beginning, not knowing then it was the first in a stream of macabre visions, the return of an old nightmare.

Kelly's charred and withered hand.

The school alight before the fire had been lit.

The dead boy, defiled and torn, his putrefying organs spread over the grass around the graveside.

Annabel. Poor little Annabel, mistaken for Gabby, her tiny dismembered fingers wrapped in a package.

And he had witnessed for the first time Estelle Piprelly's horrendous death, lying helpless on the floor, her neck broken, a trail of fire snaking towards her.

Explain that macabre run-through to a pragmatic, not to say dogmatic, Officer of the Law. Explain how he knew where *It* would be waiting for him, that the vision of a huge moon-silvered lake had unfurled inside his head like a fast-running tide, and that it was here that everything would be resolved. Such matters could not be explained or logicised: they could only be sensed, or believed in faith. Not many had that kind of faith. Certainly, for most of his life, Childes hadn't.

By now he had crossed the rough-hewn parking area, a patch scoured of shrubbery and trees, set back from the narrow road which circumscribed the reservoir to descend into the valley below the dam. He mounted the slabs that were broad steps leading onto the dam, pausing there to study the long, narrow concrete walkway with its thick, waist-high parapets on either side. The middle section was raised, low arches out of sight beneath to allow for overspill should the reservoir become too glutted with rainfall; stout concrete posts reinforced the parapets at regular intervals and graffiti etched the walls where tourists had marked their visit; dark grass fringes sprang up through wide-spaced parallel joins in the walkway's surface. Beyond the raised section loomed a water tower, octagonally shaped and set into the dam as part of its structure, where water was syphoned down to the pumping station at the base of the giant barrier.

Childes started forward, a breeze ruffling his hair. He felt exposed out there on the dam and constantly scanned the path ahead, natural moonlight somehow soaking everything unnaturally, so that the effect was surreal and colourless. The lake could have been a gently rippled aluminum sheet so smoothly solid did it appear; yet the power of the massive volume of water beneath the light-reflecting skin was ominously present, concealed but nevertheless threatening. Falling would mean being sucked down into a pitch black nether-world to be crushed rather than drowned.

He counted the narrow steps, seven in all, as he climbed to the bridge formation over the outlet arches. In the centre he waited, alone and afraid, yet determined.

Childes could hear the sea from his high position, could even make out the thin whitish plume as wave after wave broke against the distant shoreline, so clear was the night. Keen air wafted against his face as he peered over the parapet on the unflooded side. The wall below sloped outwards, a concrete basin to contain overflow at the base, a conduit leading from that underground, taking surplus water beneath the valley

to the sea. Not far from the basin was the white
pumping station and behind that another shiny flat
area, the processing plant's sludge lagoon. Occasional
lights shone further out in the valley, glowing from
homes whose inhabitants kept late hours; he envied
their unknowing snugness.

A creature winged darkly across his vision, too swiftly
erratic to be a disturbed bird; a bat, then, in accord
with the night, abruptly disappearing into covering
shadows. The soft beating of its wings had resembled
the uneven fluttering of a frightened heart.

As Childes lingered, his face a pale unlined mask
under the moonlight's glare, the visions plagued his
mind once more, assailing him with fresh intensity; not
for the first time he wondered at the malignancy governing their perpetrator. Childes' last few days had
been filled with outward mental probing, only a growing acceptance of his own unique powers giving strength
to those endeavours. He no longer resisted what he
had subconsciously known but rejected for so many
years, that personal acknowledgement flushing his
senses, lending vigour to his mysterious faculty.

He had remembered other times, insights that he
had dismissed as chance, as coincidence, suppressing
that psychic seepage, even the memory of such incidents rebuffed until now.

He had remembered the boyhood friend whom he
knew would die beneath the wheels of a hit-and-run,
the accident happening weeks later. A seldom-seen
uncle whom he realised would be cut down by a diseased heart after their last meeting, that same uncle
paralysed by coronary sclerosis months later. *The death
of his own mother, envisaged long before cancer had
ravaged her body.*

His father had treated him cruelly for that weeping
revelation, just as he had savagely beaten him afterwards when his mother's spirit had come to him, the
boy. Beaten him, Childes remembered, because his
father had blamed the boy's precognition for *causing*

his mother's death, for *initiating* her awful ending. Punishing him so badly that his nose and three ribs had been broken. And forcing him to agree through fear and, even then, loyalty, when his father had told the ambulance men and subsequent doctors that the boy, distressed by the loss of his mother, had fallen down a flight of stairs in the home.

Worst of all, in the feverish days that followed, the boy himself had come to *believe* his father's reason for mercilessly beating him, had *believed* that his premonition really had caused his mother's death as though it were some evil witch's curse; and with the recognition had also come the belief that he was responsible for his friend's car accident, that he had instigated the disease inside his uncle's heart.

His guilt far outweighed the agony of broken bones and bruised flesh and soon, when the fever that was the result of uncontrollable remorse more than injury, had broken, his mind had erected within itself a protective wall, acceptance of his psychic faculty expelled along with his own guilt, for they went hand in hand, had become part of the same.

And the infant-murderer three years ago had somehow loosened the hold inside Childes' mind, had set the precognitive process in motion once more.

Now this new killer had broken through the mental wall, turned a leak into an unsteady stream.

Childes' subconscious had even sent him back to witness his own boyhood misery, a long-hidden part of him yearning for answers. And such was the power within the boy that he had observed his older self return. The mature Childes had been the presence watching from the corner of the boy's room.

The answers, of course, provoked other mysteries, but these were of the human psyche, secrets that might never be unravelled for they involved secrets of life and the mind itself.

These thoughts coursed through him as he waited high on the dam, arousing a tantalising yet wary exhilaration, as though he were on some kind of sensory threshold. As he gazed upwards, he saw that even the moon's glacial radiance was extraordinarily puissant, dominating the night sky with a peculiar flooding vitality. Tension shook Childes' body.

He sensed he was no longer alone.

He looked behind, in the direction he had come.

Nothing there moved.

He looked ahead, towards the other end of the dam where there were more dark trees and thick undergrowth, another path from the winding road.

Something there did move.

It had watched him from the cloaking darkness and had smiled an ungodly smile.

So. At last he was here.

That was good, for their time had come. Now, under the full moon. Which was appropriate.

It moved from the trees towards the dam.

IF FEAR had bounds, then Childes considered he had reached the outer limits. He found he had to lean against a parapet to support himself, so weak did his legs suddenly become. His insides were full of wildly floating feathers, the rigid tightness in his chest disallowing their escape; even his arms were useless, their muscles somehow wasted.

It was on the dam, a black, lumbering shape in the moonlight, coming towards him, the wide, squat body rocking slightly from side to side, an awkward trundling motion that lacked any fluidity.

And as the figure approached, Childes could *hear* the sniggering laughter in its mind. A mocking laughter that iced him, imprisoned him.

Childes leaned more heavily into the parapet. *Oh dear God, its mind is in mine, stronger than ever before!*

Soon he was able to perceive moon-cast outlines in its form, reflecting off immense sloping shoulders, jumbled in the texture of curled and matted hair. The shape of a nose, a chin. The planes of forehead and cheeks. The dark slash that was a wide, grinning mouth.

It drew nearer, passing the water tower, much of its ungainly body becoming lost from view behind the steps of the raised section on which Childes stood. For a moment, only the head and shoulders could be seen.

Its eyes were still shadowed, black pits that were as deep and as full of foreboding as the lake below.

It mounted the steps, its body rising as if from a tomb, broad, wild-haired head grinning, eyes unseen, coming closer, moving nearer, its thoughts stretching forward, reaching for him. And there was something else that was disturbing about this almost shapeless mass which seemed to shuffle rather than walk, somehing that was slowly—ever so slowly—becoming evident as it advanced, drew closer and closer, to stop when it was no more than three yards away.

It was only then, when he was able to look into that broad, moonlit face and see the gimlet eyes, small and black, that realisation pounced, for when she spoke her voice betrayed nothing of her gender, the sound so low, so rasping.

'I've . . . enjoyed . . . the . . . game,' she said, each word slow and singular.

Her low chuckling laughter was as unpleasant as her voice and punched into him like physical blows. He clutched at the parapet more tightly.

The woman shuffled a yard closer and he noticed that her ankles, revealed beneath a long, voluminous skirt, were swollen, flowing over the laced shoes she wore as though her flesh were melting. An outsized anorak was spread over her upper body in untidy folds.

Childes forced himself to stand erect. His head was buzzing with confused thoughts, nausea clogging his throat. *He could smell this woman. He could scent her madness!* He swallowed hard, desperate to regather his failing strength.

All he could think of to say was: 'Why?'

The word was nothing more than a croaking sound, but she understood. He sensed, he *felt,* her shift of emotions: amusement had scuttled away.

'For her,' she said in that low, ungendered rasp, arching her neck so that her face was lifted towards the moon. 'My Lady.'

She gaped her mouth and he saw crooked, disfigured teeth. She drew in a deep scratchy breath as though inhaling the moonlight itself and when her head lowered, for one fleeting, unnerving moment, the moon reflected in those dark, cruel eyes, and it seemed as if the shine came from within, that the moon was inside filling her body, the eyes merely windows. The illusion was transient, but the vision lingered.

'Tell me . . . tell me who you are,' Childes uttered, uncertain of his *own* sanity.

The grossly-shaped woman regarded him for some time before speaking again, the brightness gone from her eyes, but replaced with a different kind of gleaming. 'Don't you know?' she asked, her words slow, but less so than before. 'Didn't you learn anything from me? There was so much I got from you, my lovely.'

He no longer leaned so dependently against the ledge. 'I don't understand,' he managed to say, striving to keep a steady tone, willing his legs to stop their incessant trembling. *She's only a woman,* he told himself, *not an 'It'. Just a woman!* But a madwoman, a small, chuckling voice in his head whispered. An incredibly *strong* madwoman, it taunted. And she knows you're terribly afraid, my lovely.

'I stole the girl from you.' The woman sniggered. Her mood had changed yet again, that shift sweeping through Childes himself, as though his senses were an integral part of hers.

'Not *your* girl . . .' she said slyly, ' . . . unfortunately. The other little girl. How the little dear wriggled, how she squirmed.'

The beginnings of anger flared inside him, a tiny flame struck in the darkness of his fear. The flame expanded, forcing back some of that darkness.

'You . . . killed . . . Annabel,' he said flatly.

'And those others.' Her voice was a low growl—a good-humoured growl. 'Don't forget all those others. Those girls were for my Lady too.'

The breeze sweeping over the dam was stronger, colder, flicking at his upturned lapels. It carried the salt smell of the sea.

'You murdered them,' he said.

'Fire murdered them, my lovely. And the woman who tried to stop me. Fire murdered the retards in the home, too. Oh how I enjoyed *that* place.' Her massive bulk edged closer and she leaned her head forward in a conspiratorial manner, silvery light haloing the matted curls of her hair. Once more her eyes lay hidden in black pits. 'Oh how I enjoyed that place,' she repeated in a whisper. 'My asylum. Nobody believed those lunatics, not their snivelling tittle-tattle. Who in their right mind *would* believe what I did to them when I got them alone? Who would credit the insane? Such fun it was, so very enjoyable. Such a pity it had to end, but you were coming closer, weren't you, my lovely? And you would have given me away. That made my Lady very cross.'

Now only one of Childes' hands rested against the concrete ledge. 'I still don't understand. What lady?'

She leered at him—at least he imagined it was some form of grotesque leer. 'Don't you know? Haven't you felt her divine force inside you? The power of the moon goddess that waxes and wanes with the moon's cycle. Can't you feel her strength in our minds? You have the gift too, my lovely, don't you see?'

'The sightings . . . ?'

She became impatient, her irritation rumbling through his own senses. 'Whatever you care to call it—none of that matters. When we share that gift, when our minds are together—*like now!*—its strength is so powerful . . . so beautifully . . . powerful.' The thought had made her breathless. Her body swayed from side to side, her face upwards again.

Her smell of insanity was rancid.

She became motionless and her head lowered. 'Don't you remember what we did with your machines? Our little game?'

'The computers?' He shook his head in bewilderment. 'You made the word "MOON" appear on the screens.'

She laughed, and the sound was threatening. '*You* made the word appear in their *minds*! Not on the machines, my lovely fool! We did it together, you and me, we made your precious girls see what we wanted them to see! And you saw what *I* wanted you to!'

Illusion. Everything was illusion; and perhaps it made more sense that way, knowing none of it was real.

'But why,' he pleaded, 'for God's sake why did they have to die?'

'Not for God's, but for our goddess's. Sacrificial lambs, lovely. And for their spiritual energy, feeble though it was in most. Interestingly strong in the woman, though, the one whose neck I broke inside the school.'

'Miss Piprelly?'

A shrug of those immense sloping shoulders. 'If that's who she was. You understand the energy I mean, don't you? I think you'd call it psychic force or some such fancy name. That energy tucked up inside here.'

A stubby finger tapped her temple and Childes shuddered inwardly when he saw how large her hands were. Powerful hands, swollen, like her body.

'But the woman's was nothing like yours, my lovely. Oh no, yours is special. I've searched inside you, I've touched your spirit. Such force, and held back for so long! It belongs to me now, though.'

She grinned and shuffled closer.

'All those others,' Childes said quickly, needing time for his anger to surge through him, to lend its vigour. 'Why did you mutilate them?'

'I tasted their souls through their inner flesh. That was the way, d'you see, my lovely? I emptied them and filled them again, but not with their own organs—oh no, their organs couldn't be returned, or they would have tried to reclaim their souls. And their souls belonged to our goddess. But I left them the stone, her physical presence here on earth. You've witnessed her earthly spirit inside the moonstone, haven't you, that tiny blue-glowing spark that's her essence? My gift to those unfortunates who had to die for her.'

Mad. She was totally mad. And she had moved very close now.

Dread, icy and clutching, held him there as she stretched one of those big hands towards him. The fingers slowly uncurled, the palm upwards, so that moonlight struck the fleshy surface.

'I've got one for you,' she whispered, smiling at all that her offer implied.

A tiny round stone lay in the outstretched palm and it might only have been the madwoman's disrupted and disruptive mind working on his, implanting the thought, the illusion—for she did have the ability: despite her madness, she did possess unbelievable psychic power—but there was an effulgence inside the gem, a bluish phosphorescence heightened by moonshine. In that glimmer he saw all the deaths.

With a gasping cry of both fear and rage, Childes slapped at the hand so that the moonstone flew into the air, a minute shooting star snuffed out almost immediately as it arced down into the void that was the dam's valley.

The demented woman, who held within her an uncanny force, stood silently before him, her hand still outstretched, her face, with its shadowed eyes, inscrutable. Childes, too, was transfixed, the air between them somehow dangerously charged, an insidiously creeping current thrumming around his body so that each hair stiffened on its own little island.

A thought burst into his mind, causing him to stagger.

Amy, sprawled writhing beyond the low wall by the roadside, her face a pincushion of glass shards, her neck unnaturally twisted against the base of a tree trunk, her mouth open with blood dribbling out.

'*No!*' he shouted.

The thought was gone.

And the shadowed gash on the woman's face was a grin.

He ducked his head into a hand as another image struck.

Jeanette, dangling over the stairway, her neck squeezed tight by the noose that was a tie, flesh puckered and swollen over its edges. Her bloated tongue slowly oozing between her lips, growing in length like some emerging purple worm, crawling down her chin to quiver over the throat that was drawn so tight. Her eyes bulging against their sockets, first one then the other plopping loose to swing against her cheeks. A trickling of clear yellowish liquid from between her legs, soaking into the white sock on one leg, falling in a broken stream into the well of the stairway.

'*It isn't real!*' he cried.

Gabby in repose, little white body unclothed and unmoving, as still and quiet as death. Her stomach cut open, sticky sweating organs breaking free, throbbing as they wriggled forth like slimy parasites. Her mouth beginning to open while these slithering things that were her existence escaped. Her fingers missing. Her feet blunted, each toe gone. She was calling for him, calling for *Daddee . . .Daddee . . . DaddeeEEE!*

'*Illusion!*' he screamed.

But the thing facing him on the dam only laughed, a deep, guttural noise that was as evil as her deranged mind.

His head shot sideways as a invisible force swiped at him. He touched his stinging cheek, feeling the hotness there. Yet she had not moved. Her snickering taunted him as cold, iron fingers jabbed at his lower body, clamping his testicles, excruciating pain doubling him over.

'Illusion, my lovely?' came her voice.

He shrieked and fell to his knees as the unseen hand turned to fire and thrust up inside his anus, piercing through, singeing the passage, reaching for his innards to melt and pulp them in its flaming grip.

'*ILLUSION?*' she demanded.

And although the agony was beyond belief, a white searing brand risen high inside him, an intense hurting that clawed his fingers and bowed his head against the concrete, Childes understood it was not real, the appalling severity driving off fear itself, and with the fear her intimidating control of his thoughts.

The pain ceased immediately with the realisation. But he was left weakened and slumped against the parapet wall. He stared up at the black looming shape that had not moved.

'Illusion,' he affirmed breathlessly.

Her anger rushed out at him like a wind squall, pressing him to the stone. A sharp scratching against his pupils blurred his sight and his fingers reached for the shrivelled contact lenses, tearing them from his eyes. He dropped the crinkled plastic onto the walkway and struggled to regain his feet, blinking away tears.

An unknown pressure tried to force him down, but Childes resisted, his hand reaching for the ledge above to pull himself up. *Not real,* he kept telling himself, *not real, not real!* Tentatively he struck out at the monstrosity in front of him. Not with his body. Not with his fists. With his mind. He aimed a blow at her with his mind.

He was surprised to see her shudder.

She came back at him and Childes reeled, his lower spine jarring against the top of the parapet. But this time the mental strike was softer, had less effect.

He heard voices, distant and somehow hollow, nonexistent. They were inside his head and as unreal as the brutal thoughts she sent him. Childes pushed at her mind again and felt her flinch. It was impossible—he *knew* it was impossible—but he was hurting her.

The voices grew louder, but still they were from within and had nothing to do with the night.

It seemed as though she were listening too, but again she endeavoured to wound him with her own secret torture. Cruel clawing fingers that weren't really there dug into his face, drawing down, jagged nails raking his skin. He felt their pressure, but not the pain. A curious vibration had began to hum through his body as though flowing through arteries and nerves, and the voices dipped and dived inside his head.

'No more,' came her rasping growl. 'Game's over for you, my lovely!'

She lumbered forward and her hands were like huge crane claws reaching for him.

Outrage helped. Childes aimed for that wide fleshy face, his fist balled into a weapon. It struck the blob of her nose, but she turned her head, lessening the damage. Blood smeared her upper lip.

One big hand swatted his away and then she was upon him, crushing his body against the low wall with her bulky weight. The breath rattled wheezingly in her throat. A rough hand went beneath his chin, lifting, pushing back his jaw so that he was sure the bones in his neck would snap. His fingers encircled that fat wrist and he tried to wrench it away, but she was too strong, too incredibly strong. He struck at her face and she merely shrugged off the blows. His back stretched over the ledge and Childes could sense the deep, empty space behind him.

His feet left the concrete floor and kicked uselessly at the obese body that held him there.

His mind went cold.

He was going to die.

Oddly, he was aware of the breeze brushing against his cheeks. And he was aware of the abyss behind. His blurred eyes were filled with the roundness of the full moon, its edges hazy to him now, as it watched impassively, lighting his upturned face with an unblemished radiance. He smelled her foul breath, harsh and heated with her exertions, as well as her body odour, stale with sweat and uncleanliness. So keenly acute were his senses that his thoughts mingled with hers, their separate psyches almost merging so that he knew her, touched the craziness that was inside, flinched back when it spasmed as if to seize. And as his mind retreated from hers, he was aware that she also heard the screeching voices, for they were within both their minds.

His balance had gone, his weight pivoted over the ledge; she held him there as though prolonging the moment.

But she was looking around, searching for the voices. She stopped. She looked towards the end of the dam, its granite structure softened by moonlight.

Childes managed to pull himself back a little while her attention was diverted. He swivelled his head, followed her gaze.

Saw the misty shapes drifting towards them.

THEY CAME from the night like wisps of curling vapour, nebulous and vague, a gauzy shifting of air, thin ethereal shapes that had little form and no substance.

Yet theirs were the voices that wailed inside Childes' consciousness.

At first they had seemed almost as one, a delicate cloud bank slowly moving along the top of the dam, but they had soon begun to separate, unthread into individual plasmic patterns, becoming different entities. Evolving into definite forms.

The woman's grip on him loosened as she straightened, an expression of bewilderment on her puffy, moonlit face. There was something more than simply uneasy surprise in her reaction, but this Childes sensed through her mind: it was an inner tremor, a flickering of fear. He eased himself from her grasp and slipped back onto the walkway, wrist muscles quivering with the effort of hauling his body over; he sank to the concrete floor, his shoulders resting against the parapet wall.

She had hardly noticed his movement, so intent were her shadowed eyes on the drifting spectres. Her brow was furrowed into deep shaded ruts and her big killer's hands were held clenched before her as though Childes were still in their grip. She took a step backwards, obese body at an angle to the approaching mists, only her head turned in their direction.

Closer they came.

Childes was weakened, as if these immaterial bodies were drawing off his strength, using his energy; but the madwoman's body sagged also, for they sucked at her spirit just as they fed off his.

He began to understand what she meant when she had spoken of the gift they shared and how strong and how *beautifully* powerful it was. But had she really known how powerful the gift could be? For it was gradually becoming evident what these slow-twisting apparitions were. Electric shivers ran through Childes and he cowered back against the wall.

The woman—*It*—the creature—the killer—was now standing in the centre of the walkway like some squat monolith as flat white light from above eerily revealed the advancing forms, their shapes becoming firm, less incorporeal, affording only occasional glimpses of the terrain beyond their discarnate bodies.

The first was small and no more than a boy. A very young boy. A very pale boy. A boy whose flesh held no blood, whose eyes held no life, and who shivered in his nakedness. A young boy whose stomach had been gouged out, shreds of skin flapping loosely over his emptiness. His mouth had opened and there were earth things inside, tiny crawling pallid grubs that always fed from graves. His decomposed lips moved and although he uttered no sounds, his words could be heard.

'*Iv i mack,*' the boy said, and those words in both Childes' and the woman's minds were slurred and ill-formed, as though the gluttonous worms feeding on his tongue also interfered with his ghostly thoughts.

'*Iv i mack.*'

('Give it back.')

'*I ont i mack.*'

('I want it back.')

His skeletal hand reached out for the heart that had been stolen from him.

The woman lurched and this time it was she who clung to the parapet.

Another immaterial figure came from behind the boy, this one, Childes discerned, a female; lipstick was smeared across her face as though a violent hand—or perhaps lips just as ferocious—had spread the redness. Mascara had run from her eyelashes in thick sooty rivers, giving her the painted mask of a demented clown, sick make-up to frighten small children. Like the boy, she was naked, her torso slit from breastbone (except there were no breasts, only runny wounds where breasts should have been) to pubic hair. Crude stitch-work had burst and objects protruded and fell from that crossed gash, hilariously funny objects, although no one was laughing, no one found them amusing: a hairbrush, an alarm-clock, a hand mirror—even a small transistor radio. She pulled at the edges of the wound like a woman closing a cardigan, afraid to lose any more items, as if those foreign objects were actually her lifeforce, her internal organs. There was baleful hatred in her smudged eyes for the woman who had so ravaged her body and had not even paid for the privilege.

That woman, dressed in her oversized anorak, put up a fat, ugly hand to ward them off.

But an old man had slipped between the grotesquely painted prostitute and the shivering boy, a lewd, ridiculous grin on his wizened face. Pyjamas hung loosely over his emaciated frame and the moon struck his eyes to give them vitality, a reflected gleam that was full of lunacy. Dried, caked blood darkened his pallid features in parts, and his head ended an inch or so above his eyebrows, sheered flat, more squirming things sucking at the protruding mushy pulp. He gibbered uncontrollably (again the sound only in their minds) as if cold air and gorging parasites were doing funny things to his exposed brain.

The woman shrieked, the cry as manic as the old man's gibbering, and Childes cringed back, refusing to believe but knowing it was happening.

Now it was the woman's turn to cry: *'It's not real!'*

The shifting figures crowded around her, pulling and snatching at her clothes, raking her face with their hands. The boy stood on tiptoe to reach into one black pit hoping to pluck out an eye.

She pushed him away, but he came back, and he was laughing at the game. She was dragged to her knees—or perhaps she fell in terror—and she thrashed her arms, all the while shouting, *'Not real, you're not real!'*

They became still and looked down at her gross, huddled bulk, the old man sniggering, the prostitute holding her stomach with cupped hands, the boy pleading for the return of his heart.

'Illusion,' Childes whispered and the woman, the she-thing—*It*—screamed at him.

'Make them go away, make them go away!'

And for a moment, as his thoughts wavered between reality and illusion, it seemed their forms did partially fade, did become insubstantial mists again. Did become nothing more than thought projections.

Until a diminutive figure pushed her way through the fluctuating images to confront the obesity huddled on hands and knees.

The little girl wore a thin green cotton dress and there were no shoes or socks on her feet, no jumper or cardigan to keep off the chill night air. One side of her hair was braided into a plait and tied with a ribbon; the other side was loose and straggly, the ribbon gone. Her cheeks glistened like damp marble and a tiny hand sought to rub away the tears. But the hand had no fingers; it ended in five blood-clotted stumps.

'Annabel,' said Childes in an awed breath.

'I want to go home now,' she said to the quivering woman, her voice small and squeaky, reminding Childes of Gabby's.

The woman raised her head and howled, a long wailing cry of anguish that was amplified over the reservoir's watery acres, swelling to become hollow and plaintive.

The boy plunged in his hand, sinking it into the woman's eye socket almost up to the thin wrist—at least it looked as if it were so to Childes. *Impossible,* Childes insisted to himself, *a nightmare only!* But when the skeletal fingers were suckingly withdrawn, dark fluid gushing in their wake, they held something round and glistening, something that was restrained by a thin stretching tendril which eventually snapped, a thread left dangling in the oozing liquid.

The woman rose, clutching the gushing hole in her face to stem the blood flow. She shrieked and wailed and screamed and begged to be left alone.

But they would *not* leave her alone: instead they pushed forward and reached for her.

She tore herself free, striking out, unbalancing the old man so that the pulpy substance and its feeding parasites inside the open container of his skull spilled out like contents from a weird Toby jug. He bent over, still grinning, still inanely sniggering, and picked up the liquefying brain from the concrete, replacing it inside the jug of his skull as easily as someone donning a hat; in truth, the gesture had all the ludicrousness of a geriatric replacing a wind-blown hairpiece.

Childes wondered if it was he, himself, who had finally gone mad.

The woman was backing away, tripping over Childes' sprawled legs as she retreated and grabbing at the parapet ledge to maintain her balance, moving towards the other end of the dam, towards the water tower, towards an escape into the trees and undergrowth where she had skulked earlier. The moonlit shapes drifted after her, arms still reaching, lustreless eyes intent on her. They followed, wandering past Childes as though *he* were the ghost, unnoticed, unperceived.

Only the small figure who had been Annabel stopped to linger by him.

Childes watched the stumbling woman retreat, despising her for the atrocities her perverted yet extraordinary mind had allowed, but taking no pleasure from this macabre retribution. One of her hands pressed against her eye socket, the fingers inky with leaking substance, but she never ceased moving backwards, shuffling away from those stalking spectres. Finally she turned her back on them, her stumbling pace increasing, nightmarish terror forcing her thick legs with their overflowing ankles into a staggering lope.

She soon came to a halt. She began to back away from the steps that she herself had risen from earlier like a ghoul from a dank tomb.

She reversed into the eagerly awaiting arms of those who had followed.

Beyond her, Childes saw what had brought her to a stop, for more ethereal figures were mounting the steps, their heads coming into view first, then their shoulders, their chests, their waists, and they were not wearing the nightclothes in which they had burned to death, but their school uniforms, the La Roche colours monochromed in the moonlight, unsoiled and uncharred by flames, although their bodies were blackened and gristled, their hair gone, skulls darkened and mangled, with exposed lipless teeth set in hideous grins and flesh hanging in rotted slivers, and Kelly pointing with a burnt and withered arm at the lumbering hulk of a woman, while her companions giggled as if Kelly had whispered some risqué joke . . .

. . . And Miss Piprelly leading them, her charcoaled head resting on one shoulder, perched uneasily there as if about to topple, her oddly tilted eyes blazing whitely from blackened bones and skin, yet full of infinite sadness, full of weeping . . .

. . . And Matron following up from behind, herding her girls, checking that none had strayed, none were lost, and all were sound and the scars and melted

tissue did not hurt, that there was no longer any searing pain, not for the girls and not for her . . .

Everything was blurred to Childes now that he no
longer had his contact lenses, yet somehow everything
was crystal clear inside his head. Clear even when
tears crept into his eyes as the crocodile file of girls,
led by their principal and tailed by their ever-watchful
matron, became momentarily whole again, their unmarked flesh glowing with life, Miss Piprelly's head
erect and body ramrod proud, Kelly bubbling and
impudent as ever, her pointing hand smooth and slender, with only their eyes still dead things. The change
was fleeting. By the time they had all climbed the
steps and were on a level with the transfixed woman,
they were charred and disfigured corpses once more.

The woman's screams were piercingly shrill as the
drifting figures converged on her, discarnate bodies
hemming her in, clutching and tearing, beating her,
raining blows that should have had no effect, yet which
somehow drew blood, somehow caused the woman,
the *beast,* to fall back. One thick arm was raised to
protect her face while her other hand still covered her
gouged eye. Childes became aware that in the background and more hazily vague, observing rather than
participating, was the figure of a uniformed man, the
blood-seeping slash at his throat matching the tight-
lipped smile on his wan face. Childes thought of the
policeman he had found slumped in his patrol car at
La Roche. Other shapes moved in the background,
but these had no definite form, could indeed have
been nothing more than mist drifting in from the lake.
But there was laughter and moaning and wailing among
those vapours.

Still sprawled against the wall, Childes watched on,
horrified and unable to move, unable even to call out.
The silent figure of Annabel stood nearby.

The woman was leaning back against the parapet,
her huge sloping shoulders stretching over the ledge in
an effort to keep away from those grasping spectral

hands. She twisted to protect her face and a stream of blood ran through her fingers to splatter against the dam's massive wall, where the flow continued to trickle down, a dark leak on a vast concrete expanse.

The next thing to happen was so fast that Childes was unsure of what he had seen—or what he had perceived, for his brain still insisted that none of this was true, that it wasn't taking place at all.

She might have attempted to climb onto the parapet to escape them.

In her wretched pain and craziness, she might even have decided to jump.

Or the figures that surrounded her might have really lifted those huge tree-trunk legs and pushed her over.

Whichever, Childes saw her huge bulk disappear and heard her scream rip through the night.

He closed his eyes, shutting out the madness, retreating into a blankness that unfortunately hid nothing. Everything was still there before him inside his besieged mind.

'Oh God . . .' he moaned. And opened his eyes.

The shapes were less defined, had become vaporous and uncertain once more. They grouped on the walkway, forms indiscernible and undulating as if disturbed by the breeze. He was dimly aware of other sounds and lights in the distance. Annabel had not moved, was near him, sad and small, her face a fading image of haunting loneliness.

Childes exhaled a sighing breath, air held so long that it had become stale in his lungs. He sagged, his head sinking onto raised knees, arms hanging limply by his sides, hands resting against the concrete like two dead animals who had rolled over and died, his clawed, upturned fingers tiny legs frozen in the air. It was over, and exhaustion claimed him as he wondered if he would ever comprehend the true and intrinsic nature of this woman who had been a devious tormenting abstraction—an *It*—to him for so long: Maniacal, certainly, a monster, too; but possessing such a strange power, a psychic force that was nothing less than demonic. He prayed that the power had been forever laid to rest.

And felt the cold insidious prickling ruffle his skin again.

Childes raised his head and looked towards the weaving mists, to where the woman had fallen. His mouth slowly dropped open, his eyelids stretched wide, and a trembling shook him as it had before.

For, even though his vision was poor, he could make out the shape of the big hand whose stubby fingers curled over the ledge like a fleshy clamp. Holding her there.

'No,' he murmured, a mere whisper to himself. 'Oh no.'

Was there a flicker of pleading in Annabel's otherwise lustreless eyes?

Childes twisted onto his knees, groped a shaking hand towards the ledge above, and pulled himself up. It seemed at first that his legs would not bear his weight, but strength returned like blood flowing into a limb that had gone to sleep, the process almost as painful.

He leaned heavily against the ledge for a brief time, then stumbled towards the clutching hand. The mists appeared to reassemble as he approached, again taking on separate forms. His legs were unsteady and he had become curiously numbed by all that had happened. When he drew near, the wispy figures parted.

They watched him, remote and impassive. The grinning old man whose skull was open to the sky. The naked boy who held something white and bloody in his frail fist, something he tried to push into the deep wound in his body as if to replace his lost heart. The bizarrely painted woman whose breasts were missing and whose belly bulged with small lumps as she pulled the sliced skin together. The schoolgirls and the matron, grisly, charred figures whose bones shone dully through gaping and mangled flesh. The uniformed man with two tight smiles, one above his chin, the other below. Estelle Piprelly, for a moment whole, unmarked, and who looked deep into Childes' eyes, an emotion passing between them.

They watchd Childes and they waited.

He reached the spot where the hand spread over the ledge to grip its inner side, the fingers seeming to oscillate with the tension of bearing the woman's full weight. He saw the fleshy wrist, the sleeve of the anorak stretched tight over the edge, disappearing at the elbow into the void. Childes leaned over the parapet.

Her round, moonlit face was just below him, slick dark liquid that reflected light shading her jaw and cheeks. One eye and a deep black leaking socket stared back at him, her other arm hanging loosely beside her as though useless.

'Help . . . me . . .' she said in her low rasping voice, and there was no entreaty in her tone.

As he looked down into her wide, upturned face, her silver hair sprayed out behind in wild tangles, he touched her madness once more, felt the crawling sickness that went beyond the iniquitous and corrupted mind which worshipped a mythical moon-goddess in insane justification for the evil she herself perpetrated; this sickness sprung from a cruel and degenerate soul, a spirit that was itself malign and rancorous. He felt and he *saw* her warped essence not in that one eye that stared up at him so balefully, but in the other deep black oozing pit that watched him with equal malevolence! And the words *help . . . me . . .* were full of taunting, alive with mocking. Childes felt and saw these things because she was in him and he was in her, and she filled him with images that were monstrous and abhorrent, repulsive and sickening, for still she enjoyed the game between them. Her game. Her torture.

But a new sensation passed through that depraved mind when his hands closed over the fat, stubby hand.

Fear stabbed those tormenting thoughts like a blade

piercing a pus-filled wound when he lifted her first finger.

A frightened moan as he prised loose the second.

A despairing, outraged shriek as he pushed at the last two fingers and she plummeted down, down, *down,* into the valley, her body bouncing off the sloping dam wall.

Childes heard the squelching breaking thud when she hit the concrete basin below. He slid to the floor of the walkway. And even before he had settled, an overwhelming relief swept through him, his being liberated from a black turbulent pressure, a confused boiling rage. He was too numbed for tears, too wearied for elation. He could only watch as the mists swirled and gradually dispersed.

Although one lingered.

Annabel leaned forward and touched his face with cold little fingers, fingers that had not been there before. Light from the far end of the dam shone through her and she became no more than a floating haze. Then she was gone, had become nothing.

'Illusion,' he said softly to himself.

THE LIGHTS came from headlamps and torches that shone at the end of the walkway. Childes looked into the glare, shading his eyes with a raised hand. He heard car doors slamming, voices, saw silhouettes appear against the brightness. He was mildly curious to know how they had found him, but not surprised: nothing more could surprise him that night.

Childes no longer wanted to stay there on the dam, even though the illusory mists had dispersed completely and no hand clutched grotesquely at the parapet ledge. The night had presented too much, and now he had to find refuge, his own peace. His head felt light from released pressure and, although he was confused, bewildered, his senses were flushed with a quiet euphoria. He needed time to think, a period for consideration, but acceptance of his sensory ability was complete and calmly acknowledged. For he was sure it could be controlled, used with restraint and intention—*she* had shown him this, although her purpose was unequivocally evil and her deranged mind had exercised a different kind of control. He rose to his feet and looked out, not into the valley, but across the reservoir itself, the moonlight glimmering off the water's placid surface, no longer sinister but with a luminous purity. Childes breathed in crisp nocturnal air, tasting the sea's faint brine, brought inland by the breeze; the air was cleansing and seemed to rid his inner self of skulking shadows. He turned and walked towards the lights.

Overoy was the first to reach him at the foot of the steps, Robillard and two other uniformed policemen close behind.

'Jon,' Overoy said. 'Are you okay? We saw what happened.' He held Childes by the arm.

Childes blinked at the lights.

'Turn those torches away,' Overoy ordered.

The two officers following Robillard went by them, the beams from their torches sweeping towards the centre of the dam's walkway. Robillard signalled for the police cars' headlamps to be switched off. The relief was instant, a heavy shade drawn against a blinding sun.

'You saw?' Childes uttered.

'Not clearly,' Robillard said. 'A fogbank had drifted off the reservoir and obscured our view somewhat.'

A fogbank? Childes said nothing.

Overoy spoke quickly, as if anxious to forestall Robillard. 'I saw you trying to save the other person, Jon.' He looked squarely into Childes' eyes, and though his gaze appeared expressionless, it barred any dissension. Childes was grateful, while Robillard looked doubtfully at his colleague but made no comment.

Unabashed, Overoy went on: 'I assume she was trying to kill you before she fell. Pity for her she was too heavy for you to hold.' The words were chosen carefully, almost as a statement that should be memorised.

'You knew it was a woman?' said Childes quietly.

Overoy nodded. 'We traced her lodgings back on the mainland. I rang you a couple of times earlier this evening to let you know, but your line was busy. I was lucky to get the last plane out tonight.'

The two policemen were shining their flashlights over the side of the dam, spotlighting the crumpled shape below.

'What we found at her home wasn't very pleasant—in fact, it was pretty grisly—but at least it proved conclusively that the woman was the killer we were looking for,' Overoy said grimly. 'The girl's body—Annabel's—was hidden under floorboards. To put her there was crazy because eventually the smell of decomposition would have given the woman away; other lodgers would have soon complained. But maybe she didn't care, maybe she already knew the game was up when she fled here. She must have been totally mad, and that's an irony in itself.'

Childes looked at the detective quizzically.

'It's how I got on to her,' Overoy explained. 'Her name was on our list of staff and patients at the psychiatric hospital. She was a nurse, and obviously as lunatic as those in her charge. Christ, you should have seen the junk at her lodgings—occult stuff, books on mythology, emblems, symbols. Oh yeah, and a small collection of moonstones, which must have cost her quite a bit. If each one was for a new victim . . .' Overoy shrugged.

'She said she worshipped—'

'The moon? Yeah, she did, one moon-goddess in particular. It was all there in her books, in her ornaments. Crazy, crazy stuff.'

Other figures were on the dam coming towards them.

Robillard spoke. 'When Inspector Overoy gave us the woman's identity, we were easily able to verify that she'd arrived on one of the ferries. She's been here for a couple of weeks, as a matter of fact. After that it was easy to locate her whereabouts on the island. She'd been staying at a guesthouse tucked away inland, far from the coast and main centres. She hadn't been seen all day, but we searched her room. Evidently, you've been lucky tonight, Mr Childes: she left her "tools of the trade", as it were, behind in the guesthouse. We found a small black bag containing surgical instruments. She obviously felt confident enough to do away with you with her bare hands.'

'She was strong enough,' remarked Overoy, 'so we learned from her employers at the hospital. They used her, apparently, to restrain their most violent patients and, according to the other doctors and nurses there, she never had much trouble doing just that.'

'Didn't they wonder why she'd disappeared after the fire?'

'She didn't. She was even interviewed by the police—she was on our list with the rest of the staff, remember? She took her normal annual vacation after most of the fuss had died down. She was insane, but not stupid.'

Maybe it would all sink in later; for the moment, though, none of what they had told him had much meaning to Childes. He stirred when he heard another voice, one so familiar and so welcome.

'Jon,' Amy called.

He looked past the two detectives and saw her only a few yards away, Paul Sebire holding her arm to support her. There was anxiety on Sebire's face, and it was directed at him.

Childes went to Amy and she raised her hands, the cast on her injured arm reflecting whitely in the moonlight. He hugged her close, loving her and wanting to weep at the sight of her bandaged face. She winced as he held her tight.

He relaxed his grip, afraid to hurt her more.

'It's okay, Jon.' She was laughing and there was dampness on one cheek. 'It's okay. I was so afraid for you.'

Over her shoulder, he saw Paul Sebire frowning. The older man said nothing as he turned and walked back to the cars parked at the end of the dam.

Childes stroked her hair, kissed the tears from her cheek. 'How did you know where to find me?' he asked.

Amy was smiling and returning his kisses. Somehow she sensed the change in him, the dark cloud that had shadowed him for so long now swept away. It was as though his very thoughts transmitted that change to her.

'We found out from Gabby,' she told him.

'From Gabby?'

Overoy had joined them, and it was he who said, 'We went to Miss Sebire's home tonight looking for you after the patrolman watching your place lost you. She didn't know where you were—'

'But I remembered you said you'd spoken to Gabby earlier,' Amy interrupted. 'It was only an idea, but I thought you might have mentioned to Fran where you were going tonight. Inspector Overoy considered it worth a try, anyway, so he rang Fran at her mother's number. She was having problems with Gabby.'

'Your daughter was in hysterics because of a nightmare she'd had,' Overoy continued. 'She'd dreamt you were by a huge lake and there was a monster-lady trying to drag you down. Your wife told us Gabby was inconsolable.'

'You knew where I was from that?' Childes asked incredulously.

'Well, I'm used to *your* precognition by now, so why shouldn't I believe your daughter?'

Gabby too? Childes was stunned. He remembered she had asked him to tell Annabel she missed her.

Amy broke into his shocked thoughts. 'There are no "huge" lakes on the island, Jon. Only the reservoir.'

'We had nothing to lose,' added Overoy with a grin.

'No, just me to convince,' commented Robillard. 'But what the hell? None of this business has made much sense to me, so why should I mind tearing across the countryside in the middle of the night up to the reservoir.' He shook his head in perplexity. 'As it happens, they were right. My only regret is that we didn't get here sooner. You've been through quite an ordeal.'

'Is it over, Jon?' implored Amy, her hand reaching up to touch his face. 'Is it really over now?'

He nodded, but the moon shone from behind him

so she could not see his face. He turned to look at
Overoy.

'Who was she?' he asked the detective. 'What was
her name?'

'She had an assumed name, we discovered, one
she'd been using for years. She called herself Heckatty.'
For some reason, there was a certain satisfaction in
Overoy's tone.

Heckatty. The name meant nothing to Childes. And
he hadn't expected it to. He wasn't even sure of what
had taken place that night. Had their spirits really
returned to haunt the creature whose very name was
so ordinary, so meaningless? Or had the fusion between their minds, his violent psychic contact with this
madwoman, brought forth imaginations that were
merely, in essence, visions and fragments of disrupted
minds.

'Illusions,' he said quietly to himself yet again, and
Amy looked up at him, puzzled.

'Oh my God,' came a voice from near the centre of
the walkway.

They turned in the direction of the two policemen
who were crouched on the bridge section of the dam
and shining their torches on an object lying between
them. One officer was taking something from his tunic
pocket to push it beneath whatever was lying there.
He rose and made his way back to the watching group,
gingerly carrying the object down the steps of the
bridge, his companion following.

Of course all their faces were colourless under the
moonlight, but there was a tightness to this officer's
features that suggested he had become physically pallid.

'I don't think you want to see this, Miss,' he said to
Amy, shielding the item he held so carefully on the
small plastic bag taken from his pocket.

Curious, Overoy and Robillard moved in closer to
look.

'Oh . . .' murmured Robillard.

Childes moved away from Amy. The other policeman was shining his torch at his colleague's cupped hands. Overoy had turned away, his face wrinkled in disgust.

'Some struggle you had,' he said sympathetically to Childes, who stared down at what the officers had found.

The bloodstained eye looked too ridiculously large to have been contained in a face. Dripping tendrils hung loosely over the side of the plastic bag and, as Childes looked down and the policeman's hands turned slightly, moonlight struck the eye's pupil. For a moment—just for a *fleeting* moment—a glint, almost like a tiny life-force, was reflected in there, and to Childes it had resembled the bluish phosphorescence that shone from within a moonstone.

Childes shivered as he turned away, and breathed in deeply, as he had only a short time before, dispersing shadows.

He slipped an arm around Amy's waist, pulling her gently to him, and they left that haunted, silver lake.

AND CHILDES wondered where this newly-accepted power would lead him . . .

DEADLY DEALINGS

☐ **A CLUBBABLE WOMAN by Reginald Hill.** Sam Connon stood pale-faced and trembling in the darkened hall of his house, the telephone in his hand. Behind him, in the living room was his wife. She was quite, quite dead. And as even a distraught husband could tell, she must have known her killer very, very well.... (138104—$2.95)

☐ **MIDNIGHT CITY by Robert Tine.** A killer who made every New York nightmare come true.... Twenty-first century New York—a twenty-four-hour-a-day beehive of humanity where every vice and crime ran wild. Someone was killing the cops one by one and only Jake Sullivan, head of a special squad of enforcers trained to stop at nothing, could foil the slaughter. (150368—$3.95)

☐ **THE OTHER DAVID by Carolyn Coker.** Two Davids. Michelangelo's great statue and now a rare "lost" portrait of the same model. Was the painting the real thing ... or merely the brushstroke-perfect invention of a super-forger? It was art historian Andrea Perkin's job to find out—but it seemed to be someone else's job to get her out of the picture. Permanently ... (139186—$2.95)

☐ **THE GREAT HOTEL ROBBERY by John Minahan.** It was the biggest hotel robbery in history and the most bizarre. Three men in tuxedos score a cool three and a half million in cash and jewels from a fancy hotel. Enter Detective "Little John" Rawlings who follows leads as slender as socialites ... until a decidedly unpretty double homicide stands the whole case on its well-groomed head.... (133366—$2.95)

☐ **LARK by Richard Forrest.** Lieutenant Billy Lark thought he had seen everything after twenty years on the town's scummiest beat, that is until his first homicide turns up a trail of grisly murders that leads to a crazed cassanova who obviously likes his ladies sexy, single, and screaming.... (141652—$2.95)

☐ **THE NEON FLAMINGO A T.D. Stash Crime Adventure by W.R. Philbrick.** Drugs, dames, death—a bubbling brew of danger in the Florida Keys. The laid-back fishing guide, sometimes private eye, T.D. Stash, finds he has a lot to learn, when his wife, an aging rock star, and a kidnapping threaten his life. (400542—$3.50)

Prices slightly higher in Canada